# Catwalk

# ALSO BY DEBORAH GREGORY

# Catwalk

**DEBORAH GREGORY**

delacorte press

Published by Delacorte Press
an imprint of Random House Children's Books
a division of Random House, Inc.
New York

Delacorte Press and colophon are registered trademarks of
Random House, Inc.

ISBN-13: 978-0-7394-9812-5

Book design by Kenny Holcomb

Printed in the United States of America

# dedication

For my purrlicious friends "Pashmina," "Angora,"
and "Nole." Thank you for stroking my fur
and helping me unleash my feline fatale.

*Meowch* forever!

# acknowledgments

*Molto grazie* to Stephanie Lane, a fabbie editor who truly earns purr points to the max. And to Lauren Heller Whitney, Andy McNichol, and Eric Zohn at the William Morris Agency. Most importantly, I must pay homage to the feline fatales who've made their mark in my life—and on the world—from Lynn Whitfield and Tonya Pinkins to Tina Andrews and Anath Garber. And to my best friend, a fashionista to the finish line—Beverly Johnson, the first black supermodel in America. Nothing will ever change that. Scratch, scratch!

# Catwalk Credo

As an officially fierce team member of the House of Pashmina, I fully accept the challenge of competing in the Catwalk competition. That includes granting unlimited access to photographers and television crews at all times during the yearlong process. I will also be expected to represent my crew to the max, abide by directions from my team leader, and to honor, respect, and uphold the Catwalk Credo:

*Strap yourself in and fasten your Gucci seat belt. By entering this world-famous fashion competition, I acknowledge that I'm in for the roller-coaster ride of my young, style-driven life. Therefore, whenever I feel like screaming my head off or jumping out of my chic caboose, I will resist the urge; instead, I will tighten a notch on my fears like a true fashionista.

**\*Illustrate your visions, but don't be sketchy with crew members.** My commitment to my House must always come first. Nothing must stand in the way of my Catwalk obligations—*nada, nyet, niente, Nietzsche!* And when someone or something presents itself as an obstacle, I promise to call upon my crew to summon the strength necessary to cut off the interference like a loose, dangling thread.

**\*Rulers are for those who rule with purrcision.** The true measure of my success will be not how I slope the terrain to fame but my ability to align my tasks and tantrums with those of my crew. I must always remember that grandiosity could land me in the half-price sale bin like Goliath—who was toppled by a tiny but well-targeted rock.

**\*Be prepared to endure more pricks than a pincushion.** Now that I've made the commitment to a goal sought after by many other aspiring fashionistas, I must be prepared for *catiac* attacks. Therefore, I will honestly share my fears and concerns with my crew, so that I can be pricked back to the reality that I am *not* alone in this not-so-chic and competitive world, nor will I achieve fabulosity solely on my own merits.

**\*Become a master tailor of your schedule.** I must face the fact that my time has now become a commodity more valuable than Gianni Versace's gunmetal mesh fabric from the seventies. Despite my daunting tasks, I must always find the time to show up for my crew and attend my bimonthly Catwalk meetings throughout the year. Together we can make our dreams come true, one blind stitch at a time.

*Floss your teeth, not your ego.** Now that I'm part of a crew, carrying on about my accomplishments like I'm the Lone Ranger of Liberty prints is not cute; neither is grungy grooming or having food crouched between my teeth. I will carry tools of my trade with me at all times, including a container of dental floss and a hairbrush, so that I can be prepared for prime-time purring and on-camera cues that may come at me off the cuff.

*Ruffles don't always have ridges.** While everyone is entitled to an opinion, I will not allow myself to become hemmed in by well-meaning wannabes outside my crew. My individual style is only worthy when it becomes incorporated into the collective vision of my Catwalk crew. I will also resist the temptation to bite anyone else's flavor to the degree that it constitutes copying, or I will be asked to pack my tape measure and head back to the style sandbox on my own.

*Pay homage and nibble on fromage.** As a true fashionista, I must study the creative contributions of those who came before me so that I can become the maker of my own mélange. I will also publicly give the fashionistas who came before me the props they're due whenever name-dropping is appropriate. Despite my quest for individual development, I must acknowledge that I will always channel influences from the past, present, and future.

*Click out your cat claws to defend your cattitudinal stance.** When others turn bitter, I must bring on the glitter. Competition always brings out the worst in foes—and even friends—because everyone will try to gobble the biggest slice of the fashion pie and no one settles for crumbs without putting up a fight.

*Always be ready to strike a pose.** Even if I am not a model in the House of Pashmina, I cannot expect to strut the catwalk without getting a leg up on the competition first and saving my best riff for last. When it's showtime, I will be prepared to do my assigned task to help bring the House of Pashmina to the finish line.

*Act fierce even when you're not feeling it.** Never let the competition see you sweat. While going through this creative process, I may feel doubts about my direction. I will feel free to bounce my ideas off other crew members, but never reveal sensitive information to outsiders! Not all fashion spies have been sent to Siberia—they hide among us, always ready to undo a dart or a hemline.

*Keep your eyes on the international prize.** As a fierce fashionista, I intend to get my global groove on by sampling style and culture around the world. In order to show my appreciation for the global access that style grants me, I commit to practice a foreign language for five minutes a day and double up on Saturdays because we're going to win the Catwalk competition and stage our style at a destination to be determined—over the rainbow! *Ciao, au revoir, sayonara!*

*1*

My younger sister, Chenille, says that I prance instead of walk. I should, since my motto is *Sashay, parlay!* Even Fabbie Tabby knows how to work it like a cat on a hot tin ramp. You can tell by the way she prances on the heels of my bare feet as I patter down the creaky hallway to the bathroom. My mom hates when I walk around without shoes on the craggy wooden floors, but I'm feeling too wiggly this morning to be on splinter patrol. Once I hit the cold faux-marble bathroom floor, I fling open the purple paisley plastic shower curtain, swiping Fabbie Tabby in the process.

"So *sari*," I apologize to my kitty sister, to whom I bear a striking resemblance. See, we both have the same ultraslanty hazel eyes, pushed-in nose with wide-splayed nostrils, and bushy sprout of golden auburn hair (mine on my head; hers from head to tail). The only way we differ: Fabbie has a plumpalicious hinie, which I push out of the way so I can squeeze sideways into the too-tiny shower stall, but then I stub my big toe *hard* on a chipped tile. Serves me right for *dismissing* my beloved boo.

I'm feeling like a bona fried frittata today for good reason. It's my first day back to school, and now that I'm a junior I'm *finally* eligible to run in the most important elections in the fashion galaxy: house leaders in the annual Catwalk fashion show competition. If I don't snag one of the five highly coveted nominations, however, then I will *not* have a reason to survive like Gloria Gaynor.

"*Oh, no, not I! I will survive!*" I screech along to the hyped hook of my mom's favorite disco song like it's a motivational mantra. Chenille swears that I sound like a cackling jackal. So *what* if I can't sing? I'm just trying to put myself on blast, okay? What I desperately need right now is a blast of hot water, because everything is about to be on like popcorn.

*Everything except the hot water,* I realize after I turn the screeching knob and watch the pathetic dribbles sputter from the shower nozzle.

"*Chenille!*" I scream at the top of my lungs, because now I'm feeling *extra* crispy. Serves me right. I can't believe I let that early-bird specialist take a shower first when I know how rickety the hot-water situation is. All you have to say are the words "broken" or "repair" and our landlord Mr. Darius's English takes a magic carpet ride to Babbleland. It doesn't matter how many times my mother complains and the repair guy futilely descends into the building's danky Tomb Raider basement.

The water situation remains chilly to tepid. The truth is, that relic of a boiler needs to be replaced with a new one from this century. And despite the fancy-schmancy name of our housing complex—Amsterdam Gardens— there are merely a few wilting shrubs on the premises. Any green thumb Mr. Darius has is from counting the thick stack of Benjamins he collects monthly in rent.

"Get out of here—*caboose babaluse!*" blasts Mr. Darius, his loud combustible rant rising from the courtyard into my second-floor bathroom window. That's precisely why we call him Big Daddy Boom behind his back.

Standing over the bathroom sink, I brace myself to swipe at my underarms with a washcloth soaked in freezing cold water and dabs of Tahitian vanilla soap. If you ask me, loitering knuckleheads like the ones Mr. Darius just shooed out of the courtyard have it easy breezy: they don't have to sweat the big stuff, like entering the Wetness Protection Program or getting nominated in the most important election any budding fashionista worth her Dolce dreams could run for.

Shivering, I hightail it back to my bedroom, catching a glimpse of plodding Chenille in her bedroom, already dressed in a gray polo shirt under her signature blue denim overalls and wearing black Puma sneakers. She's huddled over her bureau, carefully placing her precious hairstyling tools in the compartments of her gray melton cloth organizer. I scan the handygirl getup she's chosen to wear on her first day as a freshman at Fashion International, the fiercest high school in the Big Apple. I still can't believe Chenille was accepted into Fashion International's auxiliary program, designated for aspiring hairstylists and makeup artists. She should be toting a toolbox instead.

Personally, I think she should have followed in her friend Loquasia's Madden clunky-booted footsteps and applied to Dalmation Tech High School, which is directly across the street from our school. Fashion International is located on Thirty-eighth Street between Seventh and Eighth Avenues, in the heart of the most famous fashion district in the world. "You dropped a clamp," I mumble at her. Chenille studies the gray fuzzy area rug by her feet like a forensic examiner but comes up empty. "Psych," I say, deadpan.

Chenille squints at me with her beady eyes, then announces: "I'm taking the train with Loquasia."

"Whatever makes you clever," I shoot back. I walk into my bedroom, pulling out my pink sponge rollers and throwing them in my Hello Kitty basket caddy. *Puhleez,* I'd rather go bald like Shrek before I'd let Chenille touch my fuzzy goldilocks. Springing my spiral Shirley Temples into place one by one, I glance absentmindedly at the poster on the wall above my bed: Miss

Eartha Kitt poised in a black pleather Catwoman jumpsuit. One of my best friends, Aphro—which is pronounced like *Afro* and short for her fabbie name Aphrodite—gave me the poster for Christmas last year. She snagged it through a *major* hookup: Aphro's foster mother, Mrs. Maydell, worked for years as a maid on Eartha Kitt's Connecticut estate.

As you can sorta see, our household principles are divided into two distinct halves: Chenille is the yin and I'm the bling. What else could explain how she and my mother are both morning people while Fabbie and I are confirmed night creatures? I bet you Chenille shot straight up in her coffin at the crack of dusk, pecking along with the pigeons outside her bedroom windowsill until it was time to hoist her beauty-salon-cum-backpack onto her petite back and head off for her first day as a freshman.

"Pashmina!" my mom yells out. I'm naked, so I don't respond until I put on my favorite pair of pink cotton bloomers with the big cat's eye on the rear, which always make me feel like someone's got my back, or at least is watching my butt.

"Wazzup?" I yell back.

"I'm leaving twenty dollars on the dresser for you," Mom yells, her sharp voice rising above the din of the spritzing. My mom is addicted to hair spray because it provides her wigs with hurricane hold. "You never know what or who you're gonna tangle with," she warns us.

The phone in the living room rings loudly, making me jangly. Mom is not into any technological advances that soften sound. I stand quietly by my bedroom door and listen closely as my mom answers the cordless phone stationed on the Plexiglas end table. Suddenly, she gets an extra crispy tone in her voice: "I can't believe you're calling here before nine!"

I cringe, praying that it's not one of my crew.

"I don't know. . . . I *said*, I don't know, okay? I'll send it when I can," my mom says in a tart voice to the intrusive person on the other end.

My stomach wigglies rotate like they're on a spitfire grill. I realize that Mom has hung up on yet another creditor. She thinks we don't know, but they've been hounding her lately like a basset on a bone mission. Suddenly, I feel guilty: if Chenille and I weren't too old to be sharing a bedroom, we wouldn't have had to move to a bigger apartment. Like a *chatte noire*, I retreat stealthily to my bedroom, which Mom and I have spent the whole year pinkifying from floor to ceiling, including the wooden dresser we found on the sidewalk. Every weekend last year, Mom, Chenille, and I took the subway downtown to the Upper East Side to hunt for furniture discarded like empty cans of tuna by the resident snooty-patooties.

I snap the back closure on my petal pink bra, then carefully ease my skinny legs into my pink fishnet pantyhose, but I can't seem to dissolve my guilt. We're always stressing about money. That's why I'm motivated to get a part-time job pronto—hopefully from the job board postings at school. Of course, I know my mom wanted to move out of the Boogie Down Bronx for her own reasons: to be closer to her job and maybe even to get away from Grandma Pritch. My throat still automatically constricts every time I think of her forcing gooey oatmeal down my throat when we had to live with her. Mom left us with Grandma Pritch when I was three years old and didn't come back to get us until I was five.

Now Grandma Pritch is living all by her lonesome in the Edenwald Projects on Baychester Avenue, across the street from where we used to live. She's so old her eyes are going; last week she tried to take a shower in the hallway closet, then caused a ruckus in her building, claiming someone had swiped her shower stall! Shoot, she may be old, but Grandma Pritch *still* gives me the fritters.

My mother, who most people call Miss Viv, is an assistant manager at the Forgotten Diva Boutique, a plus-size clothing store (with *snorious* clothes for old-school customers) on Madison Avenue and Seventy-second Street. She was a sales assistant for a long time, but two years ago she got a promotion, which is how we were able to move into this three-bedroom apartment on the verge of a nervous breakdown. But I'm not un-grateful: as long as I have my own bedroom, I don't care if the ceiling collapses, because I'll just carry on like Chicken Little—dust myself off, then sashay through the soot, okay?

Chenille's modus operandi, however, is more like the Road Runner's, because it's only seven o'clock in the morning and she's already stationed by the front door for a hasty exit.

"Bye, Ma," she shouts before she slams shut the heavy metal front door.

I wince at the fact that Miss Wannabe "Snippy" Sassoon left without saying goodbye to me. I'm so over her, or maybe it's the other way around, because it seems that the taller I've become, the less Chenille is feeling me. Maybe it's the fact that we're now two grades apart even though I'm only one year older. (I was in the IGC program in junior high for intellectually gifted children [I hate the way that sounds] and skipped eighth grade.)

Suddenly, I realize that Chenille has the right idea about time management: it wouldn't be a bad idea to get to school early today. I hold up the new outfit that Felinez and I worked on for two weeks.

"Wow, this is the whammy-jammy!" I exclaim.

It's my ode to cheerleader chic: the pink pullover knit sweater has the letter *P* glued on the front and pink pom-poms hanging off the bottom edge and will be worn over a pink checked pleated wrap skirt fastened on the side with a giganto pink safety pin. Felinez also put a fuzz ball on the toes of my pink pleather boots: if you look closely you can see roll-around eyeballs pressed into the center of the fuzz ball. The pièce de résistance, however, is the matching shoulder bag. Using pink mop fibers, Felinez made me a bag that shakes ferociously like a big, bouncy cheerleader pompom. Staring in the beveled antique mirror, I put on my CZ (cubic zirconia) bling: first, my favorite eBay snag, a black Naughty Girl Lolita watch with floating pink crystals inside; then my French Kitty rhinestone cat pendant primed inside with Frisky perfume and dangling on a Mexican silver chain. My mom gave me my latest kitty *cadeau* for my fifteenth birthday last May. One day, I'll be able to wear bona fide *blang*, like a Hello Kitty diamond pendant by Kimora Lee. I stuff my pink satin meowch pouch into my purse—it's a little drawstring pouch that Felinez and I came up with for carrying essentials. You can wear it on your wrist or on your neck, or put it in your purse. Even Fabbie

Tabby has one—she wears it on her collar. Inside is one quarter, her phone number, and some biscuits, in case she ever prances too far over the rainbow.

Now I grab my hot-pink Kitty decal–littered notebooks and head to my mom's room to retrieve my designated ducats. My allowance is skimpier than I hoped for, but I'm determined to stretch it longer than my Chinatown-find fishnets, which are cramping my crotch area, okay.

I walk into the kitchen, where Mom is already stationed in her favorite little niche, drinking a cup of Belgian Blends mocha and reading yesterday's *WWW, Women's Wear Daily*, which she brings home from the boutique every night. She never eats breakfast and I don't either—even though she yells at me for doing the same thing she does.

"Please change the litter already," my mom instructs me without looking up from her newspaper. She is now dressed in the tailored attire associated with her "Miss Viv" professional personality—a hot-pink wool blazer, black wool trousers, and a black turtleneck sweater, most likely cashmere, which she craves. (There was a reason why my mom named both her daughters after luxury fabrics, pashmina and chenille, okay.) It's my job to take care of Fabbie, and one that I do gladly. Chenille obviously is not a cat person, and my mom has enough to deal with.

"Is that jacket new?" I ask Mom, checking out her outfit while I open the refrigerator and take out the carton of pink grapefruit juice and my *Vogue* magazine (I like to keep my fashion as fresh as my juice).

"I told you not to leave your magazines in the refrigerator," Mom snaps without looking up. Now it's my turn to ignore her while I indulge in my favorite morning ritual—sipping and flipping. I don't know why she acts so janky about my storage habits—it's not like we're running a gourmet garage in the refrigerator. See, my mom is a medi-okra cook, which is why we mostly eat take-out chow. Besides, she's so tired from working that she doesn't have time to cook.

Humming, I continue gulping juice and scanning the pages of my cool magazine until I get my fill of Juicy Couture, Gianni Versace, and Kate Spade.

"You excited about today?" asks my mom.

"I'm hyped," I respond. "I've got to get nominated."

Mom looks puzzled, which makes me realize that she doesn't remember about the Catwalk competition. She was just asking a general question, like it's my first day in kindergarten and I'm gleeful about showing off my new Princess Potty Mouth lunch box. (Awright, I did love that thing—stuffed it with PB&J sandwiches till the hinges rusted off.)

I realize that now is not the time to stand mute like a dummy (Catwalk code for mannequin). "Don't you remember, all I talked about last year was I couldn't wait until I was eligible to run for house leader nominations in the Catwalk competition? Hello—well, that time is now!" I shriek, trying to stimulate Mom's brain cells, which must be suffocating underneath her Beverly Johnson frosted shag wig.

"Okay, don't get huffy with me. What happens if you get nominated?" Mom asks warily.

"The five candidates with the most student votes get appointed house leaders," I explain carefully, hoping my mom will grasp how important this is to me. "*Then* I get to pick the students that I want to be members of *my* house—the House of Pashmina."

"So what else do you get besides that? I don't like the idea of you spending all that time involved in nonsense. You could get a part-time job and bring some money into this house," my mom says, tipping her hand. Now I see why she feigned an amnesia attack—she was hoping I'd forgotten all about my little dollhouse dreams. Well, I'll show her—time to bring out the hot-glue guns!

"I know it may not seem like much to you, but I could snag a one-year modeling contract with one of the five big model agencies. All of them have representatives attending the Catwalk competition fashion shows in *full force*," I say, zapping her hard.

Mom knows Fashion International's policy on modeling as well as I do. They have a not-so-tacit agreement with the model agencies not to sign students under sixteen, and even then, only students who have competed in the Catwalk competition are eligible. But the real prize is that every year at least three student models from the winning house are given one-year, $25,000 modeling contracts. So why shouldn't I keep my eye on the grand prize?

"And how much is this gonna cost me?" Mom asks, turning defensive.

"The Catwalk Committee provides each house with monthly expense funds. And I'm in charge of the budget—and submitting the monthly expense reports to the Catwalk director," I counter, my face flushed.

"Yeah, well, I know how these things work. Just remember that my money is funny right now," Mom says sternly.

"I know," I say, exasperated.

⌐ ⌐

"Geez, *I know*," I repeat to myself, barreling down the stairway. When I get to the first-floor landing, I'm blindsided by the latest graffiti scrawled on the wall in screaming red letters: TREVA AND TINA 4REAL. *Get a life*, I moan inwardly. I gallop like a moody mare across the courtyard, then catch myself and switch into my sashay for the rest of the long stretch to the sidewalk. That's what's digable about being your own fashion representative: whether you live in a brokendown palace like I do or on a fabbie estate in Connecticut like Eartha Kitt, when you step out into the urban jungle, the only thing people see is your style.

"Pashmina!" Stellina screams, jarring me out of my schemes and dreams; I didn't see her crouched on the bench across from the monkey bars.

"How ya doing, Pink Head?" she giggles, calling me by my nickname. "That outfit gets *major* purr points!" Ten-year-old Stellina cups her tiny hand into a cat's paw.

I howl involuntarily because it's funny to see myself mimicked by someone with such purrlicious potential. Stellina is one of the poised posse of kids who live here and look up to me because I want to be a model. They really gobble up every Kibble 'n Bit of instruction like I'm serving it à la mode.

"How come you sitting out here?" I ask. Stellina and her best friend, Tiara, went away to a Fresh Air Fund camp for most of August. But now it's back to school, so everybody is springing into action.

"I'm waiting for Tiara—her mother left for work already, so she snuck back upstairs to change her clothes into something more bling-worthy," Stellina explains, rolling her eyes. I feel bad for Tiara because her mother must be color-blind: what else could explain her forcing her daughter to mate checked skirts with polka-dot turtlenecks?

At least that's one drama I don't have to deal with: my mom doesn't stress about my dress—even if the creditors are about to knock on our door.

"Whatchu up to?" Stellina asks, panting like a puppy for the 411.

"I got ants in my pants about getting nominated for house leader," I reveal.

"Oh, that's jumping off today?" she asks earnestly, then squinches her nose. "You mean the fashion show thing, right?"

"*Oui, oui.*"

"What do you mean by house—you go to some-body's house?" she asks.

"No. It's like—um, we call it a house—a fashion house." I'm struggling to figure out how to explain it in terms she would understand. "You know, like the House of Baby Phat or the House of Prada."

"I got you," she says wisely. "So it's Prada or *nada*!"

"I hope so. The winning house gets to say *sayonara*. If I don't win, I'll be watching eggs fry on the sidewalk for another summer," I lament. Judging by the puzzled expression on her face, I realize that I have to explain further. "The winning house gets a trip somewhere over the rainbow."

"I got you." Stellina nods knowingly. "I wanna go back to camp next summer. It was real fun. But all that swimming was hard on my press-and-curls!"

"Awright, I'm out."

"See ya, supermodel!" Stellina says with a final sigh. "Can I be a model, too?"

"No doubt," I assure her.

As I descend into the subway, I indulge in my favorite fantasies: in the first, I'll spot a model clutching her portfolio, on her way to a go-see; in the second, I'm spotted by a famous photographer or agent or some other Big Willie fashionista who thinks I'm already ripping the runway, but they just can't help asking, "Are you a model?" I haven't seen one model yet, but I bet they ride the iron horse because it's the best way to get around, given the gridlock. I stop to dig absentmindedly into my pom-pom purse for my Fashion International MetroCard, and some harried passenger torpedoes my leg with an oversize shopping bag that must be loaded with bricks, because my knees buckle involuntarily.

I turn to look at the offending "bag lady," but she doesn't even say sorry. Luckily, my fishnets are intact and I make it to school in one piece, clutching my Hello Kitty necklace like it's a good luck-charm, confirming my one true belief: in the fashion jungle, only the accessorized will survive.

## FASHION INTERNATIONAL 35TH ANNUAL CATWALK COMPETITION BLOG

New school rule: You don't have to be ultranice, but don't get tooooo catty, or your posting will be zapped by the Fashion Avengers!!

YOU'RE NOT KATE SPADE, SO DON'T THROW SHADE. . . .

While some of us are planning on participating in the Catwalk nominations today, others have let it be known to the powers that "busy bee" that they won't be participating in the nomination process today. For the broken record, there is a reason why only junior and senior students who major in Fashion Buying and Merchandising, or Fashion Marketing, and have maintained a 3.5 grade point average or higher are eligible for the prestigious position of house leader. As Catwalk Director Fabianna Lynx (Ms. Fab) has explained, house leaders must possess strong management, planning, budgeting, and executive skills. Therefore, it doesn't make dollars and sense for someone who likes to doodle all day (yes, I'm talking about Illustration majors!) or get their click on (wannabe Francesco Scavullo photography majors) to be in charge of a Catwalk house. On the other hand, someone who prefers snapping their fingers like a general and keeping their team members' egos in check would soar in such a position. So why don't we all manage our own inflatable

egos and show up to today's first Catwalk general assembly meeting to
participate in the task of nominating
*qualified* candidates? Still don't want
any part of this democratic process? Sorry to hear that, but may
I suggest dropping out of school
altogether? Then perhaps, one day in
your player-hating future, you can ob-
tain a GED by visiting the Web site
www.thatsyourproblemnotmine.com.

9/8/2008 07:30:22 AM
Posted by: Spadey Sense

# 2

I can't believe that the school year has just begun and Shalimar Jackson is already back in business with her horse and phony show, jamming up the security check-point line in the process. This time Shalimar is pretending that her four-legged constant companion J.B. *still* has a Limited Access Fashion Pass when everybody knows the Fendi fiend was banned last semester. But leave it to Miss Jackson to crank out a Coty Fashion Critics' Awards performance before she even snags a house leader nomination.

"He *does* have a pass—I swear! I left it at home cuz it got sucked into my Dirt Devil by accident and I haven't had time to get it out of the lint bag!" whines my biggest Catwalk rival. Petulantly, Shalimar stomps her foot in protest, but instead the clunky heel of her brown lizard "Shimmy Choo" lands on the precious toes of Willi Ninja, Jr., as he tries to cut the line.

"*Ouch!*" snaps Willi, whose feet will no doubt be insured by Lloyd's of London one day, given his star status in voguing—our fave phys ed class.

"My bad," quips Shalimar. "I thought I was light on my feet."

"Yeah, well, you're *heavy* on my corns!" retorts Willi, another Catwalk rival.

The crowd in line snickers like bloodthirsty spectators at the Colosseum in ancient Rome, except in this case, it's the House of Ninja against the House of Shalimar—*coming soon to a runway near you!*

Our favorite security guard, Flex, is more interested in a certain someone's departure. "Shalimar, let's go," he commands. "If Ms. London sees J.B. in the mix, I'm gonna lose my job." He motions like a drill sergeant for the too-short model wannabe to step out of the conga line. We all dig Flex because he's like his namesake and doesn't get supa bent about drippy incoming Mambolattes or the sharp paraphernalia that other schools consider dangerous objects but ours considers merely tools of the trade.

After all, this is Fashion International High School, and we're desperately determined fashionistas who are more interested in taking a bite out of the big time than taking a bite out of crime. Don't get me wrong: fashion school is not a fairy tale. There are many times when clashes, crises, and competition make us wanna click out our cat claws and slice each other into grosgrain ribbon. However, the only physical violence I've ever witnessed within these lime green, cobalt blue, and hot-pink walls was during my freshman year when Chintzy Colon, who happens to be standing in back of me in the line, sliced her index finger with an X-Acto knife in fashion marketing class. At the time, we were all busily crafting promotional materials that were abracadabra fierce for our dream business plans when a certain senorita lived up to *her* name by "cutting the corners" too closely on her fold-out brochure. Led by her bloody finger, Chintzy fled to the Fashion Lounge, crying hysterically, like a five-year-old being chased by a Weeble balloonicle in the Macy's Thanksgiving Day Parade.

I turn around deliberately to check out this *lesser* Catwalk contender. Chintzy averts her eyes from mine as if she is still wincing from last semester's macabre memory, but I'm not swayed by her deception. It's no Victoria's Secret to me why she spent last year networking, noshing, nose-grubbing, and numbing her tootsies: the Chintzy cherub is angling for a dangle despite her phony protestations—"*Oh, you think I could get nominated, mija?*"—echoing down the halls.

"*Hola*, Pashmina. *Que bonita*. Those are bootylicious," Chintzy coos, staring down at my feet. Her gushing proves my *punto*: she's definitely on hype patrol.

"*Muchas gracias*," I reply, since I can't return the saccharine-spiked compliment. Chintzy is wearing a white vinyl miniskirt, which to me is like kryptonite—white induces inertia followed by fashion death if worn after Labor Day. I twirl one of my bouncy ringlets, frazzling the curl like I always do when I'm nervous. I'm not stressing about Shalimar, because I know she's a *shoe*-in. Both of Shalimar's parents work on Wall Street, and let's just say the business of Benjamins must be booming right now, judging by Shalimar's extensive Choo collection.

Chintzy, on the other hand, doesn't have a dad—I don't mean like my situation, because she has met her dad—but I know he doesn't visit—and her mother is a secretary at Avon and raising four kids solo. (On Career Day, we all had to go around and share, but afterward Chintzy kept the 411 flowing like true confessions.) Nonetheless, Chintzy has me worried. Obviously, she's not as crafty as Zorro with an X-Acto knife, but she knows how to sprinkle on that Splenda smile to land enough votes to edge me out of the top five. Suddenly, I fast-forward: I can already see Chintzy during our election campaign, her table crowded with jumbo pans of juicy chorizos—Latin sausages—and glass pitchers of Puerto Rican virgin sangria in an attempt to get everybody punchy enough to put her name into the ballot box. Maybe I should be taking notes, because Chintzy's affable nature worked like a *brujería* spell on our fashion marketing teacher. Even after Chintzy bungled her brochure for her business plan for ChicA Public Relations, she still snagged the same grade I got for mine—a disappointing B-plus. My ego was squashed like mushed plaintains.

"Wazzup, Miss P.P.! Work your initials, Churl. That sweater is off the hinge-y!" Willi squeals, posing like a prom queen, since he cut the line courtesy of his girl, Dulce, who is five Prada pumps ahead of me. Dulce turns to glare at me with her Spadey sense; if you see Dulce, you see her red patent-leather Kate Spade tote bag clutched to her side like a life preserver.

"Thank you, Mr. N. You are what's up, okay?" I hurl at the sneaky Ninja.

"*Soooo*, inquiring minds need to know. Are you *in?*" Willi taunts me.

"In there like swimwear," I shoot back with my best poker face, even though I don't know whether Mr. Twirl Happy is referring to the Catwalk competition or voguing classes—both of which he thinks he has locked up. And he freakin' does. Willi Ninja, Jr., is, after all, the adopted son of voguing legend Willi Ninja, who brought the fun underground modern dance form to our school curriculum. Suffice it to say, I'm green with Gucci Envy that his heir apparent was born with a pose at his elbows instead of a pacifier in his mouth. Mr. Willi is luckier than Miss Piggy: I mean, they both get to be the ham and eat it, too! I, on the other hand, don't even know my father's name. Sometimes I think: How am I ever gonna compete with that kind of legacy?

"*Pobrecito,*" Chintzy announces sadly. She's eyeing J.B., who is wearing a white satin cape draped around his tiny shoulders as he exits with Shalimar, who has finally given in to Flex's command to step off. Another round of snickers emanates from the crowd in approval of Shalimar's grand finale. J.B.—James Brown—is Shalimar's hyperactive Maltese. He's aptly named for his fast-moving, feverish footwork, reminiscent of the late Godfather of Soul himself. Unfortunately for Shalimar, J.B.'s jaws are just as quick as his feet: last June, he chomped on Ms. London's Fendi briefcase, prompting his ban from school. What a psycho Twinkie he is.

"Take a bow," I mutter under my breath, secretly eyeing the dynamic duo's exit while I pretend to be staring at the prominent square lime green sign perched on the wall directly to my right: NO VOGUING IN HALLWAYS, PLEASE.

Obviously, Fashion International isn't like any other school. That's why exchange students from all over the world vie for admittance to this fashion mecca, where there are more perks than the Mega Millions lottery: the coolest guest lecturers, a Fashion Café with an international menu that prohibits split pea soup because of its dreadful color, and a hands-on curriculum that includes model appreciation and voguing classes. Properly behaved purse-size pets are even permitted to attend with their student owners as long as they pass the only tests they're required to take: a charm barometer and weigh-in by Principal Confardi, who then grants a Limited Access Fashion Pass, which means the pets are allowed everywhere in school except in physical education classes or the Fashion Café. During those periods, pets must be checked into the Petsey Betsey Annex downstairs—an animal lounge with trained attendants funded by designer Betsey Johnson.

But not all pets are deemed acceptable, as witnessed by another prominently placed sign in the hallways: NO PET SNAKES PLEASE. *The only reptiles we want to see are on your purse!*

At long last, I feel the tickly paw scratch on my neck (my crew's secret Catwalk salutation) that I'm craving. I turn around to see Angora, who has slithered into the line behind me. Chintzy doesn't seem to mind, because she just shoots me an apologetic look, like she's used to making way for budding supermodels.

Like me, Angora has got her own agenda. That's why she majors in fashion journalism: so she can become a model *and* fashion personality; in other words, a bona fide "model-blogger." I can already picture her frame by frame on a *Rip the Runway*–style show like the one supermodel Tidy Plume hosts on the Teen Style Network. If you don't know who Tidy Plume is, then just hand in your All Access Fashion Pass *pronto soon*, okay. Tidy is a *major* Victoria's Secret model, so major that it's written into her contract that she must *always* close their annual fashion show wearing the blinged-out Fantasy Bra—diamond-encrusted, sometimes to the tune of eight hundred karats and $6.5 million.

"What's the matter, *ma chérie?*" Angora asks, seeing the pained look on my face. Angora may be near-sighted, which is why she always has her glasses—baby blue cat's-eyes trimmed with a delicate scattering of crystals—perched on her upturned nose, but she registers everything like a human scanner. Like right now. I gently tug at my fishnets, but she intuitively deciphers that I'm feeling kaflustered about the tall task ahead of me today—that is, getting nominated as a house leader.

"You need a tutu to do ballet, but anyone at any time can *wiggle*," Angora snickers, yanking my fishnets up after we walk past the security checkpoint. Angora loves to talk in sound bites—obviously honing her fashion-hosting skills.

"*Meowch, mijas!* Sorry I'm late," screeches Felinez, bouncing toward us, her wild dark hair flapping as much as her red cheerleader-style pom-pom purse. Although she is clutching the new looseleaf notebook she crafted over the weekend, husky Felinez still manages to ensnare me in an octopussy grip. "I missed you, Pink Head," she coos.

I giggle because we just saw each other, but that's just the way Felinez is. "Lemme see," I say, peering at the cover of the red vinyl–bound looseleaf on which she decoupaged a Barbie postcard framed in red crystals. " 'Every morning, I wake up and thank God for my unique ability to accessorize,' " Angora coos, reading the inscription. "That is *très* adorable."

Obviously, the postcard speaks volumes about Felinez's career goals. She couldn't breathe unless she was making something—and for me, Felinez is the ultimate accessory. We met in kindergarten at P.S. 122 on Tremont Avenue in the South Bronx. Even back then we were a couple of funky fashionistas—making fun of all the wee wee wannabes, snapping on their corny outfits like I was baby Dolce and she was Goo-Goo Gabbana, when we were just budding style gurus still nibbling on Gerber's. I had trouble pronouncing Felinez's name back then, so I started calling her Fifi, and the nickname has stuck ever since. By the time we were nine, Felinez could already turn a sow's ear into a silk purse with all the stuff she found in the garbage. To this day, Felinez would prefer to take a Dumpster dive in a back alley than a trip to a shiny shopping mall. I hate that we're not in the same grade anymore because I got skipped, but I stop myself from saying it. Instead, I hold her tight and mumble, "Nothing is gonna tear *us* apart, Miss Fifi!"

"This is what you two spent all weekend doing?" interrupts Angora, eyeing our matching shoulder bags and pleated skirts. Her blue eyes are opened so wide, they look opalescent.

"*Oui, oui*, croissant!" I say, imitating Angora. She's from Baton Rouge, and I just love the way she lays on her Southern drawl like greasy sweet peppers in a French flambé. Angora herself is a tasty mélange of French Canadian and Choctaw Indian, with a dash of Cajun thrown in for spicy seasoning.

"Well, I figured we're gonna need more than a few cheers to get those votes today," Felinez says, wincing while she tries to pull her skirt down because she's self-conscious about her adorable chubby legs. Felinez is my inspiration—*por vida*, for life. But I know why she stresses so much. It was just a few years ago that we were shopping on Thirty-fourth Street at one of those tiny boutiques—as in the sizes were too small for Felinez and she couldn't fit into this pink thermal top with cute red cherries on it that I had also tried on. I will never forget the hurt expression on her face: it was the first time Felinez felt more like a float in the Puerto Rican Day Parade on Fifth Avenue than a yummy sundae with cherries on her top.

"Tell me you didn't weigh yourself again this morning," chides Angora.

Felinez pauses for a second—like she's Chintzy and going to give us the PR version (as in publicity, not Puerto Rican, which is half of what Felinez is)—then realizes that she's talking to her crew and lets out a fart as well as the truth.

"Sí, sí, I did," she says, embarrassed.

I know my best friend's ritual by heart: every morning after she pees, she takes the scale out of the oven in the kitchen and puts it on the floor and weighs herself naked—but not before she moves the scale around on the floor like an Ouija board until she finds that magical spot that tips the indicator to a lower number. Then she puts the scale back on the warm grate in the oven, slamming the oven door in disgust, vowing never to weigh herself again.

"Did your parents leave yet?" Angora asks. Felinez's parents are in a band called Las Madres y los Padres, a Latin hippie group that pays homage to the love-and-peace music from the sixties. They're always on the road, doing gigs on cruise ships and wherever else they can pocket a groovy paycheck.

"That's why I'm late!" Felinez says, exasperated. "My mother kept me up all night, changing her mind a million times about her costume! First it was a pink ruffled top with purple paisley bell bottoms, then she was like, 'No, *nena*, make me a yellow top to wear with a miniskirt!' I was like, 'Yellow is not *lo mejor color* this year unless you're Big Bird on tour, *esta bien?*' Oh, she drives me *tan loca!*"

Of course, Felinez is the one appointed to make the "freebie" costumes for Las Madres y los Padres. Luckily, her father and the other male band member aren't as outfit-obsessed as Felinez's flamboyant mother, who calls herself Madre Cash and is *muy* demanding. Madre Cash wears the kookiest hippie-style costumes you've ever witnessed, and when they return from their world tours, she works Felinez like Spinderella on her over-worked sewing machine.

"I can't believe she kept you up like that, when she knew you had to go to school," I say, flopping my purse on the floor so I can dig for one of my gooey gloss wands.

Felinez gasps. "*Mija*, you know it's bad luck to do that! If you wake up broke tomorrow, you'll be sorry!" she scolds me.

"Yeah, well, I have a news flash for you, Senorita Fifi. Your *brujería* prediction must be retro, cuz I woke up broke *this* morning!"

Felinez laughs nervously. She takes *brujería* very se-riously. I also know that she's so happy to see her parents when they come back between their gigs that she'll do anything to keep her mother in stitches—literally.

"I know, *mija*, but that's not what made it worse. You'd think Michelette would help. No, she's sitting there watching the same episode of *Betty la Fea* a million times!" Michelette is Felinez's older sister, the one who actually takes care of Felinez and her seven-year-old brother, Juanito. Michelette works in a video store and can rent all the movies she wants, but instead she's obsessed with the Colombian soap opera. Their cousin in Bogotá tapes the new episodes of *Betty la Fea* and sends them to Michelette at least once a month. In return, Michelette tapes the episodes of the American version—*Ugly Betty*—and sends them to her.

"Should we wait for Aphro?" asks Felinez.

"Nah—I've got to get inside a bathroom stall *pronto soon* to fix my twisted fishnets so they can stop cutting off my circulation because they're not long enough, which is the short story of my five-foot-ten life!" I say, unleashing a mouthful. We're all nervous about today.

"Okay, let's get ready to Tanqueray," Angora says, pushing open the hot-pink door to the Fashion Lounge, then sniffing the air. "New Stick Ups."

I smell the fresh aroma, too, even though I can't place the scent.

"Orange blossom with a tinge of *santal*. Perfect for *moi*. God, I've missed this place!" Angora says, staring at our favorite sign on the freshly painted hot-pink wall, adjacent to the row of pale pink porcelain sinks with shiny gold faucets. Unlike most of the signs around our school, this warning is delivered in three languages so there can be no misunderstanding:

WEAR A SCARF, BUT DON'T BARF, PLEASE!

POR FAVOR, USA LA BUFANDA, PERO NO GRUNYAS!

S'IL VOUS PLAÎT, PORTEZ DES ECHARPES, MAIS NE VOMISSEZ PAS!

"This weekend, Daddy and I went to the *supermarché*—and finally got an odorizer for my room. Now I can smell magnolias every morning," Angora informs us.

I love how she makes a trip to the supermarket sound like a Parisian experience. Unlike me, Angora has a dad she loves. It took a lot of wrestling, but her mother unwillingly let her only daughter come live with her dad, Beau Le Bon, in the Big Apple. He is a supa-cool cartoonist and creator of Funny Bunny—you know, the goofy rabbit that tells jokes when you press his stomach.

"Is the odorizer shaped like a bunny?" I ask. I'd be surprised if her dad let her buy anything normal. Their whole house looks like an Easter treasure hunt—from rabbit salt and pepper shakers to porcelain eggs from Bergdorf Goodman.

"No, but he made me hop to the counter carrying it," Angora chuckles, shaking her head.

"You look so pretty in that top," Felinez says to Angora, who's wearing a fuzzy scoopneck sweater with short sleeves. She always manages to look so cuddly.

"Yeah, it's just the right salmon color—like expensive smoked lox, instead of Bumble Bee!" I heckle.

"Five purr points," coos Felinez. Purr points are our ratings system, used for everything from boys to bustiers.

Angora plops her book on its edge till it teeters over. "What's that?" Felinez asks.

*The House of Gucci,*" Angora, who reads voraciously, states. "What a *frothy* bunch. Far more eccentric than the Addams family. I mean, when they got into a fight, they threw five-hundred-dollar handbags out the window!"

"Yeah, well, the only house I'm interested in right now is my own," I mutter nervously.

"The House of Pashmina. Well, I'll be *dirndl!* I love the sound of that," Angora says, blinking rapidly, then posing, reminding me of the test shots she did when we first met freshman year in modeling 101. Angora posed with her white Ragdoll cat named Rouge, and they almost looked like sister and brother with their matching blue eyes and pristine auras.

"There's no way a certain person is getting

nominated," Felinez starts babbling, under her breath but loud enough for inquiring minds to latch on to.

I look toward the stalls just to make sure no one is eavesdropping. I mean, the walls in our school really do have pierced ears.

"Just transpose the letters in her name and you'll come up with the two words that best describe her!" Angora says smartly.

I pause for a moment trying to catch on, but I come up blank. "Chin and Neitzche?" I ask, chuckling.

"No, I wasn't talking about her," Angora corrects me.

"Well, I was," Felinez says. She *despises* Chintzy.

Suddenly, I catch Angora's spelling drift: "OH!" I snicker, cupping my paw to touch hers in recognition of pure genius at work. Felinez realizes at the same moment that Angora is referring to Shalimar.

"*Sham. Liar!*" we screech in unison.

"Awright, it's showtime," I say, signaling for us to go our separate ways. I'm off to textile science, while Angora is headed off to voguing 101. It has taken me two years to convince her to strut her gait. "Promise me you'll pose instead of pout," I say, trying to encourage her. I know Angora could vogue if she would stop feeling so insecure about freestyling. "Just dig into your spicy heritage!" I assure her.

"Thank you for that genealogic encouragement,

*chérie*, but I can't move like you!" Angora says, already starting to pout.

"Ah—you promised," I warn her.

"Okay voilà!" she retorts. "Just keep expecting miracles to be whipped up like soufflés!"

I run off to my class, with Angora's taunt teasing my eardrum. I guess I do expect miracles. Shouldn't everybody?

## FASHION INTERNATIONAL 35TH ANNUAL CATWALK COMPETITION BLOG

New school rule: You don't have to be ultranice, but don't get tooooo catty, or your posting will be zapped by the Fashion Avengers!!

ENUF WITH THE SUPA-DUPA SUR-PRISE . . . ??

Anyone who claims they wannna be in the Catwalk competition for reasons other than the prestigious perks should cross the street to Dalmation Tech—and let us normal fashionistas speculate about the goodies that will be bestowed on winners this year. So far, we've heard that Louis Vuitton, Ooophelia's, the Limited, and Radio Shack are providing gift certifi-cates. As for the designer mentorship, it will most likely be with a certain flower empowered mogul. That's right, someone who knows a showroom intern at Betsey Johnson says calls with Catwalk Director Fabianna Lynx were exchanged and the Flowered One will also be one of this year's judges. (This scoop is bona fide despite the fact that the intern in question was fired for swip-ing samples.) As for the hush-hush destination for this year's trip, *you can* stop ruminating about Gay Paree before you crash your "model" airplane into the Eiffel Tower. The Catwalk committee would *never* pick the *same* destination two years in a row. *Bon-jour!* We've also heard about the top-secret communiqués written in invisible ink passed around among

Catwalk officials all summer that revealed such sensitive information. So now that we're back to school, let's get back to Fashion Journalism basics, shall we? If you know the *who, what,* or *where* about the above, then decipher the code for us before we read you!

9/15/2008 8:00:02 AM
Posted by: Fashionista1005

# 3

By second period, I'm ready for my close-up at the Catwalk general assembly meeting. Angora, on the other hand, is ready for a meltdown. I wait outside Studio C to retrieve her from voguing 101, but she bolts out, staring blankly ahead like a zombie. She doesn't even register my gagulation over the tastiest Toll House morsel in fashion town exiting before her. This fashionista is taller than most of the guys, which means he's model material, as opposed to the rest of the shorties at our school. I discreetly check out his chiseled cheekbones and the zebra-striped mink hat plunked on his head, both of which hype his purrlicious appeal. So does the portable supersonic sound system he's carrying under his arm. Much to my chagrin, however, Shalimar suddenly appears next to the beauty with a boom box, ready to suck him up like sushi.

"It was a thousand-dollar ice cream sundae!" Shalimar brags, peering into his piercingly blue slanty eyes, which are framed by thick blond eyebrows. It's obvious that Shalimar is still searching for a new taste sensation despite the fact that for her sixteenth birthday, her parents took her to Serendipity 3 restaurant on the Upper East Side, where she got to indulge in the world's most expensive sundae. All morning, I've been hearing dribbles (but seen no nibbles, mind you) about this Golden Opulence Sundae: five scoops of Tahitian vanilla ice cream covered in 23-karat edible gold leaf, then topped with chunks of rare Chuao chocolate.

"Is there *anything* she won't devour?" I whisper to Angora. "I can't believe you didn't tell me you were taking a voguing class with the Mad Hatter!"

Angora is too vogued out to care about the latest object of my ogle. "If one more person asks me why I'm not in intermediate voguing with *Pashmina*, I'm going to hold a press conference!" Angora marches away quickly, sending Morse code distress signals with each clomp of her powder blue suede UGG boots. By the time we hit the second floor, she's out of breath and has to rest by the Hall of Fashion Fame passageway.

"Are you okay?" I ask. Angora's asthma goes into full throttle when she's kaflustered.

"I'm just fine and dandy. I hid in the back of the class so Mr. Blinghe wouldn't call on me. I think I need a chin splint from hiding my face in my palm—that's all," Angora says, struggling to regain her normal breathing.

"It was just the first day—and I'm sure Shalimar's shade didn't help," I offer.

45

"Oh, *plissé*! I can forget about modeling in a Victoria's Secret fashion show, okay? I don't need Je-T'aime's crystal ball to read the *Women's Wear Daily* headline of the future: Angora prance? Not a chance!"

Je-T'aime is Angora's dad's Creole psychic from Louisiana. He doesn't make a move without her. In Angora's case, I decide to coax the wilting magnolia into putting one UGGed foot in front of the other. If I get elected, I'll need my star model to be prance-ready by spring, and that's why I'm hoping that voguing classes will help Angora unleash her inner feline fatale. According to Willi Ninja, the unspoken fashion rule is: if you can vogue, then you can work the runway for points on the Dow Jones, okay.

"If I didn't think you could be as fierce as Tidy or Tyra, I would tell you to move back home with your mother and master the art of hyping hush puppies!"

*"Perch. Prance. Payday!"* Angora giggles, repeating another of my mantras. Then she pulls out her inhaler to rebalance her oxygen intake. "His name is Zeus," Angora adds nonchalantly.

"What was he doing with the beatbox?" I ask.

"He's a deejay—'hip-hop addict,' that's what he called himself. Mr. Blinghe made us introduce ourselves because 'voguing is about connecting with others,'" Angora repeats wearily.

"Does he want to model, too?"

Angora nods.

"Now, there's a new hyphenate," I offer.

"What do you mean, *chérie*?"

"A model *and* a deejay. What should we call him?"

"Speaking of hyphenates, take a look at this one," Angora says, perking up. She whips out the *Little Brown Book*, the magazine for Bloomingdale's insiders. (Her father's Funny Bunny antics have their perks now that parents are dropping carrots on his likeness, sold at Toys 'R' Us.) Angora opens to the page featuring Nacho Figueras, an Argentine polo player and the face of Ralph Lauren's new men's fragrance. *"Purrr,"* I hum approvingly. "A professional polo player *and* a model. I think Zeus is tastier, though. Oh, I got it—what about 'model-spinner'?"

"I like that," Angora says, smiling sweetly at the photo collage of Tidy Plume.

"Your eyes are prettier because they peer deeper into the soul," I coo to Angora.

"Her breasts are bigger though. I want those breasts, *chérie*," Angora counters.

"It's an indisputable facto that A-cup means A-list."

"Then add an addendum to our Catwalk Code: B-cup means more Benjamins!" Angora quips.

"Sounds like a *booby* trap to me."

Senior-year design major Nole Canoli and his five-member entourage turn the corner and walk ahead of us into the Fashion Auditorium. Elgamela Sphinx, the model in the bunch, towers over the rest of them and breaks out her supermodel-in-training smile. "Hi Pashmina and Angora," she coos.

As for Nole Canoli, the word on the street is he could be the next Gianni Versace. That means, a designer who is bling-worthy. Nole has a pudgy round face set off by his thick black Gucci glasses. He also has an egg-shaped head that probably glows in the dark because it's so giganto and closely shaven. Oblivious to our presence, the bling-worthy one walks into the auditorium. "It's turning into a real Macy's Thanksgiving Day Parade," I observe.

Angora nods knowingly as I reminisce about my fave cartoon balloons. When I was five years old, my mom finally rescued us from the gingerbread house before Grandma Pritch cooked Chenille and me in her oven. I started kindergarten a few weeks later, and on Thanksgiving the three of us went to the Macy's Thanksgiving Day Parade. I held my mother's hand tight because I thought if I let go maybe she would float away. My little hands were freezing, but I was in heaven watching all the gigantic balloons travel by. Sonic the

Hedgehog. The Weebles. Snoopy. The only one miss-ing was my favorite, Miss Piggy.

Angora nudges me from my childhood memories to clock Nole Canoli in action. "Anyone with that much hot air *has* to be deflatable." Nole air-kisses Liza Flake, who attends the Fashion Auxiliary program for hair-styling. Every chance she gets, you can spot her whip-ping out her turquoise faux crocodile portfolio, which is filled with test shots taken by photographers who use hairstylists, makeup artists, and fashion stylists to trans-form the models being tested into primp-ready posers. Rounding out the Canoli entourage are makeup artist Kimono Harris and hairstylist Dame Leeds, both in the auxiliary program. "Mini Mo," as the supa-petite blusher is called by her friends, always wears China red lipstick and her dark, straight hair is cut in a geometric precision bob, sorta like Aphro's (except Mo's hair requires no "assisterance" from Revlon Realistic Relaxer). Probably the most pampered member of Nole Canoli's entourage, however, is Countess Coco, whose tiny head topped with a foxy mane sticks proudly out of the black Prada bag thrown over Nole's right shoulder. She's a purebred Pomeranian with bulging eyes and equal attitude.

Speaking of entourage members, as we descend into the doorway of the auditorium, Aphro, who is seated midway, finally waves us down like a desperate housewife in Times Square trying to hail a cab. Even from rows away, we can hear Aphro's armful of silver and gold bangles jangling to their own fashion jingle.

"*Scratch, scratch!*" coos Aphro, sitting next to Felinez. They both extend their cupped hands and we all cross paws. Then Aphro unleashes one of her signature snorts—a laugh so hearty it sounds like a happy hog lapping up slop at its trough. It's part of what makes the mighty Aphrodite such a purrlicious Babe. Aphro majors in Jewelry Design and invented her own hip-hop moniker by adopting "Biggie" as her middle name. She wants to start a jewelry company called Aphro Puffs. Let's just say that the self-proclaimed "model-blinger" takes the advice of our marketing teacher, Ms. Harness, very seriously: "You're never too young to start branding yourself."

Angora and I plop down in the cushy hot-pink theater-style seats next to our crew.

"Okay—time to thread the needle," Aphro pipes up, which is Catwalk code for taking care of business. "Let's take bets. What's the supa-dupa surprise gonna be—a person, a place, or a *thang?*"

"Winner gets a Mambolatte," Felinez chimes in.

"Oh—all right. I think it's gonna be a person. A special mentorship with someone like—ooh, I got it— a French designer in Paris, like Yves Saint Bernard!" Angora says satisfied.

"Um, I think it's gonna be a place," Felinez says

50

confidently. "Like the Catwalk winners get to stay at the Four Seasons Hotel in Paris, where they'll plan a party?"

"Right! Y'all are all wrong! It's definitely a *thang*—like the Queen of England donating her royal jewels to the winning team, *ayiight*," quips Aphro.

"So *sari*," I counter, ready to throw mystery into the mix, "but it's none of the above."

My crew gives me the look that I know all too well: *Whatever makes her clever!*

Despite my excitement about what's about to jump off, I lean on Angora's shoulder and sneak a yawn.

"Pash—if I tell you something, you won't get upset?" Angora says, leaning closer.

I respond warily, "Wazzup, buttercup?"

"You need a spritz," Angora says, palming her vial of Bitty Kitty fragrance into my hand.

"I should have known that Tahitian vanilla soap wasn't going to hold up," I whisper. "I had to take a bird bath this morning because the hot water went to a hootenanny, leaving me high and dry."

Angora smiles at me, but I'm so embarrassed that I can feel the eye on the backside of my bloomers blinking in discomfort.

"God, I'd like to undo Mr. Darius with a seam ripper!" I mumble.

"Not to worry, *chérie*—only I can tell you smell," Angora whispers into my ear.

"Thank you for the blast," I say, spritzing on more of the Bitty Kitty fragrance before handing it back to Angora.

Yet another Catwalk opponent, Chandelier Spinelli, and her best friend, Tina Cadavere, scurry to grab seats in our row. Two steps in, Chandelier slides back out apologetically, like she's forgotten something terribly important—"Forgot her false teeth maybe," I whisper to Angora. Flinging her suede cutout scarf once around her neck, Chandelier unwittingly whacks Tina on the nose. "I'm sorry, Miss *Fluff*!" she squeals. Tina lets out a round of heckles as the dizzy duo scurry to another aisle.

"Tina the Hyena is on the loose," Angora observes. When we were freshman, Chandelier was real cool with me until she started throwing shade—as in Gucci twisted horsebit–hinge eyeglasses. By sophomore year, she went from tore up from the floor up to chic chitty-bang-bang with Nole Canoli and his crew.

"All I wanna know is how Miss *Chan-de-lee-ay* started hanging with Guccis?" shouts Aphro drawing out the pronunciation, which garners snickers from the nearby seats.

We shush Aphro in unison, but to no avail.

"Someone tell me please, then I'll shut up!"

"Maybe her father got promoted to head nurse,"

Felinez offers with a giggle. In sociology, Chandelier mentioned that she lives with her father and that he's a male nurse at a hospital in Brooklyn.

Aphro twirls the ends of the purple chain wrap draped around her neck like a detective meditating on clues. She designed the scarf from knitted links intermingled with chain mail; unwrapped, it would trail for miles. Aphro was in the same modeling 101 class as Angora and I. Hands down, Miss Aphro is the best catwalker among us, which is why the anointed strutter will be choreographing our fashion show. See, scoring points in the Catwalk competition depends as much on the choreographed posing and prancing as it does on a house's fashion theme and scheme.

At last, the auditorium has filled up with students who want to put their dibs in. Our principal, Mr. Mario Confardi, skips onto the stage with his signature sprightly gait. He smoothes down his fuschia silk tie, which contrasts sharply against a pale pink shirt and superbly tailored dark gray gabardine suit. Everything about our steely principal spells professional, which is why I suddenly sit up straight in my chair and poke Felinez to do the same. Mr. Confardi steps to the mike in clipped choreographed motion, his every move revealing the hidden Confardi code clearly deciphered by the most perceptive fashionistas among us. Loosely translated, it means: *I'm serving it up like pancakes, so you'd better grab my guidance while it's hot!*

Standing like a model on the catwalk patiently posing for the photographers stationed below the ramp to capture fashion shots, Mr. Confardi waits for our catty chatter to cease without having to signal us. That's also Confardi code. Our top fashion dog may be short with a slight build, but he is *très* commanding—and chic. Take his wardrobe: he's aways Dolce down in the suit department but pinches his pennies for Prada when it comes to his footwear—usually baroque brown lace-ups with perforated and stitched toes.

"Good morning," Mr. Confardi announces in his piercing voice. "Glad to see you could make time in your busy schedule to place your nominations—including you, Countess." Mr. Confardi motions to Nole Canoli and Countess Coco, who is clearly on the fast track to divadom, judging by her well-placed paw on the armrest.

Mr. Confardi continues with the words we are all waiting to hear: "Welcome to the nomination process for house leaders for the Thirty-fifth Annual Catwalk Competition."

We all clap. "Bring it on!" someone shouts. I turn and catch Anna Rex's stone-faced profile: that long aquiline nose and dark straight hair pulled back severely into a ponytail. Not one facial muscle registers excitement, not even a twitch. On last year's Catwalk blog, one of the house leaders claimed they vetoed picking the stoic one as a model because she is obviously a Botox-injection regular. While that rumor has still not been verified, one thing is true: Anna Rex maintains a 4.0 grade point average without breaking a sweat. There are five Anna Rex disciples—all super-skinny, with an obvious clique code that requires them to always wear black and never smile in public. It's also no secret that Anna Rex and her calorie-conscious cronies are the reason why the school implemented its no barfing policy in three languages. They never eat in the Fashion Café, but they can be seen outside the school smoking tiny clove cigarettes, supposedly hand-rolled in Dutch Teepees by a Surinamese Indian Chief, or so claims the snobby one.

A hush washes over the auditorium as Mr. Confardi continues his shrill spiel: "Our founding principal, William Dresser, had a unique vision when he created the charter for Fashion International forty years ago. He wanted an educational environment where a passion for fashion could truly flourish."

Speaking of unique visions, I can't help my wandering eyes, which search the crowd for just one more peek at Zeus. Not a zebra stripe in sight. My fashion lights are dimmed.

"Our founding father also created the format for the

Catwalk competition so that the most talented of our students could walk right into a fashion career—almost literally—after they graduated," Mr. Confardi continues. "To facilitate this process, the five competing Catwalk houses must be helmed by a committed leader."

Angora, Fifi, and Aphro turn and beam at me like I possess the key to fashion *paradiso*. I blush instinctively.

After Mr. Confardi winds down, he announces: "Now for the driving force behind the Catwalk competition, Ms. Fabianna Lynx!"

As we all clap, Ms. Fab grandly walks up the steps onto the stage with her pampered, pudgy white bichon frise, Puccini, hot on her heels.

"Sashay, parlay!" Aphro shouts out. It's giggles all around. As if on cue, Puccini plops his fat white extra-furry body down on the stage like a pancake next to Ms. Fab as she proceeds to adjust the microphone stand to accommodate her six-foot-tall stature. More giggles.

"Check the outfit," I whisper. Ms. Fab's style can be spotted from the last aisle in the auditorium: today she is wearing a leopard-print ankle-length denim dress with leopard-fur trim around the scoop neckline, and calf's-hair leopard-print mules with red piping. Puccini is wearing a matching outfit—a leopard-print denim coat—minus the mules. We all know that Ms. Fab makes both their outfits because, as she says, she wouldn't be

56

caught dead shopping at the Forgotten Diva, no offense against my mom.

"I heard she used to carry secrets for the Soviet Union in her lynx muffler," Angora offers about the so-called Lynx legacy, which fascinates us all.

"I bet she was the most furbulous double agent to grace the Kremlin," I concur.

Ms. Lynx looks ready to speak, so we wait with bated breath. "Good morning, my fellow fashionistas!"

*"Good morning!"* we shout back.

"Candidates nominated today will be eligible to run in the Catwalk elections. And next week, you will cast your ballots at the Catwalk election. The final five will be responsible for selecting their team members, delegating duties, and presenting a style vision that will culminate in one of the five full-concept fashion shows, which are held at Bryant Park."

Angora and I take a deep breath. We are definitely at the starting gate. Let the fashion games begin.

"Okay, shall we begin placing nominations?" Ms. Lynx says, looking down at Puccini as if he will be contributing. "Oooh, Puccini, don't you just get goose bumps at this petticoat junction?"

Puccini lifts his head and peers at Ms. Lynx, then drops his chin back on the floor with a defined *plop*.

"I had the honor of becoming the Catwalk director

twenty years ago, when our founding father was still here," Ms. Fab says, then takes a pause, which Aphro feels compelled to fill.

"*And* we heard you were sleeping with him!" she blurts out.

Sometimes I think Aphro has Tourette's syndrome. What else could explain why things just slip out of her mouth like hazardous emissions?

"He may be gone, but I believe he's watching with pride," Ms. Lynx goes on spookily, luckily not having heard Aphro. "*Okay.* I now move for nominations to begin. Raise your hand if you second."

Hands fly up, and I feel the excitement buyers must feel sitting at a Sotheby's auction, waiting to get their bid on with their numbered paddles.

"Farfalla and Sil Lai will assist with nominations," Ms. Fab explains as her two assistants ascend to the stage.

Nole's hand flies up first. "I nominate Chandelier Spinelli."

"I second that," someone else says.

Chandelier blushes and accepts the nomination.

Everybody claps, including Angora, who can't help herself; after all, her mother runs Ms. Ava's Etiquette and Charm School in Baton Rouge. Meanwhile, I keep my hands to myself and instead try to gauge my odds of beating Chandelier to be one of the top five contenders.

I also hide my disappointment that Nole nominated *her*. Aphro, Angora, and Fifi are oblivious. They hold their hands high like they're totem poles.

Farfalla calls on another student.

"I nominate Chintzy Colon," someone says.

"I second," says another.

Both Chintzy and her Splenda smile accept to a strong round of applause. Now I'm starting to sweat. Chintzy got nominated before I did?

Both Willi Ninja, Jr., and Shalimar Jackson also get nominated. Finally, Angora gets her nomination in. "I nominate Pashmina Purrstein," she announces loudly.

"I second that!" Aphro yells out.

After all the usual suspects and a few long shots such as supa-shrilly Chantez Winan get nominated, Ms. Fab asks the question we've been waiting for. "I move that we close the nominations. Does anybody second?"

A sea of voices second Ms. Fab's motion.

Sil Lai reads the list of Catwalk house leader candidates. "If you are one of the thirteen candidates that I just called, you have one week to launch your campaign. The election will be held next Monday," she explains. "At that time, all students will be eligible to cast a ballot. The day after Election Day, the poll results will be posted outside the Fashion Café. Please read the Catwalk competition rules and regulations *carefully*."

Ms. Lynx sashays back onstage, grinning like a spotted Cheshire cat. Sil Lai runs center stage to hand Ms. Lynx the Big Willie bronze statue. Ms. Lynx holds the Big Willie statue like it's an Academy Award—and to us, it is.

"This is what you will work so hard for—our school's ultimate symbol of promise, potential, and dedication. Each year, a Big Willie is bestowed upon the winning house. Good luck to you all!"

Ms. Lynx waits for the thunderous rounds of applause to die down. "I'm sure each and every one of you is also familiar with the $100,000 prize and college scholarships that will accompany this prestigious award—thanks to our generous corporate sponsors. What everyone has been dying to know, of course, is this year's destination for the all-expenses paid two-week trip."

I sit up in my chair, my appetite whetted for more than a Mambolatte all of a sudden.

"The winning team will be whisked off to . . . Firenze, where they will stage their fashion show as the opening collection in *Pitti Bimbo*!"

"Italy! Knew it!" I scream, cupping my hands to Angora. Firenze is Italian for Florence, where the junior fashion collections—Pitti Bimbo—are held every summer.

"But hold on. We do have one extra perk this year

that has managed to stay hush-hush on the plush," Ms. Lynx goes on. "Someone please hand me the note written in invisible ink!" she giggles, motioning to Farfalla, who eagerly marches toward her with a satin leopard tote. She plops it into Ms. Lynx's outstretched left hand.

"Break it down!" Aphro shouts, because she can't stand the anticipation anymore. None of us can.

We watch as Ms. Lynx opens her spotted tote like it's Pandora's box, but all she pulls out of it are a pack of leopard tissues. Coughing, Ms. Lynx puts her hand to her ample chest and waits for her throat to clear before she resumes speaking: "For the first time, we have an unprecedented surprise."

"*What is it!*" someone screams.

We all burst out laughing. "Let me catch my breath, will you?" Ms. Fab insists. "Okay, okay. I am incredibly pleased to announce that for the first time in the thirty-five-year history of the Catwalk competition, you will have more than just memories to savor, because this year the entire process will be taped, then televised by the Teen Style Network!"

"Omigod!" Aphro shouts, like a supa-giddy contestant on *The Price Is Right.*

I drop my jaw like a sun-kissed guppy, then announce, "I *think* I won the bet!"

Amid a cacophony of screams and shout-outs, Ms.

Fab smiles before she explains that film crews will have unlimited access to Fashion International.

"I expect everyone to come to my office and sign a waiver. If you don't sign a waiver, you cannot be captured on tape—and I know everyone is dying for their close-up, right?" coaxes Ms. Fab. "Oh—the episodes will begin airing next spring. But please be advised, our faculty has absolutely no control over the footage the network uses, so please do *not* prance to my office putting in requests!"

Suddenly, I freeze. "What does that mean?" I say to Angora. She squinches her nose and smiles.

"We are counting on *every* student—whether you are a Catwalk House member or not—to remember that you are indeed a representative of Fashion International and are expected to carry yourself like a true fashionista," Ms. Fab warns.

Now I tug Angora's fluffy sweater sleeve. Her blue eyes are beaming so brightly they look like metallic Christmas balls dangling from a well-lit, overdecorated tree.

"I can't do this," I moan.

"What do you mean, *chérie?*" Angora asks.

It's easy for Angora to get excited by the possibility of roaming cameras. I shudder thinking about a camera crew following me home to my dilapidated neighborhood. "Great. Maybe they can tape the drug dealers on

114th Street while they're engaged in a transaction!" I gripe.

"So what?" Aphro says with a shrug. So what? At least Mrs. Maydell keeps their home spotless. "Don't let 'em come to your house."

"That's right, *mija*," seconds Felinez.

"Well, we have to get into a house first before we can worry about them following us home," Angora advises. "Let's just take one Baby Phat step at a time."

"Right now, we're taking one Baby Phat step into the Mambo Hut and buying you a Mambolatte!" Felinez says.

"Afterward, let's hit the job board—and pray," groans Aphro. "I've got to make some money."

"I hear that," I moan.

"Me *tambien*!" Felinez joins in.

Chandelier throws a glare in our direction. "Fasten your Gucci seat belt, girls, because we're in for the roller-coaster ride of our style-driven lives," I predict.

"That's good for our Catwalk Credo," Angora advises. I whip out my pad and scribble. Then I poke Aphro to watch Chandelier as she air-kisses Nole into oblivion.

"Oh, Gucci hoochie, *puhleez*!" Aphro chortles.

For once, we don't poke Aphro into silence.

## FASHION INTERNATIONAL 35TH ANNUAL
## CATWALK COMPETITION BLOG

New school rule: You don't have to be ultranice, but don't get tooooo catty, or your posting will be zapped by the Fashion Avengers!!

BLING BLING IS THEIR THING. . . .
Some misguided soles circle around their hoop dreams instead of facing them head-on. No, we're not talking about the electronically tainted types at Dalmation Tech populating those skanky basketball courts in hopes of channeling video-gaming addictions. We're talking about certain fashionistas right here at Fashion International who have banded together into posses based on the bling quotient of their baubles and bangles. One so-called *purrlicious* posse comes to mind: we see them every day, prancing around our bubble-gum pink hallways with primp-ready purpose, intent on reinventing the fashion wheel with their kitten-size talent. So far, these feline flashers number four, which is why we have aptly dubbed them the "Bling Quartet." Perhaps it's time to define the real meaning of the term "fashionista"—an emblem most of us wear like a badge of honor because we value its connotation of a person with fashion humility who relies on the *established* and *enduring* design icons from Pucci to Gucci for inspiration. My advice to real fashionistas who are *serious* about earning their street cred on Seventh Avenue: stay away from

the Bling Quartet's glare, or you'll get a sunburn. And don't be fooled by their bling ambition, which they believe will outshine the rest of us at the Catwalk competition. We know who is the 23-karat topping on *this* opulent fashion sundae—and who is *definitely* not the cat's *MEOWCH*!

9/17/2008 4:00:03 PM
Posted by: Shimmy Choo to YOU

# 4

One week after the Catwalk nominations, it's time to hit the campaign trail. The thirteen house leader candidates, as well as our "committee members" (aka our closest crew), have been allowed to exit last period earlier than the "civilian" students so we can set up our Catwalk election tables in the corridor on the main floor. Despite the twenty-minute grace period, time is not on our side. When the bell chimes at three p.m., it will be helter-skelter as the fashion locusts descend on our tables to get up close and personal with the candidates—and the freebies. Then at five o'clock sharp, the schmoozefest will be officially over so everyone can cast their ballots at the voting booth set up in the Fashion Annex.

Despite my sweaty underarms and pounding heartbeat, running my Catwalk election campaign is more fun and ghoulish than celebrating Halloween. Not only do we get to wear costumes for the occasion, but we've also had our share of tricks *and* treats.

Speaking of tricks, Shalimar Jackson and her jaded

cronies sneak up the back stairwell, flinging open the fire exit door so quickly that they alarm us with their caco*phony* of terror. I don't mean to stare, but Shalimar's stretchy Lycra dress is so short she looks like a peacock plucked of its plumes. Her equally hard stare makes me feel embarrassed about the back alley location of my election station. Okay, so it's not really in a back alley, but my table is pushed so far into the corner of the dimly lit hallway that if I turned my back and accidentally lost my balance, I'd probably knock open the fire exit and go tumbling like Alice in Wonderland down the stairwell into a rabbit hole.

"Bling, bling, bling!!" heckle Shalimar and her best friend, Zirconia, running past us.

"*What* was that?" I ask, stunned by Shalimar's latest shenanigans as her bubble butt bounces off to her election table, which is in a prime retail location at the end of the wide and brightly lit intersection.

"I didn't want to mention it, *chérie*, but someone posted an entry on the new Catwalk competition blog, referring to us as the Bling Quartet. I guess we're supposed to be, um, supa-show-offs," Angora reports hesitantly.

"Did Rouge rip out your tongue? I mean, *now* you're telling us this?" I ask nastily.

"What happened? I didn't know the Catwalk blog was already up," Felinez demands.

Neither did I. I'm so mad at Angora for not keeping our ear to the street. "You're supposed to be the reporter, so start reporting!" I advise her sharply. I may have a few blind spots—like my hissy catlike temperament—but that doesn't mean I like being blindsided by a Shimmy Choo–wearing chortler. "Who was it, do you know?" I ask, even though I don't want to know.

"Take a Gucci guess," Angora says.

I snatch the paper place marker with my name off the bare table in disgust so we can begin setting up.

"We might as well be positioned behind a scaffold. Then at least we could put up a sign, 'Open During Construction,' " I gripe.

"I'm telling you I think somebody bribed *somebody*—that's what's up," huffs Aphro.

Angora breaks into a skeptical smile.

"We're not pulling your weave. It's true!" Aphro continues. Angora is naive about the wicked ways of the Big Apple. "Trust, Kentucky Fried Chicken is not the only source of greasy fingers in this gritty city."

"Oh, come on, *mijas,* it's the last day," Felinez says, rubbing my shoulders.

I throw the kitty tablecloth on our table with extra vigor. Angora runs her hand gingerly across the tablecloth, an adorable hot-pink faux fur fabric trimmed with winking cat's-eye sparkling decals. Sometimes, Angora seems so fragile—her delicate touch, her soft nature. Maybe that's why I can't help pushing her around. I don't mean to, but I guess that's *my* nature.

"Chérie, I'm merely a kitty in the city just like you—clawing my way to the top. Why don't we work together?" Angora says, her eyes blinking rapidly because she's upset.

My nerves are on edge because Chintzy Colon has just plopped some homestyle Boricua hors d'oeuvres on her table, which is adjacent to ours, and the aroma is overwhelming.

"We *would* have to be set up next to her chorizo factory!" moans Felinez.

Anna Rex's black lace–swathed table is to the left of Chintzy's, and she doesn't seem too happy with the pungent odors, either. The sight of Chintzy's edible wares must be causing her sensory overload. I can tell by the deliberate way Anna keeps folding her promo pamphlets, as if she has obsessive-compulsive disorder. Anna turns up her nose, whispering furtively to her disciples, who are as skinny as she is and also dressed in black. She's probably nervous about her whole campaign going up in smoke, even though in Anna's case that wouldn't be such a bad idea.

Meanwhile, Moet Major, whose table is to the left of Anna Rex's, prances up and down the hall, showing off her new black satin baseball jacket with HOUSE OF MOET embroidered on the back in golden letters.

"A little presumptuous, no?" I hiss.

Felinez shakes her head in agreement. She's freaking out, too: she worked so hard over the past week supplying us with our treats—namely, matching babydoll T-shirts with our slogan emblazoned on the front in fuchsia letters: STYLE SHOULD MAKE YOU PURR. Felinez also made Angora a blue catsuit so stretchy it yawns and a purple one for Aphro, as well as matching catty masks with tinted plucky whiskers. Now Angora is opening up her powder blue travel bag on wheels, chirping away anxiously—another one of her nervous habits.

"You dragged that on the bus?" Aphro asks, impressed.

Angora hates the subway and the scurrilous furry friends who hang out on the train tracks like crew. As a matter of facto, she won't set foot down under unless she's with us; otherwise, she travels everywhere on the bus. Considering the route Angora takes to school—straight down Broadway—it's not a bad idea. She lives with her father on Eighty-ninth Street off Riverside Drive, an area that has the added green benefit of Riverside Park right by her tootsies. Even after two years, Angora is still getting used to the city and all its noise.

The mention of a bus has obviously jarred her memory about her morning jaunt. "Have you ever been on one of these new, super-long buses? I mean, I don't know about all that snaking around," Angora starts in. "Those buses are sooo long, they scare me. I actually don't think the front of the bus knows what the back is doing all the time." Angora sways from side to side to make her point as she pulls a huge bag of furry items out of her bag. We watch in amazement. She really should be a reporter. I could even see her doing the weather: *It's raining Dolce and Gabbana booties today,* mes chéries!

"What have you whipped up like a soufflé today?" Felinez asks, imitating Angora.

"Okay, I thought this would be *très* adorable— they're fur balls for the wrist or the hair. They go with our feline fatale message," Angora says, her eyes widening, which means she wants our approval. I pick up one of the fluffy pink pom-poms on an elastic band with a paper tag attached to it that says in tiny letters: EARN YOUR PURR POINTS TODAY.

"Fur balls, get it? Rouge tried to eat one this morning. Like the ones she spits up aren't big enough!" Angora's cat, Rouge, has a finicky system: she is constantly coughing up something or sniffling from allergies, and only bottled water touches that finicky tongue.

Felinez spurts out what I'm thinking: "*Mija,* this must have cost a lot, no?"

Suddenly I feel guilty. Angora is down for our cause, so how could I snap at her even if her father does have

71

funny money to funnel for furry excesses. I guess I would be jealous if Angora didn't despise her psychotically perfect control freak of a mother so much.

"They kept me up all night," Angora says proudly.

"*Tan* coolio," coos Felinez, arranging the fur balls on the table so we can get on with our flow.

Suddenly, the cackling from the corner table reaches a high pitch. I glance down the hallway and stare involuntarily at Shalimar as she shimmers away in her metallic gray turtleneck minidress. Her friend Zirconia is wearing a matching sweater dress in vanilla, all the better for showing off her matching bubble butt.

"Leave it to the knit wits to put the emphasis on 'sachet' instead of 'sashay,' which carries more clout in my prop portfolio, okay," I observe, watching carefully as the bubblemint twins pile ivory sachets on their table.

"Hold this end," Aphro says, nudging me back to our duties. I grab the end of the hot-pink banner with our election campaign slogan in spotted pink letters—STYLE SHOULD MAKE YOU PURR—and step onto the chair so we can tape it above our table.

"*Purr*fecto!" Felinez says, nodding approvingly.

Stepping down from the chair, I put the basket of pink satin meowch pouches on the table just in time to catch another back stairwell entry.

"How you doin'?" asks this guy, his face settling into what looks like a permanent smirk.

"Feline groovy," I respond, handing him a meowch pouch, which causes him to snicker sweetly.

I have never seen this goofy cute guy before, but apparently Felinez has, because she greets him by his name. "Hi, Ice Tray!"

Before he can even respond, she shoves a pamphlet into his hand and starts our spiel: "You can earn your purr points today by voting for Pashmina Purrstein!"

"I can do that," he says, breaking into a grin that reveals his giganto rabbit front teeth. Running my eyes up and down his downtrodden decor like a human scanner, I take in his graffiti-tainted hoodie and Hefty Bag–gy jeans that are falling so far down his butt you could make a deposit in his coin slot.

Angora greets him with her usual charming curiosity. She is so nice to everybody. I have to thank her later for keeping her eye on the prize: voters.

"Where did you get your name?" Angora asks, using a technique we learned in Salesmanship: always focus on something about the customer to stimulate interest.

"It's my tag," he says proudly.

"You mean, like your design label?" Angora quizzes.

"Nah—more like for my art."

Suddenly, I realize that Ice Tray is referring to the

intricate doodlings left behind by grafitti artists on practically any surface in the Big Apple that will take to spray paint. All the buildings in Amsterdam Gardens are "decorated" by taggers. For all his blustering, Mr. Darius has never caught anybody defacing the property, and of course, he's too cheap to get the walls repainted.

"It's *très*—you know, like French?" he explains proudly.

"Oh," Angora says, beaming.

"Wazzup with your name?" Ice Très asks Angora.

"She looked like a goat when she was born—without the horns, of course," I quip.

"Oh, you mean cuddly—like *you*," he teases.

"Actually, my mother thought it was a pretty name for a girl with good breeding—she is very proud of her French heritage, by way of Canada," Angora interupts.

"What about *your* name?" Ice Très asks me.

"My mother wanted her daughters to live in the lap of luxury, I guess," I say, shrugging because I realize it sounds pretentious. It sounds more endearing when Mom says it.

"*Ayiight.* Well, I'm trying to get to Paris in a few to study art," Ice Très informs us.

Now I wonder what he's doing at our school, but he clears that mystery right up—at least geographically.

"I just moved here from Hamilton, Washington.

We had to outrun the Pineapple Express," he says. I have no idea what he's talking about, but Felinez perks up at the sound of an exotic dish. "See, we was always getting flooded out. Tropical water coming up from Hawaii made the river situation a little too hectic round our way, so my family got tired of that and we moved here."

Felinez listens with sympathy as he continues, "Thought about going to High School of Visual Arts, but everybody knows the honeys are over here!" Ice Três chuckles, winking and blinking again—at me.

"Wow, that's deep," I retort, impressed—not—at how he turned a natural pineapple disaster into a shallow move for honey dipping.

"I know, right," he says mischievously. "Nah, on the real, I wanna open my own company, Fashion Thug, you know, with hand-painted denim joints and whatnot—and jeans that fit big booties *specifically.*"

Felinez winces and makes a face behind his back like, *Don't do me any design favors, graci-ass!*

I take a closer look at the graffiti on his jeans, checking out the details, which causes Ice Três to jump on an explanation like a firefighter with a water hose. "These are from PRPS—you know, it's pronounced 'purpose.' I got a lot of their joints from Pieces on 135th. Their wash is *sick!*"

"Pamphlets, please," orders Aphro, signaling that

our chat with Ice Très is over. Time is tick-tocking away.

"Awright, check y'all later." Ice Très breaks out.

After he walks away, Angora says approvingly, "I think Mr. Ice Très is *très* smitten with you."

"*Claro que sí*. Nobody is ever smitten with me!" Felinez says, pouting. "Not when you two are around."

"I'm sorry, but I am not interested in members of the thugeration," I say offhandedly, even though I think with the right makeover Ice Très could be even tastier than a croissant. But Felinez is right: whenever guys come flocking like geese, they treat her like she's a hologram. What's up with that?

Aphro, however, is oblivious to Felinez's feelings: "So is that a no on a hug from a thug?"

"Yes," I say firmly.

"Yes to a hug, or no to the thug?" Aphro continues.

"Yes—I mean, no!"

Luckily, the bell rings. "Showtime!"

Watching the students pour into the hallway, I tap my feet impatiently. It will take them forever to snake down the corridor to us—especially now that Chintzy will be plying potentials with chunky chorizos! I also can't help but notice how many guys stop to congregate by Shalimar's scentsation. Even Ice Très stops to do a buffalo stance. Shalimar pushes one of her sachets up to his nose, causing him to break out in his rabbit grin. Now

I know he's not a true artist; if he were he wouldn't have fallen for Shalimar's sham (and I'm not referring to her pillows, either).

"Maybe we should have padded our booties for the occasion," I say, wincing.

"Someone is green with Gucci Envy," chides Angora.

As usual, Angora is on *punto*.

"Maybe I'd better rethink my position on, um, aspiring visual artists," I say pensively. "After all, I am originally from the Boogie Down, where graffiti art was born on the cars of the IRT subway line." Staring at him with my mouth open, I wonder if Ice Très sensed that I wasn't digging his doodlings. "Close it!" Aphro shouts.

"You talking to me?" queries Zeus, who I didn't see hovering in back of me.

"No—not you!" shrieks Aphro, letting out a snort.

Now I want to gaspitate over zebra stripes, but instead, I quickly snap into election mode. "Hi, I'm Pashmina Purrstein and I'm running for Catwalk house leader."

"I'm Zeus," he says, grinning. I try not to stare at his chiseled cheekbones. Zeus, on the other hand, is trying to show me his artistic side. "I dig your slogan— 'Style Should Make You Purr.' I can do a lot with that visually—I'm a graphic artist. We have three cats, too."

"Who's 'we'?" I ask, wondering if he means his

family. I'm always curious about other people: if they have more than I do—like a real father, or even a mother who *maybe* talks about their father sometimes, hello.

"Oh—my mom and dad. And I got two sisters. You'd dig my mom; she's crazy about cats. My dad was upset when she brought the third cat home. But she was like 'What do you want me to do? Cats are like potato chips, you can't have just one!' "

Angora laughs loudly. She just loves sound bites. Zeus stands like a statue and rests his left hand on the back of his hat, which I gather now is like his security blankie. "I'm serious. I could do a lot with your catty theme—um, visually. I major in display and whatnot."

"Yeah, you said that before," I say, nodding. But before I can continue, Zeus fills me in on the rest of his credentials like he's auditioning, when I'm the one trying to snag a vote—and maybe even more than that.

"I'm also a deejay, so I could hone in on your whole vibe—you know, laying down rap over tracks."

I'm not surprised by Zeus's allegiance to hip-hop— anybody could spot the flavor he savors. "Yeah, Angora told me you're a deejay. But you're a model, too, right?"

Zeus blushes *big*-time, staring down at his sneakers. Definitely Adidas. "Yeah, I'm trying to get a hookup with Vanna Snoot. She's a customer of my father's," he admits like he's embarrassed.

"Straight up?" interrupts Aphro like he said the

magic password. Vanna Snoot owns Snoot, Inc., the fiercest model agency in New York. As if reading our minds, Zeus elaborates. "My dad owns a custom tailor shop on Fifty-ninth Street under the bridge."

"I think I've seen that shop," I say. His dad's shop is next to the Snoot agency. We've all canvassed the block hoping to get a glimpse of the goings-on inside Snooty Central, which is housed in a three-story pink building with gilded window shutters that beckon like an attraction at Madison Square Garden on Halloween: scary but inviting.

"My dad makes a lot of clothes for her—and the models, too," Zeus continues. "Anyway, he's trying to get me an appointment. He showed her a Polaroid—I couldn't believe he did that, man."

"Can he get you an appointment?" I ask.

"She wants to know—can you get us an appointment, okay?" Aphro asks him point-blank.

"I hear you. Word is, Vanna doesn't see anybody," Zeus says, undefeated. "And you know the policy about students from Fashion International."

I sigh knowingly. The only model wannabes from our school who get snagged by agencies are winners from the Catwalk competition.

"See, that's why I want to lead a house," I confide. The reason we're all hyped about Snoot, Inc., is that they break new faces.

I wonder if Zeus is a "friend of Dorothy's." Not all the guys in our school are gay, contrary to the snick-erings from the bozos across the street. Like Ice Très so aptly put it: everybody knows the fiercest honeys go to Fashion International.

"Um, you know about our theme?" Angora asks Zeus.

"Yeah, I can see it," Zeus says astutely.

"And we're definitely catering to the Kats and Kit-ties!" I say, interrupting her.

"Well, you've got my vote," Zeus says, beaming.

After he leaves, Angora announces: "Wouldn't it be great to have him in our house?"

"Well, I've got to get elected first," I say, staring longingly after Zeus's shadow.

Now Nole Canoli and his best friend, super-exotic Elgamela Sphinx, stand swooning at Chandelier Spinelli's table. Nole holds a pair of her giveaways—chandelier earrings, of course—to Countess Coco's furry, pointy ears.

After a few more snickers, Nole's entourage marches down the hall.

"Oops, here come the cattle," Angora says, beam-ing. My eyes lock with Nole's, and he looks like a deer caught in the headlights. I know he's voting for Chan-delier Spinelli, but I break into a grin and hand him a fur ball anyway.

"Ooh, that would look so cute on Countess's

collar!" coos Elgamela, who wasted no time dangling Chandelier's sparkly giveaways from her own perfect earlobes, further accenting her Arabian princess aura. Today, she even has an amber crystal stuck in the middle of her forehead.

"Oh, that's my version of a Bindi!" she explains giggling, catching me staring and tossing her long, dark wavy hair. Suddenly she's fascinated by something we have, too. "What's that?" Elgamela asks, pointing to the pink satin meowch pouches.

"Felinez makes them," I announce proudly. "They're called meowch pouches and you can wear them on your wrist or around your neck. And you *are* such a feline fatale."

"Here, *mija*, take one!" Felinez says, shoving one in Elgamela's hand. She hesitates for a second, which prompts Aphro to chortle. "Girl, we know you're voting for *Chandelier*, but don't be bashful when it comes to booty!"

"Spoken like a true pirate," Nole says, giggling.

After they leave, I feel a twinge of sadness. "I wish we could snag Nole for our house, no?"

"Pash, I thought you said you despised his gawdy Gucci tendencies?" Angora asks, quoting me verbatim.

"Yeah, well, I'm prepared to believe his hype. Everybody says he's gonna be the next Versace," I offer, pouting.

A student interrupts our little huddle and I automatically snap into vote-for-me mode. "Hi, I'm Pashmina Purrstein. I'm running for house leader."

"I know who you are. My textile science class is next to your runway class. I saw you in action, too," the girl says, giggling. I scan her quickly and notice that she's hiding behind her big black sweater—kinda like Felinez used to before she began expressing herself bigtime.

"Um, you know anything about our style philosophy?" I ask her gently.

She shakes her head in the negative.

"What's your name?"

"Janilda."

"Look, Felinez and I have had it up to here with the plus-size clothing market. We're even sick of that distinction. New millennium girls kick it in every size—and that's what the House of Pashmina will be featuring in our fashion show," I say proudly.

Janilda's pretty eyes brighten.

"And that's not just for the Catwalk competition. My career goal is to open a chain of stores—Purr Unlimited—that will break boundaries by offering our fly private label collection in every size."

"We're gonna be like that Florida orange juice company—own the land, the growers, the oranges!" Felinez shouts.

"You got your strategy *down*." Janilda chuckles.

"You never met Felinez before?" I ask, surprised.

"Um, no, I've seen her around," Janilda explains.

"Oh—when you said textile science—"

"Yeah, but I *major* in textile science."

"Oh. Felinez majors in accessory design, but she will be my right hand, my partner in our enterprise. And, um—"

"But aren't you, like, going to be a model? I mean, a major model?" Janilda asks.

"For true." Because I understand that not everyone is up on our whole modelpreneur philosophy, I break it down further for Janilda.

"You are *major*!" she coos when I finish. "I like that—'modelpreneur.' Well, you've got my vote!"

Janilda bounces away.

"We're gonna be the Ben and Jerry of the fashion *mundo*—scooping up profits, *big-time!*" I coo after her.

Angora and Felinez cross paws with me on that one.

But just when I think I can celebrate my victory, along comes Chenille.

"Hi, Chenille!" coos Angora, shaking a fur ball against the front of Chenille's overalls.

Chenille looks down at the fur ball positioned at her ample chest, then grabs it and even reads the slogan before announcing to me: "Oops, you missed a spongie." My mouth drops open as I clasp at my curls, searching for a runaway sponge roller. *"Psych,"* Chenille hisses.

*Where's Grandma Pritch when I need her?* I think, glaring at my sourpuss sister.

"Um, gotta go. See you later," Chenille says dourly.

I watch Chenille waddle down the hall in her baggy denim overalls and suddenly I get a flashback to the sixth grade. One day after class, I saw Chenille standing in the hallway, gabbing away with her friends, with my favorite black crochet shoulder bag flung over her shoulder like it was hers. I was so pissed that I walked up to Chenille and took my bag off her shoulder, turning it upside down, dumping all her stuff on the floor. Chenille's arms started flailing all around, but that's where the advantage of being a foot taller came in very handy. I just pulled her hair and kept her at arm's length. Too bad a school monitor appeared out of nowhere and escorted us both to the principal's office. Obviously, the principal was none too happy when she figured out that we were sisters. "You two should be ashamed of yourselves!" she hurled at us. I wasn't, but Mom was. She said that I was selfish and didn't even reprimand Chenille for borrowing my bag without asking me. Ever since then, I guess you could say my sister and I have been on a Rocky Road binge.

"Well, so much for Ben and Jerry," I muse out loud.

*"Chérie,* she's gonna vote for you," Angora says.

"She'd better do my hair—for free!" Aphro chortles.

"If I were you, I'd spend my ducats on a *real* hair-stylist," I hiss back. The magic hour is upon us and I start packing up our toys so we can go home.

Aphro senses my discomfort and throws a fur ball at my head. "I'm just gonna *weave* that one alone!"

## FASHION INTERNATIONAL 35TH ANNUAL
## CATWALK COMPETITION BLOG

New school rule: You don't have to be ultranice, but don't get tooooo catty, or your posting will be zapped by the Fashion Avengers!!

TRUE PIRATES <u>LOVE</u> THE "BOOTY." . . .

Last night, thirteen Catwalk candidates plied us potential voters with stylin' spiels and swag before we headed to the Fashion Annex to cast our ballots. The campaign antics may be over, but the drama quotient is about to quadruple seven times a Pucci scarf square once the election results are posted on Thursday! In the meantime, I feel compelled to break down last night's booty (and I'm not referring to Shalimar in that skintight Silverado Express dress either, which made her look like she was having chipmunks in reverse!). After I chomped on Chintzy Colon's chorizos, which were exactly how I like my fashion—*hot, hot, hot!*—I proceeded to angle for a pair of danglers from the candidate with the highest fabulosity factor, Chandelier Spinelli. Now, that's when I couldn't help but overhear *another* candidate complaining about the expenses incurred for her "She Shells." If Chantez Whining, oops, Winan, wanted to make a *splash,* she should have been asking herself: "Is this bootylicious enough for ya, babe?" I was not born yesterday, so I can tell when someone's freebies have been lifted from the dirty shores of

86

Jones Beach—for free—thereby counter-
acting the whole inherent pleasure
of receiving goodies and giveaways!
Obviously certain candidates should
keep a dictionary right by their Lee
press-on nails so they can look up the
definition for the word "swag" and
start appreciating its acronym: *stuff
we all get* (and deserve)!!

9/23/2008 10:45:34 AM
Posted by: Miss FLUFF

# 5

The next day I sniff my underarms and detect the distinct smell of Swiss poodle. In one hour, the names of the five elected house leaders will be posted outside the Fashion Café. I'm bouncing off the walls worrying about the results, which is why I shimmied out early from physics so Felinez and I could rendezvous in the Fashion Lounge.

"How come walking up and down the bathroom doesn't make time go faster? Newton was a *fig*," I complain nervously.

Felinez is more concerned with fashion reality than the laws of motion. "What is that stain, *mija?*"

She is pointing to the ashy white ring on my brown suede fringed moccasins. "I can't believe it!" I shriek.

"You stepped into water with alkaline properties," Felinez says in her distressed Boricua accent.

"Alka-*what*? The toilet in my house overflowed this morning!" I cry in disgust. "I *had* to sop up the water so I could take a shower. If I waited for Mr. Darius to come, we would have floated away in a tsunami!"

Felinez knows firsthand the fringe benefits of living in a brokedown palace. "Really, *mija*, he is the worst landlord. You should report him," she advises.

"To whom?" I counter. "Note to fashion self: shower with sheep in my sleep instead. It'll be safer!"

Right now, I hope Felinez also knows how to remedy my ruination. I was psyched about debuting my Power-to-the-Prairie outfit today, from the brown faux suede fringed miniskirt to the beaded ceremony necklace. "All this in the hopes of snagging a pow wow in Zeus's tepee," I moan, stroking the embroidered succotash headband I tied around my forehead after I tamed my frizzy hair with Elasta QP Glaze, which is Miracle Whip for girls like me who are knotty by nature. Trust, it's the only way I'm able to work my native plaits.

"I knew you liked him!" Felinez squeals.

"Oy, wait till he sees me. He's gonna call me Dances in Toilet Water!" I predict.

"Don't worry, I got the Nu-Hide cleaner from leather class in my locker. I can fix it," Felinez assures me.

"Thank *gooseness* my best friend is such a GENIUS!" I quip in my goofy voice. "Let's go by your locker, then hit the job board before the zoo lets out."

Speaking of animals, Chandelier barges into the bathroom with Tina the Hyena. Chandelier, however, is acting more like an anxious antelope. She gallops to the sink and stands so closely to me that the blast from her breath opens my pores. "Who needs Bioré strips when you're around," I mumble under my breath. Instead of apologizing, she stares at me wide-eyed like her pupils are adjusting to the reality of competing in the food chain.

"I thought of you," she says, rubbing lipstick from her teeth, "when I was getting a root canal yesterday."

"Silly me. I thought having capped teeth made excavation a moot point," I counter.

Chandelier stares down at the ring around my footsies, then cuts to her Gucci loafers, then to Tina, like she's doing a Woodbury Common outlet commercial. "Exclusive edition," she declares to Tina.

"*Puhleez*. They grind those out like Parks sausages!" I retort angrily. Felinez snickers loudly as we flee the Fashion Lounge. "God, she's such a primping *predator*."

After we zap the water stains, we dash for a ducat alert at the job board. I send a text message to Aphro and Angora to meet us outside the Fashion Café later for the "showdown at the okie-dokie."

Meanwhile, Felinez is fretting about her Italian homework. "*Io sono malata*," Felinez says, reading from her notebook. " '*Malata*' means 'sick' and not 'mulatto'?"

"Mos def."

"How do you say 'mulatto,' then?"

"I don't know, but I bet you in Italian they say something less slavery-oriented," I shoot back. Every

Black History Month, my mom makes us watch *Roots* together, and inevitably she blurts out, "I hate that word, 'mulatto.' " Probably because that's what I am, even though she never told me.

"God, I can't wait till we go to Italy," Felinez says, psyched, then cringes. "If we win, I mean."

"We'd better," I retort, echoing our Catwalk Code: *Act fierce even when you're not feeling it.*

Felinez smiles assuredly.

"Let's sashay by Ms. Fab's office," I whisper to Felinez, in an effort to quelch my own anxiety.

*"Por que?* What for?"

"Maybe we'll get first whiff of the It List," I say sneakily. Creeping closer, we get a whiff, all right—of a conversation not meant for our ears. "That's a good idea for reaction shots," advises Ms. Lynx, her voice of authority trailing into the hallway. "But you should stick around the Fashion Café afterward—and do try today's special, jambalaya gumbo. I hear it's divine."

"Any reason why?" asks an unfamiliar voice.

"There's nothing like Cajun peppers to put blush back in your cheeks. Oh—you mean—well, you'll see," Ms. Fab adds emphatically.

We stand still like undercover fashion spies trying to decipher Ms. Lynx's cryptic instructions.

Seconds later, four scruffy-looking men and one petite woman pop out of Ms. Fab's office. I freeze when I see the familiar logo on their equipment bags: TEEN STYLE NETWORK. I quickly examine my ceremony necklace like I'm searching for hidden hieroglyphics. Luckily, the crew seems too distracted to notice us. The lady has a pixie haircut and is dressed in grungy sneakers, jeans, and a green camouflage jacket. She points at one of the neon signs in the hallway: LEAVE YOUR CORNS ON THE COB. NO BARE FEET, PLEASE.

"Jay, get a shot of that," she orders, motioning to one of the guys hoisting a camera bag.

Jay hops to the task.

"Omigod! Ay, *dios mio!*" Felinez shrieks, once we're out of earshot. "Do you think Ms. Lynx is on the jinx?"

Instinctively, I know what Felinez is referring to. For the past twenty years it's been a secret tradition at FI to kick off the Catwalk competitions with a quickie voguing battle known as a pose-off once the leaders have been chosen.

"Don't be *radickio*. *If* she knew about our pose-off, we'd all be banned to Style Siberia," I shoot back, but my shuddering shoulders aren't so convinced. See, end-of-season markdowns aren't the only thing fashionistas can count on: disobey any of Fashion International's cardinal rules—like "no voguing in hallways"—and suspension is imminent. The loophole that fashionistas have hidden behind for twenty years, however, is this:

nobody said *anything* about voguing in the Fashion Café. People who already have props wouldn't understand why we would risk suspension for something that seems so silly, but they don't understand. See, we can't control the outcome of the Catwalk competition, but at least *we* decide how we're gonna set it off.

As we approach the job board, another thing becomes Swarovski crystal clear: we also can't control the competition for all the job postings. "This is a mob scene. We might as well be standing in a line for a fashion show at Bryant Park!" I huff.

"I know, *mija*. You'd think they were giving away swag!" Felinez groans, trying to jockey for space in the huddling masses. I reach into my purse to retrieve my pink pen and jab Diamond Tyler in the chest. Turning swiftly to meet her gaze, I'm relieved that her Victoria's Secret push-up padded bra with revolutionary patent-pending technology obviously softened the impact of my intruding elbow. (During gym period, I saw her in the cute scallop-edged "Secret" in the locker room.)

"I voted for you!" Diamond blurts out.

"Now, that's what's up," I respond gratefully, but I can't help but notice that Diamond has a serious case of ring around the eyes.

"Is everything cool?" I ask her.

"I was up all night with Crutches," she says, and

seems relieved someone noticed. Crutches is Diamond's cat, who was born with weak legs and has trouble walking.

"I've been taking her to swimming lessons, and the muscles in her back legs are getting stronger, but she was moaning all night cuz I pushed too hard," confides Diamond.

"Yeah—but it'll be worth it. Crutches'll be sashaying in no time!" I chuckle.

"That sounds more like Fabbie," Diamond offers shyly, a troubled look clouding her misty green eyes. "God, I never have any luck with these jobs. I think I'm gonna try the animal shelters."

"Really? You mean volunteering?" I ask. What I really want to ask her is, doesn't she need the seven dollars an hour like we do?

"*Mija*, this one looks good," Felinez says, interrupting the currency exchange. She points to a posting for the Betsey Johnson boutique.

"Omigod, I would do a kitty mambo in my bloomers just to work there," I concur. Diamond grins at me like she wishes she had my gusto. Little does she know that it comes from having nothing to lose but my hopefulness. Felinez continues to scan the postings for an assistant schlep job in any designer showroom, which would be primo for her.

"Oooh, this one," I say, pointing to a posting for

Ruff Loner showroom assistant. "No ducats, but internship credit."

"No way, José. I don't care if I have to fold the same pashmina scarf fifty times as long as we work together!" Felinez testifies like a preacher.

"Stick to a showroom," I protest, pulling out my cell phone. "It's time you put your pattern-making skills to a test."

"If I can't work with you, then I'd rather spend all my time making the accessories for our fashion show," Felinez declares defiantly. "At least *that* freebie means a chance at flying the Friendly Skies—for free!"

"Hold up, Tonto. Let's wait and see if there will be a House of Pashmina, then I'll demand you devote your every waking *minuto*," I advise her, positioning myself in a corner for privacy so I can get a leg up on the competition. Just to make sure, I suck in my stomach.

"You think they're gonna see your flat stomach on the phone?" Felinez asks, whacking me in the midsection.

Shooing her away, I speak in my professional voice. "Um, hello, I'm calling from Fashion International." Meanwhile, the girl on the other end informs me in her brittle British accent, "We're not taking any more applicants at the moment. *Not* from Fashion International."

Humiliated, I hang up. "Do you think she could tell

on the phone I'm black?" I ponder out loud because I can hear my mother's voice ringing in my ears. She got played back in the day trying to snag A-list jobs. And even when she did get hired at two-star boutiques, she was constantly reminded that the cocoa color of her skin stood in the way of a payday or promotions.

Felinez, however, snaps me back to reality—literally. "No, Pocahontas, I don't think so!" she says, yanking one of my braids to make her *punto*.

"Well, Miss Prickly Pennyweather didn't know how fabulous we are!" I gripe, writing down more job postings in my notebook, but I decide to wait until later to resume cold calling so I can put on my cheerful voice.

Despite our layover at the job board, we arrive outside the Fashion Café before the Catwalk announcement is posted. Some of the usual suspects are posed in place.

"Wazzup, pussycat!" yelps Ice Très. He has a chartreuse messenger bag slung over his shoulder. It's tagged with his wannabe brand, FASHION THUG in silver metallic letters. I gaze at his sly smile and realize that he may not be as tasty as a Toll House, but he is definitely crunchy. Maybe it's time to yank Shalimar's silver spoon. That's what up, until Zeus rolls up on us. Today, he's carrying his sweet sound system with a purpose known only to us. "I'm ready to crank it up," he confesses, crossing paws with Ice Très.

I stand with a hand on my hip, checking them out while they start riffing about an assignment in Illustration, then switch to the subject of sneakers. Suddenly, Zeus realizes that I'm being left out of the mix. "We're serious sneakerheads, ya dig?" he explains.

Meanwhile, Shalimar must also be digging Ice Très, because she rolls right up. "I thought you were waiting outside biology for me?" she asks him boldly. I marvel at her sudden switch in taste sensations: obviously Zeus is no longer the cherry on top of her "opulent" fashion sundae.

"Oh, I thought you said chemistry," shrieks Ice Très, guffawing like Roger Rabbit on helium.

Speaking of infectious laughs, Angora and Aphro finally arrive on the fashion scene, too. Aphro lets out a signature snort to release her anticipation. "It's time to flip it like burgers, baby, *ayüght!*" she yelps.

"No doubt," adds Ice Très, getting his flirt on, until Shalimar puts his moves into deep freeze.

"Can I talk to you for a second?" she asks him in her best Mrs. Softee voice, pulling him aside.

Ice Très shrinks inside his hoodie, smiling coyly as he's dragged to the sidelines.

"What's up with that?" Aphro asks me.

"Shalimar is obviously *hood*winked," I say offhandedly, trying to keep the situation Lite FM.

"I wonder what she put in those sachets? Maybe we should have taken a whiff," adds Felinez.

"Probably some of that Frankenstein stuff," Aphro says with conviction.

"Frankincense," Angora says.

"Whatever." Aphro snorts again, becoming fascinated with the burnished metal symbol on my ceremony necklace. "Oooh, what's up with this?" asks Aphro. She loves symbolic trinkets from around the world.

"I think it stands for 'unity' in the Iroquois tribe," I say, trying to remember. I got it last year at Ooophelia's, but I haven't worn it yet because I wanted to work it with the right cultural theme, like I always do.

At last, Ms. Fab's assistants, Farfalla and Sil Lai, approach with the important papers in their hands.

"And the winner is!" Aphro says, jumping up and down. Everybody giggles. Except for Shalimar. She stands with Ice Très at her side like she's a presidential *shoe*-in. Now Aphro squirms her way up front while I stand pondering whether Ice Très is feeling Shalimar over me.

"No way, José," Felinez says out loud, resting her paw on my forearm to balance herself as she stands on her tippy-toes to no avail. "Can you see?"

"Not a whiff," I reply as Sil Lai posts the It List on the pink velvet board.

"Chérie, I can't see either," Angora adds, squinting.

Chandelier Spinelli squeals. "Guess Miss Piggy can see," I observe, clutching Felinez's sweaty paw. By now, Aphro has managed to elbow her way to the front of the fashionmongers and yells out loudly to us, "*Pashmina Purrstein, that's what I'm talking about! We're in the house. We're in the house.* Omigod. Omigod!!"

"*Yes!*" I scream, raising my cupped hand in the air.

"*No!*" someone screams through their cupped hands like they're maneuvering a bullhorn.

"Oh, snap!" yells someone else amid a round of hyena heckles. I don't turn to glare at the source of the dis. Instead, I let Felinez envelop me in a bear hug. Then I close my eyes and press my head down against her fuzzy hair.

"We did it, *mija!*" Felinez says, gurgling against my chest, clutching me tighter. I inhale the sweet scent of Fanta orange soda that always clings to Felinez's clothes. Sometimes I fiend for Fanta because of Felinez, but I've only seen those delicious orange cans in one place: "Uptown, baby, where they sip it down, baby!" I sing in my goofy voice.

Felinez giggles, then says, "Stop, *mija*. You're giving me cramps!"

I let go quickly. "Oy, I can't take two floods in one day!"

Felinez doubles over in laughter or pain; I'm not sure which, so I shut up for a *segundo*. Now Felinez's face turns red.

"I'm just playing!" I say, hugging her again. "Seriously, I can't do anything without you—not since I'm six." This time when I open my eyes, Chintzy Colon is standing nearby, staring at me, her eyes wet from fresh tears like she's a newly crowned beauty pageant contestant.

"Congratulations," I coo, over Felinez's shoulder.

"I didn't get it," Chintzy says, wincing. Then she hides quickly behind her Snap-On Smile. "I'm happy you won, though. You deserve it, Pashmina."

Now I feel janky about snapping on her. Chintzy can be cool, even if she's fortified by artificial sweeteners.

"I hope you'll choose me to be in your house," Chintzy says.

Felinez grabs my hand, so I slither away without responding, and we make our way to Aphro. I make sure, however, that we end up right near Zeus just in case he wants to beam me up.

"See, told you I voted for you!" Zeus says enthusiastically, then motions with his index finger to the lunchroom. "I'ma check you inside."

I grin like I'm flattered even though I was hoping he

would drop a few more corn niblets in my direction. Fe-linez senses my longing and pulls my sleeve like a ventriloquist so I'll gush on cue instead and not miss my five minutes of fashion fame. "God, I feel like Miss America!" I say.

"Don't say that, *mija*. You'll jinx yourself—cuz they always get caught in scandals!" Felinez warns me.

"Well, maybe I'm taking notes for my own scandal!" I declare joyously, staring at my name, the third on the list, before I make an observation that causes my smile to crumble like blue cheese. "Why is Shalimar's name first?"

Shalimar Jackson

Willi Ninja, Jr.

Pashmina Purrstein

Anna Rex

Chandelier Spinelli

"Because it's in alphabetical order, Miss Paranoid!" Angora says, wrapping her arms around me.

"Oh, right!" I respond, just in time to spot another sore loser: Moet Major who has cleverly folded her black satin baseball jacket emblazoned with HOUSE OF MOET over her arm.

"That's what they have sample sales for," Aphro says, referring to the sales where designers discard their surplus stock to make way for the next season.

"Yeah, I guess she let the cork out of the bottle

big-time," I reply. Nonetheless, I feel bad for her, because that could have been me, so we hustle inside the Fashion Café and step to the counter.

"How's the shrimp?" Felinez asks chirpily.

"So fresh, it'll crawl on your plate by itself," Velma, the crabby food attendant, shoots back.

Felinez takes a plate, then advises me to try the crab salad—so she can taste it, of course.

"No thanks, it sounds too itchy." Instead, I turn around to scratch my deep desire: to see Zeus, who is perched at a table with his sound system on top of it. He beams at me from across the room. "He's braving the fashion frontier!" I say excitedly.

While I'm busy ogling Zeus, all eyes are on Willi Ninja, Jr., who has just pranced into the Fashion Café, grinning from ear to ear, with his crew in tow. Doting Dulce stands to his side, meting out her Spadey sense. She clutches her red patent tote like she's a fashion victor.

Suddenly, I overhear Shalimar explaining our private pose-off to Ice Très in a voice louder than a boom box: "We never know when the pose-off is happening until a few hours before. I'm telling you, it's kept more top-secret than the designs for Barbie dolls, which are kept locked in the Mattel corporate vault!" she shrieks.

"I wish someone would lock her up in a vault—on time delay—and eat the key!" I grumble at my gumbo.

"Would you listen to Miss I Wanna Be Down? She'd better get that *bourgie* tone back in her voice before her parents cash in her stock options," Aphro observes accurately.

"I can't believe she's digging him," I say, puzzled.

"*Puhleez.*" Aphro hmmphs. "She's just sprinkling him to show us she can can."

Secretly, I wish Ice Très would spread some of his sprinkles around again, like he did during elections. "I wonder what she really put in those sachets," I repeat, shaking my head as Shalimar continues to babble:

"The trick is to hang loose and be ready for the signal. Like with musical chairs. Cuz once the hankie is dropped, you're supposed to stop whatever you're doing and start posing for points."

"She did *not* say for points," Aphro blurts out in disbelief. "She is such a shamorama. And always gotta explain everything in such big 'O' detail."

Leana, the other Fashion Café attendant, starts in: "You lucky I don't know how to vogue—cuz I'd show y'all how the real heffas shake it!" Cackling loudly, Leana drops a dollop of gooey gumbo on Shalimar's plate.

I turn just in time to catch the Last of the Mohicans: Nole Canoli and his crew making their timely entrance. His late arrival signals that the pose-off is about to be on. Dame Leeds looks around the café like an undercover spy, then snags a broom and runs to the door. He slides the broom sideways into the door handles, securing them. Now that the door is barred, absolutely no one will be allowed to enter the Fashion Café until the pose-off is *finito*.

"So much for the Teen Style Network," I say with relief.

The crowd breaks out into a loud round of claps and piercing yelps. Nole and his crew join Chandelier and Tina at their table, letting it be publicly known where his allegiance stands. After exchanging air kisses, Chandelier cuts her slice of pizza with a plastic fork and knife, like she's Princess Kryon at a socialite luncheon.

I'm too excited to sit down, and I can't afford to take my eyes off Willi Ninja, Jr. None of us can. We're waiting for our five minutes of fame.

In true dramatic form, Willi Ninja, Jr., signals the chef to hook him up with the special. "But don't worry about a napkin, cuz I'm gonna use my hankie! *OOPS!*" he yells loudly, dropping his white cotton hankie with a flourish on the floor, and falling into a vogue step before his body hits the shiny pink-and-gray linoleum.

Zeus cranks up the music: bold lyrics delivered in the falsetto voice of a male singer over the spaced beats of hip-hop music.

*"This is house, my house! In my house we work our*

*theme like the Dream Team. The theme of my house is more than a feeling. It's homage to house maximus à la mode. It's an attitude I'm taking straight to the bank. Homage to house maximus. Bank on my house. Next to Gucci, they get loosey. Next to Prada, there's nada. Next to my house there is victory maximus. Homage to house. For real fashionistas. Because that's what's up. You must obey the rules in my house, so repeat after me. This is house, my house! And this is my homage maximus. Pose struck!"*

The music vibrates with thunderous bass as all the students in the lunchroom break out in elaborate poses to profess our undying love for fashion. My lungs are filled with pride as I quickly observe that every single student has stepped to the Catwalk challenge. As usual, some of the more dedicated voguers have elevated their posing to a higher level by jumping on top of a lunchroom table. I stay on the floor so that I can meet Willi's gaze as he challenges each of the other four house leaders—including me. Ninja, Jr., approaches me, utilizing the clean, sharp movements inspired by martial arts that earned his legendary father the moniker he passed on to his adopted son.

Screams of "Work, supermodel or be worked!" are heard over the hypnotic hip-hop beats.

I beam at Angora, Aphro, and even Felinez, who is no slouch in the voguing department. She has her own salsafied ways of moving, which I love. Angora moves carefully, but I can tell she is serving her soufflé, as she would say. One day, I know that Angora is gonna break out and vogue like a real supermodel. I know she can.

I try to quickly take it all in: Willi Ninja, Jr., approaches Chandelier's camp. Nole is holding Countess Coco and voguing, beaming like a proud fashion papa. Elgamela Sphinx gyrates her hips like a dreamy genie rising from a bottle. I know Elgamela is going to make the fiercest catwalker, and I feel a twinge of sadness that she won't be in my house. Now I cut my eyes over to Shalimar, who is voguing with Ice Très. Once his eyes meet mine, he slithers toward me and vogues in my face, trying to press his body against mine. I block him with my outstretched arms, pushing him away. Shalimar's shady eyes rest on me, so I decide to go with Ice Très's flow just to set her off.

"Twirl!" Aphro shouts, watching Willi Ninja, Jr., who has just picked up Elgamela. In return, she stretches out her arms with complete abandon. After he puts her down to a round of applause, Willi Ninja, Jr., picks up the hankie and stretches his arms in a final pose, signaling the end of our pose-off.

Zeus turns off his tasty track, "Homage to House." Then Dame Leeds removes the broom from the doors to the Fashion Café, but not before we get off another round of victory claps. For one more year, fashionistas have pulled off our private pose-off without prying eyes upon us.

"Major purr points for Miss Angora," I say proudly.

Once the doors are swung open, the Teen Style Network crew waltzes in. Their timing is perfect—for us. Zeus zooms past me with his sound system tucked under his arm, obviously on his way to his locker to hide the evidence. "Did you lace those lyrics yourself?" I shout after him.

He nods in the affirmative and hustles over quickly. "I'm honored to have been a part of this. I've never seen anything so tight before!"

"Well, you get major purr points for mixing," I profess. Now that it's official, I *have* to lure Zeus into my house. The top cat in the hat could seriously hook up the music for my fashion show.

As if reading my mind about plucking potential candidates for my house, Zeus offers, "Have you seen Dame Leeds's portfolio?"

"No," I say, wincing. Zeus seems tight with Dame Leeds, but Dame Leeds leads to Nole Canoli, and that fashion trail can only lead to Chandelier Spinelli.

"You know Dame?" Aphro asks, impressed. She rests her head on my shoulder, still out of breath from posing.

"For a minute," Zeus says, fiddling with his hat.

"He never talks to us," Aphro says matter-of-factly.

Dame Leeds's ears must be buzzing like a yellow-jacket, because he motions for Zeus to come over. Zeus shrugs and humbly says, "I'm glad you dug the track."

As Zeus trails off, Aphro yells after him: "I think she digs more than that!"

I shove Aphro like a harried passenger on the IRT: hard and with no regard.

## FASHION INTERNATIONAL 35TH ANNUAL
## CATWALK COMPETITION BLOG

New school rule: You don't have to be ultranice, but don't get tooooo catty, or your posting will be zapped by the Fashion Avengers!!

PUERTO RICAN PRIDE IS MORE THAN A PARADE

After the nominations for the house leaders were posted yesterday, there were five winners and eight losers. Like in all elections, there were mucho factors at play—such as fashion, foes, and just plain forgery. Sorry, but call me a stickler for creative arithmetic, *esta bien*? For example, everybody knew Willi Ninja, Jr., was going to be nominated—he was even given the honor of dropping the hankie for our pose-off. If you ask me, that's not what a real election is supposed to be. I mean, I'm not into hating or anything, but just because someone has inherited his pedigree from a parent who was a voguing legend—even if said legend did model in fashion shows for Claude Montana in Paris—that doesn't make him qualified to be the best house leader, *esta bien*? What about candidates like Chintzy Colon or Sarabelia Rodriguez, who couldn't possibly win because they don't have the same kind of street cred or, for that matter, enough Latin constituents to shoulder the vote? Does that mean they aren't qualified to lead a house? *Yo pienso que no.* I don't think so. Latin influence on fashion extends way beyond Carmen Miranda wearing fruit baskets on her head, even if that was a popular theme with drag queens like Tropicana and Flotilla de Barge in last year's Puerto Rican Day Parade. Doesn't anybody care that in the thirty-five years since the Catwalk competition began, there hasn't been one Latin house leader elected? Not one? *Por que*? Doesn't that go against the multicultural mission that our school's founding father, William Dresser, had for Fashion *International*? This is why I'm strongly advising fashionistas with a conscience to use the Teen Style Network coverage this year to voice our pride in all things multicultural. Then maybe next year a Latin candidate will stand a chance of getting elected and being noticed for more than just her tasty chorizos! Must Latin talent always wear bananas on their heads to get noticed? *Parate,* okay? Stop signs are red for a reason!

9/25/2008 10:35:44 PM
Posted by: Cha Cha Heels

110

# 6

The hallways are buzzing like beehives from the success of our pose-off. Even Ice Très is trying to store honey for the coming winter. "You posed for purr points. I'm digging it, pussycat," he coos, winking coyly at me as Aphro and I sashay down the hall.

"Then why don't you come to my house?" I offer boldly. If Shalimar wants a pillow fight, let the goose feathers fly.

"You haven't seen my portfolio, but you want me in your house?" he counters coyly.

"Rewind. This is prequel to a sequel, hopefully. I said *come* to my house, not *be in* my house. And bring your portfolio if you want. We're having a preinterview strategy meeting," I explain, then hit him with the time and locale like a professional house leader.

"Okay, your crib, I got you," Ice Très says, accenting his nod with another wink.

I try to pretend that I'm just scouting talent, which I am—*sort of*.

Meanwhile, Aphro's trying to suppress a smile, but

Ice Très's goofiness is even melting her sugar cane shell, not that she'll admit it. "That's a *lot* of winking and blinking, if you ask me," she says, and hmmphs as we exit the apiary.

"Who's asking?" I gently nudge Aphro down the stairs and squeal, *"Showgirls!"* Last Saturday night we all watched this *scandalabrious* movie on TV at her place about two competing Las Vegas show-girls prancing around with the most awesome plumage on their heads. Anyhoo, one of them pushes the other down a flight of stairs to secure star status in the show. Sure their ways are wicked. Just like the fashion biz.

"Well, it could lead to a hoodwink, that's all I'm saying." Aphro continues. I ignore Aphro because I'm feeling hyped by the fact that Ice Très accepted my pre-screening invite. "Purr points. He's good." I giggle, marveling at Ice Très's dead-on imitation of *moi.* "M.O. to the I."

Aphro and I head to the job board for more cold calls, but after fifteen calls, "chilly" would be a more appropriate word.

"What a buzz-kill. Don't they know I'm the leader of the House of Pashmina?" I gripe to Aphro while I force myself to keep dialing for dollars.

*Finally,* we get an appointment at Loungewear Lulu, a flagship boutique on West Broadway off Grand, which manufactures its own line of leisure and loungewear—or so explains the nasal person on the other end of the phone.

"I've never heard of this designer before. Have you?" Aphro asks me, twirling one of the feathered ends of the sequined purple lariat artfully wrapped three times around her long graceful neck, setting off the short, chic, sharp lines of her Cleopatra bob.

"No, I can't say I've seen Lulu riffing about ruffles on the Teen Style Network," I declare, "but that's what I dig about the fashion biz—another day, another designer."

Chenille walks past us, barreling toward the exit. "Hey, Chenille. Was you at the pose-off?" Aphro asks.

"No, but I gotta *pose my way* to a client," my show-off sister announces proudly.

"Well, sashay to a payday," I suggest sharply. Chenille takes my hint and saunters on her merry way. Secretly, I feel a twinge of Gucci Envy that my younger sister is snagging ducats before I do, but I say, "I don't understand how she plans to get into one of the houses if she can't even represent at the pose-off."

"I know. It's *unbeweavable*," retorts Aphro.

"Bet this. I won't be calling on Shrek's secret assistant to be in my house—and she can take that to Banco Popular," I sassyfrass.

My cell phone does a ringy-ding. "It's my mother

calling again." I assure her that I'll be home by six o'clock to let Mr. Darius in to fix the toilet. But I protest, "You think he coulda came this morning?"

"Never mind that. It's not like there was anybody home who needed to *use* the toilet," my mom gripes in the agitated tone she gets when she deals with Mr. Darius.

"Well, it's a good thing Fabbie didn't have company," I joke, but Mom is not in the mood, so I quickly change my iTune. "Don't you want to know where I'm going now?" I ask teasingly, then blurt it out before she responds. "I have a job interview in SoHo!"

I should have known, however, that my mom would take this info to negative town: "Can't you find something further uptown? I don't like the idea of you traveling so far, especially at night."

I stand still, tapping my foot, listening to my mom as she drones on about the sharp increase in predators on the prowl for pubescent flesh.

"Well, I guess I'm lucky I'm not wearing my red hoodie today to tempt the hungry wolves," I retort, anxious to eighty-six this conversation. Instead, I succeed in further pissing off my mother, who drops the latest crime statistics before she releases me from her rant.

"*Bad* kitty! I *should* be declawed," I grumble after snapping my cell phone shut like a Venus flytrap.

"What you *shouldn't* have to do is deal with Mr. Darius," counters Aphro.

I shrug, unfazed. "Frankly, I think Big Daddy Boom should watch a few reruns of *Flip This House* and pick up pointers. Consider yourself lucky Mrs. Maydell is a home*owner*."

"Actually, she ain't, and *Mr.* Maydell lets us know every time *they* get into a fight," Aphro says, and provides a gruff demonstration: *"This is my house—I'm the one making the mortgage payments around here so y'all better straighten up and fly right!"*

Mr. Maydell is kinda scary; according to Aphro, he's always ready to rumble with her younger foster brother, Lennix, for the slightest infractions.

I feel a breeze by my ear as Chandelier and Dame Leeds whiz by us, chomping on strategy cuds like hype-hungry cows. "I've got all the members I need to win. Getting the rest of my team together is going to be easy breezy," Chandelier brags.

"I heard that, Miss Thing," agrees the dramatic hairstylist. "And you know I'm going to work it for points on the Dow Jones. I'm thinking we should feature short hair so we can angle the dangles—chandelier karats!"

I try not to cringe as I concede that Dame won't be working his dangle-proof drama for our house.

"What about you, Miss Pashmina?" Chandelier

turns and asks me in her taunting voice. "Who's down with feline fatale? *Meowch!*"

Aphro and I pretend we don't hear her, so she continues dropping lines from her brag book. "Don't know why I'm bothering going on this job interview, because I know it's already mine!" she says with assurance, then pecks Dame on both cheeks like they do in Europe.

"Snag it, Gucci girl!" shrieks Dame, pecking back before he hurries down the hallowed hallway.

"Oh, bye, Miss Aphro . . . scratch, scratch!" Chandelier singsongs before grandly descending down the stairs to the doorway of the main entrance, where the attention deficient can get stroked by the ogle-ready Dalmation techies who linger outside after school.

"Why she always putting me on blast?" Aphro asks, her eyes blazing.

"Because she knows you call her Gucci hoochie behind her back." I giggle as Aphro and I walk toward the less frequented Eighth Avenue exit, for those of us whose own initials are enough, like Bottega Veneta.

"*Chan-dee-le-ay* better not be going on the same job interview we are." Aphro groans in protest as I fling open the door.

"Don't even trip—" I start in, ready to squash her doubts, but squash my riff instead when I spot the Teen Style Network crew crouched right outside the pink wrought-iron gates. By reflex, I adjust the headband plastered to the center of my forehead. The lady hones right in on us like a heat-seeking fashion missile. "Hi, I'm Caterina Tiburon. I'm the field producer for Teen Style Network—assigned to cover the Catwalk competition," she announces, confidently extending her right hand. Her handshake is firm and forceful in contrast to the soft, rumpled condition of her drab, baggy khakis and pocket-plenty camouflage jacket. Secretly, I wonder if Caterina Tiburon has gone AWOL from the U.S. Army. She isn't exactly what I expected a producer from the Teen Style Network to look like.

Before I respond to her courteous introduction, I tug down my mini from the micro end. "Hi, I'm Pashmina Purrstein."

"You're one of the house leaders, right?" she asks rhetorically, her eyes darting around at the other students coming out of the building.

"Yes," I say proudly.

"We knew she would get elected," Aphro chimes in. "True talent always rises above the din of the sales bin!"

I keep the Silly Putty smile plastered on my face despite the fact that Aphro sounds like one of the shady fabric merchants on Orchard Street—desperate to move bolts of raw silk that will unravel as soon as you get them home.

Caterina smiles faintly, then cuts right to *her* yardage requirements. "I'd like to get you on camera."

I freeze, but luckily my lips move. "Abso—um, yeah . . . of course," I say, fussing with my headband again.

"Not now," Caterina clarifies, excusing herself; then she whispers to Jay and a tall guy crouched next to metal cases of camera equipment. After she finishes, the tall one comes over. "By the way, I'm Boom," he says, extending his hand. I wonder what they're up to, but the way Boom cracks a smile puts me at ease.

"I'd like to schedule some time with you—I'm interviewing all the house leaders," Caterina says firmly.

"Um, okay. We can do it tomorrow, whenever you want. We can meet in Studio One downstairs—right next to the Hall of Fame?" I offer.

"If you don't mind, I'd like to see you in your natural habitat first. This is the more candid up-close-and-personal take before we get into the nuts and bolts—of fabric—of the competition," Caterina continues. I can tell she's trying to make a joke because she senses my hesitation.

"Nuts is right," I joke back, then get embarrassed that Caterina might get the wrong impression of me.

"Look, it's just establishing shots," Caterina continues, using production lingo. "I already have an appointment with Shalimar Jackson. We're going over to her apartment to tape her at seven o'clock while she holds a meeting for her social club."

Now my apprehension is bona fried. Shalimar is going to be shot in her Limoges-laden penthouse with the members of a *bourgie*-woogie organization, all of whom go to private schools like Huxley, Baumgiddy and Tense. That makes the fur on the back of my neck stand at attention.

"Um, okay. Lemme check with my mother first," I say, stalling. "I know she usually has her bridge club on Wednesday nights. I'll call you on the cell as soon as I clear the schedule?"

Caterina hands me her card, and I scribble my cell number on a page and tear it out of my Kitty notebook. "I look forward to it," she says.

After they leave, Aphro says, "You are so shady."

"What was I supposed to say—Spades?" I quip. Spades is a card game that my mother plays with gusto, but Hector, her quasi boyfriend, hasn't been around lately for her to even do that. Aphro and I played with them once, since it requires four players.

"What's the name of Shalimar's social club again—Hansel and Gretel?" I ask sarcastically.

"Jack and Jill," answers Aphro. "You got elected house leader for a reason. You don't have to front for anybody."

"Yeah, but you gotta come over."

"Let her come over Thursday. I mean, you did invite Ice Très," Aphro points out.

"Now, that's a plan." Why not have the Teen Style Network shoot us while we're having our first prestrategy meeting? "I mean, we gotta get the Catwalk flyer together to post on Friday."

Now that the Catwalk house leaders have been chosen, I have to begin interviewing and snagging some more fierce members for our house.

"You're definitely gonna help me with some catworthy choreography?" I ask Aphro, getting ten poses ahead of myself.

"I got you," Aphro says as she reflects on the bold moves from the pose-off. "Did you see Elgamela? I didn't know anybody could do that with their belly button."

"Too bad she won't be doing that for us," I lament, reflecting on the sad fact that Chandelier has snagged our favorite model. "Well, we'd better scurry on down to SoHo."

"I don't 'scurry.' I take the subway like the rest of the animals in Manny Hanny," Aphro quips as we descend into the gloomy underworld. Dramatically, Aphro sidesteps the puddles of dirty water scattered on the grimy, slippery floor of the train station. "Well, I guess you ain't the only one who sprung a leak today."

"This is true, but I pity the peeps who don't have access to the iron horse like we do," I say, like it's a consolation prize. "Gets you wherever you're going—pronto."

Aligning with my predictions: fifteen minutes later we arrive in the puddle-free, pricey shopping strip on West Broadway.

"SoHo is *sweet*," proclaims Aphro like a fashion mantra. "Definitely the spot for Purr Unlimited."

I gaze longingly at the endless stretch of stores ahead. The first three blocks on West Broadway are the most important retailwise, and for this privilege, boutique owners pay a premium rent. "Sixty dollars per square foot!" I exclaim.

"Sixty times at least five hundred square feet for even the smallest store. Do the math—that's serious sweating each month," adds Aphro. I know she secretly hopes to have a store, too, for her Aphro Puffs jewelry line. Something small and tasty like the Tarina Tarantino jewelry boutique on Greene Street—my fave, of course, since she's a devotee of Russian Hello Kitty.

"All Big Apple landlords are *greedy*," I announce like it's a revelation, at least to me, which makes me feel the pressure about picking slots for Catwalk house members. "Since we can't have Nole Canoli, we gotta think of another designer who can fulfill our vision," I fret.

Aphro stares blankly at the gray blazer and slacks in

the window of the Banana Republic store. "Meanwhile, *they've* obviously got enough bananas to open yet *another* one."

"What about Diamond Tyler?" I ask.

"I know you dig her animal sensibilities," Aphro says, like she's hesitating.

"Yeah, but she is a *good* designer."

"We've just got to look at portfolios, that's all there is to it," Aphro says, shrugging. "I dig Nole's stuff, but I can't say I've really checked anybody else, that's all I'm saying."

I hate when Aphro does that. For somebody who riffs raw, she can flip the script and act so cagey. I know she digs Nole. Who doesn't? Hello! I'm so busy fuming at her that we walk silently for the next three blocks. When we get to the fourth block on West Broadway going west, we stop in front of a store obstructed by a scaffold. I can't see the building number we're looking for. "This has got to be it," insists Aphro.

"Nah, it *can't* be," I snap, staring at the pay-less-and-look-it outfits propped in the window. "Are you sure this is the right address?"

"There's a sign, right there," Aphro huffs, pointing at the small block-letter sign displayed in the corner of the window: LOUNGEWEAR LULU.

My attitude sinks to the level of my moccasins.

"Should we even bother going in?" I ask, turning meek at the sight of unchic.

"We made an appointment. What if they call the school and tell them we didn't show up?" Aphro points out, attempting to push the door open to no avail. I press the buzzer instead, which chimes with a spooky echo.

"Almost all the boutiques in the Big Apple have buzzers because boosters are always mopping instead of shopping," I remind her. Boosters then sell the stolen merchandise through an underground network, which costs the retail industry billions in lost revenue. "But I bet this is not a mopping stop on their itinerary."

Once we're buzzed inside the fun house with the distorted designer duds, I examine the rows of packed racks of clothes directly in front of me. Front and center of one rack is a white jumpsuit covered with hordes of invading sequins. "I think Chintzy would like this. It could go with her white go-go boots," I observe glumly.

On the top of each rack are hand-blocked signs with the word SALE! in glaring red letters. *Subtle*. This is the kind of store, my retail instructor would say, that conducts sales all year round. Seemingly out of nowhere, a tiny, frail woman with ashy white skin and even ashier long hair appears from behind a mirrored door. She's wearing a long black empire-waist dress.

"What can I do for you two ladies?" she asks in a squeaky voice, approaching us slowly like a zombie from *Dawn of the Dead*.

*Escape!* I want to squeal, but instead I announce that we're from Fashion International. The scary lady's eyes widen, or so I think, until I look closer and realize that this is their perpetual state. Some of my mom's best customers at the Forgotten Diva boutique are also afflicted with the same Popeye pupils—no doubt the handiwork of an overzealous plastic surgeon.

"I'm Lulu Fantom," the lady says, breaking out into a fit of giggles and revealing teeth that look like they've trotted on the yellow brick road.

After we tell Lulu our names, she breaks into another round of giggles, which makes me wonder if she's making fun of us? I hate when people trip about my name. So does Aphro. But when Lulu asks us about our majors at school and we tell her, she giggles again. That's when I realize we're probably witnessing her signature snorkle.

"I design my collection myself," Lulu starts in as she proceeds to show us around the store, confirming our worst fear: she is, indeed, the designer behind the duds in this haunted house, established in 2004—the same year designer Faux Sho' introduced his fake Mongolian lamb maxicoats that had women looking like Swamp Things.

"I can't keep these in the stock," Lulu continues, proudly showing off a pair of ivory gaucho pants with white sequins up the side. "I just love this fabric."

"Is it muslin?" I ask in disbelief.

"Yes, I just love it; it gives the illusion of linen at half the cost," she boasts.

In my opinion, muslin is the hillbilly of fabrics, but I decide it's best to keep my thoughts to myself. Cuckoo Lulu continues to gush over a few more of her "signature pieces," before she makes it crystal clear that the tour of her haunted house is over. Even though neither of us is interested in blemishing our supa-scanty résumés with a stint at Loungewear Lulu, I feel insulted when we're ushered out of the store without so much as a half-meant *I'm looking at lots of applicants, but I'll be in touch. Toodles!*

Once outside, we adjust to the letdown. "I think she's running a *bootique*, not a boutique!" I exclaim, getting depressed.

"She was definitely peekaboo scary!" Aphro adds.

"How about we try a few more real boutiques while we're down here?" I suggest.

"No doubt," Aphro responds cheerfully.

By the fifth real boutique and apologetic round of "Sorry, but we're not hiring," the two of us are ready to click our kitten heels and head home. "I hope Felinez didn't get kicked to the curb like we did," I say as we walk quickly to the subway station on Spring Street. "We gotta at least look in the window," I say, and Aphro knows exactly what window I'm referring to. We turn onto Greene Street so I can swoon at my favorite store. "Ooh, look at the new bag candy!" I say, staring hungrily at the lipless Pink Head of the rare Russian Hello Kitty cameo pendant dangling from a lucite beaded choker. "Oy, I can't believe I don't have one of these yet."

Aphro shakes her head at me. "My jewelry is gonna be more fierce."

Now it's Aphro's turn to swoon, so we stop for a *segundo* in front of the Jimmy Choo boutique. "Shimmy Choo," I groan, using the Catwalk code name for the former Malaysian cobbler whose sought-after heels help everyone from Beyoncé to Lindsay Lohan sashay to stardom. "I sure could use a little shoe therapy right about now," Aphro says, prompting me to whip out my cell phone and call Angora for feline support.

"Stop sole searching, *chérie*," Angora hisses through the receiver. "We live in a cold, cruel world. That's what my mother says anyway, and she's always right."

⌐ ¬

By six-thirty, I wish I could say the same thing about my mother, because it's obvious I rushed home for no reason. Mr. Darius has stood me up. *Again*. I'm so annoyed I could scream from the rooftop. And I would if the door up there wasn't locked with prison-issue chains. My cell phone rings and I run to my bedroom to grab it out of the brown suede fringed messenger bag I was carrying today. Fabbie is plopped on top of my bag and she won't budge. "Move the caboose!" I yell, then toss her like a salad, but I've already missed the call. I'm worried that maybe Mr. Darius called my mother or something. I don't want her to think that I wasn't here holding down the fort like a true Apache. But I see from the missed call prompt that it was Felinez, so I hit her back.

"What's up, pussycat?"

Felinez alternates between barks and screams into the receiver before she blurts out to a salsa beat, "Ruff! Ruff! I got a job. I got a job!"

"You'd better work, supermodel!" I scream into the receiver, before I register an alternate reaction: *God, how come Felinez got a job and I didn't?*

Felinez is so busy babbling about her new position as an assistant to the assistant at the Ruff Loner showroom that she doesn't notice that I've missed a salsa beat.

"And I get to recatalog the patterns from all the past seasons," she babbles on, before she finally pauses for a breath and says, "*Mija*, how did it go in SoHo?"

"Well, let's just say SoHo was so low I had to hurry home and lick my wounded paws," I joke.

Suddenly, there is a loud rapping on the door. "Hold on!" I yell, scrambling to get by Fabbie, who now is sashaying ahead of me to the door like she's a fluffy Goodfrill Ambassador.

When I open the door, Mr. Darius stands like a stone statue, not moving even a facial muscle.

"Um, hi Mr. Darius. Are you going to fix the toilet?" I ask, holding the cell phone to my chest.

"No. I come tomorrow. There is flood in the basement. We gotta fix," he says unapologetically.

"You gotta be kidding!" I shout, losing it. "You gotta fix the toilet. My mother is coming home soon."

"You try the thing," he says, motioning with his hands like we're playing a game of charades.

"The plunger?" I guess.

Mr. Darius ignores me. "Try fix it, maybe."

"No, it doesn't work!" I blubber. "When are you going to fix it?"

"I come tomorrow," Mr. Darius says, clearly annoyed, being led by his protruding stomach as he walks away.

"Hello! What time?" I balk, stepping into the hallway in an attempt to stonewall him.

"I don't know," Mr. Darius says, shooing me away.

"I gotta know what time," I insist.

Mr. Darius's eyes catch a tiny twinkle as the corners of his mouth turn up involuntarily. "Okay. Okay?"

"Six o'clock," I command, pointing to the face of my French Kitty watch.

Mr. Darius nods his head slightly, then waves his hand like he's shooing me away again.

"Oy," I groan, closing the front door. Then I resume my Catwalk leader mode, getting back on the phone and filling Felinez in on the Teen Style crew sighting after school.

"Omigod. I wish I was there!" Felinez says. She ran off to her appointment at Ruff Loner before Aphro and I left to go down to SoHo. "So, are you calling her back?"

"Calling who back?"

"The producer. Caterina. You said she wanted to see you in your natural kitty habitat?" Felinez reminds me.

"She did not say that!" I giggle. "Oh, right. Lemme—Omigod, I just thought of something so shady, I may go into total eclipse!"

"What happened? *Que paso?*" Felinez screams in anticipation.

"Operation: Kitty Litter," I respond, deadpan.

"Ay, *dios mio*, what are you up to, *mija?*" Felinez says, with a giggle.

"Operation: Kitty Litter" is the code name we invented and have used for all our covert secret operations since grade school.

"Aphro is right: we get the Teen Style crew to come

over and shoot us having our first preinterview strategy meeting. *And* I tell Mr. Darius to come over at the same time to do the repairs," I explain.

Felinez gets quiet.

"Blue Boca? Come on, don't you get it? They could get him! On camera, I mean. Maybe he'll think it's the fashion police or something! At least he'll be embarrassed when I hit him over the head with the plunger!" I crow, trying to jump-start Felinez's enthusiasm. Blue Boca is a nickname I gave Felinez one summer when a heat wave so blazing struck the city that all she did was suck on blue ices that turned her tongue spooky blue. "I just want to see the look on Mr. Darius's face when Caterina instructs Boom to stick a camera on him. *Comprendo?*"

"*Mija,* maybe he'll get really mad," Felinez warns.

True to my stubborn nature, I ignore her apprehension. "Operation: Kitty Litter is a go. Signing off!"

**FASHION INTERNATIONAL 35TH ANNUAL
CATWALK COMPETITION BLOG**

New school rule: You don't have to be ultranice, but don't get tooooo catty, or your posting will be zapped by the Fashion Avengers!!

WHO'S AFRAID TO PRANCE TO A PAYDAY? . . .

Not all students at Fashion International fantasize about becoming a supermodel or a "modelpreneur," as the most ambitchous among us like to call ourselves. Some of us are intent on fashion domination by using our managerial skills and creative vision. Take me, for example. Nothing matters more to me than providing a platform for my unique take on style from a gay perspective. That's why I feel qualified to lead a house in the Catwalk competition—NOT because I happen to be the best voguer in school! Yes, my adopted father, vogue legend Willi Ninja, was responsible for providing the student body at Fashion International with a more appropriate physical education elective than basketball, fencing, and calisthenics classes. Although he is no longer with us, we should all continue to express our gratitude for his making such a valuable addition to our curriculum as voguing classes, and sparing us from being subjected to the bouncing ball and other boring antics associated with butch sports. However, I feel compelled to clarify what voguing actually is, given what I witnessed during yesterday's pose-off. Voguing is a dance form that originated in Harlem ballrooms back in the day, and it combines various techniques from the martial arts, jazz and modern dance, gymnastics, and yoga, among other disciplines. And thanks to the dazzling voguing displays presented by Elgamela Sphinx and Miss Aphro Biggie Bright, I'm going to add belly dancing and hip-hop to the eclectic beat-driven blend. Beyond this, there is also an exquisite execution that distinguishes it from other dance disciplines. Voguing is structured around distinct hand and arm movements, so the trained voguer must keep time with the beat of the music as well as accentuate various changes in rhythms. Therefore, simply primping and POSING to the beat is only ONE aspect of voguing. Also, for the record, Jody Watley and Malcolm McLaren, NOT Madonna, were the first two recording artists to feature true voguers in their music videos. Nonetheless, the Material Girl received maximum exposure because of her blonde ambition, if you catch my drift. Given my posing pedigree, all I would have to do to gain the same exposure would be to pull down my pants and stick my butt out of the school window!! Contrary to shady belief, I have no intention of following in my adopted father's footsteps like his godson Benny Ninja, whom I revere completely, and who thankfully may be joining our school's faculty (no disrespect to Mr. Blinghe). But, see, I intend to dance to my own fashion beat because I don't have to pose for a payday. Now if you don't mind, I must get ready for my Teen Style Network close-up, then win the Catwalk competition. Click. Dial tone. Good-bye!!

9/30/2008 12:45:45 PM
Posted by: Twirl Happy1992

# 7

Staring at the sign-in sheet in the reception area of Ms. Lynx's office, I shriek when I see that Chandelier Spinelli has already booked her time slot for Studio C to conduct interviews for team members. Sure, she may already have Nole and Elgamela in the Gucci bag, but she still has to enlist talent for her house like the rest of us: by *any means necessary*. Channeling Zorro, I boldly scrawl my name on the sign-in sheet in the slot for Tuesday from four to six p.m. Then I plop down on one of the gilded chairs with the leopard seat cushions to wait for the blank team member forms that I'll need to submit after I have selected all my house members. But first, Farfalla has to win *her* battle with the temperamental Xerox machine.

"*Madonna, ancora! Ma, venga!*" Farfalla yelps, shoving the paper tray into its compartment. Pressing the Start button to no avail, Ms. Lynx's dramatic assistant turns to coaxing: "Oh, *please, per favore, va bene?*"

I smile at her, embarrassed, then avert my eyes to

the spotted plaque hanging on the closed door of Lynx Lair: WEAR FASHION, OR BE WORN.

Still no Xeroxes, so I scan the wild inhabitants of Catwalk Central: the bobcat heads mounted on the walls, the carved cheetah bookends standing menacingly on their hind legs, and, crouched in the corner, the leopard ceramic statue with the gaping jaw.

Suddenly, the door to Ms. Fab's inner sanctum swings open, and out pops another predator. I stare down at the leopard-skin area rug sprawled by my feet as Chandelier's babble spills into the reception area. "I can't believe I got the job!" Chandelier squeals, tossing her stiff, spritzed hair that's like an overtamed lion's mane. Then, turning toward Farfalla, Chandelier grandly announces: "I got a job at Betsey Johnson!"

Like a well-trained fashionista, Farfalla feigns bright-eyed interest even though she's preoccupied with her Xerox crisis. *"Bravo!"* she chortles.

At last, Chandelier floats into the hallway on her fashion-job cloud while my mind starts spinning like a dreidel. How did Chandelier snag a position at Betsey Johnson? What was she doing in Ms. Lynx's office?

Ms. Lynx steps out of her lair and looks at me quizzically. "Just waiting for forms," I inform her.

*"Dov'e* Sil Lai?" Ms. Lynx shoots to Farfalla.

*"Lei andata in giro per il tuo cappuccino, ma espero che ritorna subito!"* frets Farfalla.

The commanding Catwalk Director continues speaking to Farfalla in Italian. By now, I'm lost in translation, so I sit mesmerized fantasizing about living *la dolce vita* in Italy for two weeks in July.

"*Ecco, finalmente!*" Farfalla says, refueled by the humming sound of Xerox copies ejecting into the tray.

*Finally* is right. Now I'm armed with the necessary forms. "*Grazie!*" I say, then hightail it into the hallway, but not fast enough to avoid Chintzy.

"Oh, hey, wazzup," I say, bracing myself.

"When are you interviewing?" Chintzy asks eagerly.

"I thought you wanted to be in Shalimar's House?" Yesterday I watched while Chintzy stood Splendafied by Shalimar as she dangled a hookup with Grubster PR, one of her father's investment clients. Of course, the conversation went hush until I faded to fuchsia down the hallway.

"No way, José," Chintzy responds.

"My flyer will be up tomorrow, okay?" I say, stalling. "Right now, I gotta hustle and flow to the Fashion Annex to do research for a quiz!"

As I clomp in my pink classic Swedish wooden clogs down the stairs, I'm so preoccupied with Chintzy's sudden desire to walk feline that Zeus spots me first.

"I knew it was you!" Zeus says, his pale blue eyes squinting at me like I'm a magical looking glass.

"Oh, I guess you heard my herd," I say, embarrassed.

"Where you roaming?" Zeus asks, chuckling.

"To the library to check on zebra migration patterns," I jest.

"That's always interesting."

"Nah—actually, another kind of pattern. Tartans for textile science. I still can't tell the difference between the Barbecue Plaid and the Braveheart!" I reveal.

"Oh, the last one's easy—check out Mel's kilt," he advises, but realizes by my blankety that I don't get it. He quickly adds, "In the movie?"

"Right." I nod, trying to picture the Scottish plaid in question, but all I can envision are Mel's bushy calves. "Are you into kilts?"

"Could be," he answers.

I decide it's time to bite the catnip. "You'd be an asset to my house—whether you bared your legs or not."

Zeus breaks into his squinty-eyed grin again.

"We're starting our preinterview strategies tonight at my house at six *sharpo*," I babble, holding my breath. "Consider yourself in if you can make it."

My cheeks start burning. Why did I put him on blast like that? Shrieking inside, I decide to take it back. "You probably have something more important to do, like scrubbing your sneaker collection."

"Nope. Consider me in there like swimwear," he says calmly.

"Oh, I get it—it's Posture Like Pashmina Day," I quip, scribbling my address on a sheet of paper in my Hello Kitty notebook. Then I get embarrassed because I don't want to spill the refried beans about Ice Très.

Zeus squints at me like he wants to ask what I meant, but instead he just riffs, "No doubt."

I hand him the scribbled-on paper and he breaks out, explaining that he has to head uptown.

Right after school, Felinez, Aphro, Angora, and I have to head downtown to the Alley Kat Korner on Avenue A to buy some kitschy items for our first close encounter with a camera: pink-frosted cupcakes, paper plates and cups, and pink popcorn. "These kernels will pop for the camera." I giggle while Angora picks out posies.

Operation: Kitty Litter is about to jump off at six o'clock tonight at my apartment. That is, if Mr. Darius and the Teen Style Network crew show up. In the meantime, we get busy pinkifying my crib.

"Does Zeus know about Operation: Kitty Litter?" Angora asks as she places the flowers in the metallic blue floral vases she's supplied for the occasion. I'm secretly grateful she left her dad's rabbit vases at home where they belong.

"Um, no. And hopefully Mr. Hairiest Darius is on his way," I say.

"I'm glad you didn't tell him. As Ms. Ava says, sometimes the truth is just plain inappropriate."

"No wonder enrollment in your mother's etiquette school is so high. Fiberoni coaching along with napkin placement. *Quel resistable*," I add, imitating Angora and throwing our prized pink faux fur tablecloth over the scratched wooden dining room table. "Zeus was psyched about coming over."

"Angora, the flowers are beautiful. *Que bonita!*" Felinez says, sniffing the bouquets of pink roses and delicately spotted yellow Peruvian lilies. Angora has arranged bouquets around the living room and left one as a centerpiece on the dining room table.

"These are my mother's favorite—the Dreamland Bouquet. I should send her a bunch to christen her new home on Hysteria Lane," Angora declares, going on to explain the indignities her mother has to endure "living in a smaller house, like less fabbie neighbors. Speaking of Fabbie, where is my little darling?" Angora keeps cooing until Fabbie Tabby hops onto the couch and waits for Angora to come and pet her to death. It's a ritual they have.

"Anybody up for a sip and a flip?" I ask, grabbing the jumbo bottle of ginger ale out of the fridge and the *Vogue* magazine nestled next to it.

"Hit me, Pink Head," Aphro says, lunging at the *Vogue* like it's the Holy Grail. "Yo, would you buy a magazine if I were on the cover?"

"Yeah—*National Geographic*!" I reply, wondering about another model with cover potential. "I can't figure out if Zeus is on the loose?"

"Well, he's gotta be gay, straight, or *très* taken." Angora smiles, then shrugs. "My mom was also giving me dating advice last night on the phone."

"From the woman who still thinks spam is canned lunch meat? *S'il vous plaît!*" I heckle, taking a swig from the bottle of ginger ale, then belching with gusto.

Felinez grabs the bottle from me and takes a swig. "That is so ghetto!" Aphro squeals.

"No, it's not! Ghetto is when three people take swigs from the same bottle—not two!" Felinez counters.

"Well, then ghetto couture is inviting Ice Très over," I slide in nonchalantly.

"I thought you invited Zeus over?" Angora asks, blinking at my boldness.

"Yeah, well, I like them both—and according to the game of Spades, whoever has the two of clubs wins the kitty!" I giggle, meowching Felinez.

"Explain?" Angora asks.

"We gotta teach you Spades," I reply, making a note to my fashion self. "Once the cards are dealt, whoever has the two of clubs gets to pick up the six cards left on the table, which are called the kitty. Then they can discard any six cards they want," I explain. "So maybe I'll be doing the discarding!"

"*Mijas*, the real question is, why would a tasty *sabor* like Zeus wanna join our house?" Felinez interrupts.

"He digs our theme and our dream—and hopefully me too," I say wistfully. "That reminds me. Chintzy Colon also wants to join our house."

"No way, José!" Felinez objects.

"She could be an asset," I counter, because I'm not at all surprised by her reaction.

"I'm telling you, *mija*, she's a sneaky senorita!" Felinez says, taking a bottle of pills out of her purse.

"Okay," I snap. "Note to fashion self: shelve this discussion until later. And what is that you're trying to shove in your blue *boca*?"

I grab the bottle out of Felinez's hand despite her protestation: "Michelette took them—they really work!"

" 'Burn, Baby, Burn'?" I say, scanning the label. "Do you see what that says? 'These statements have not been evaluated by the Food and Drug Administration.' "

"Maybe they don't have time to evaluate everything!" Felinez argues.

Aphro lets out a snort. "You need to stop."

"That's easy for you to say. You're skinny. What about me?" Felinez blurts out.

She is freaking. "I hope you can keep it locked down in front of the camera crew," I warn her.

"*Por que no*? Why not? You're gonna show them the leaks in the ceiling! All you wanna do is embarrass Mr. Darius! Why shouldn't I show them my cracks? Pudgy, *pobrecita gordita* Felinez! Your best friend—*por vida!*"

"Fifi Cartera, I cannot cope right now. Can you please put a baste stitch in your ego until we can mend it properly later?" I beg my best friend.

Suddenly, there's a knock at the door and I'm so relieved to be off kitty pity duty that I lunge for it. I fling it open only to see my favorite zebra-striped mink hat. Zeus catches the kaflustered expression on my face. "I'm still invited to be a member, right?" he asks, smiling.

"Abso-*freakin'*-lutely!" I say, flopping my arms around his carved muscular torso, which is hard as stone, probably from his skateboarding antics out on Monyville, Long Island. I get my blush on—again. The rest of my crew senses my seismic reaction like they're earthquake experts, so I try to render their reading inaccurate by turning the dial to Lite FM: "How did you get up here without ringing the intercom?"

"Oh, right," he says, wondering if he did something

wrong. "These two little girls let me in. They ran up to me in the courtyard, and asked if they could feel my hat!"

It figures. Everybody wants a piece of Zeus for conservation. "Don't tell me: Stellina and Tiara, right?"

"Yeah. They're really hyped," Zeus says, nodding.

"They are our resident models-in-training," I explain, then babble on about my plans to open the House of Pashmina fashion show with trot-ready guest tween models.

Zeus keeps nodding, then looks at me like he didn't see me earlier. "I dig this look. It's different from the other day?"

"Yeah, this is my Diehard-Dutch-Girl look," I say, blushing, then patting the front of the cotton flowered kerchief tied on my head.

"By the way, how'd your interview go at Betsey Johnson?"

I freeze. So does Aphro. We look at each other like, *Where'd he get this tiddy from?*

"Ice Très told me," Zeus pipes up, sensing static. "I guess Shalimar told him?"

"What *what* in the butt?" Aphro blurts.

Zeus doubles over laughing from Aphro's outburst.

"Um, I think what Aphro is trying to say is, we did not have an interview at Betsey Johnson. Chandelier got that job, anyway," I say, trying to keep the situation static free. Zeus nods, puzzled. Now the intercom rings. I answer it and hear Caterina's voice. "I'll be right down," I inform her chirpily.

As I walk out the door, Angora comes to close it behind me. "I can't believe Ice Très isn't here yet."

Angora purses her lips. "He'll be here."

"Handle her," I whisper, this time nodding toward Felinez. Angora winks and nods. Fifi is definitely stressing. But she's right about one thing: maybe I *am* more interested in pulling a prank than taking care of business. Suddenly, I start having second thoughts. Well, they're here and I have to explain somehow why my building looks like the "before" shot on *Extreme Home Makeover* while Shalimar's looks like the "after."

My neighbor, Mrs. Paul, walks out of her apartment and joins me at the elevator bank, clutching the faux tortoiseshell handle on her vintage purse like she's carrying a pitchfork inside. Mrs. Paul never smiles, at least not at me.

When the elevator comes, Mrs. Paul gets in first. "It's hot in here. Or is it me?" I ask, flapping my crocheted babydoll tee against my chest for ventilation.

"Don't get lippy with me," Mrs. Paul mumbles.

"Right," I say politely, fleeing from the elevator as soon as the door opens to the lobby. I can't help it; my clunky wooden clogs clop heavily onto the faux marble floor. Stellina and Tiara bolt to the front door and announce to the camera crew, "Pink Head taught us how to vogue! You wanna see?"

"Who's Pink Head?" Caterina asks, amused.

"Me. It's my nickname," I explain. "It means a friend of felines who worships at the altar of pinkdom." *Pink Head, Blue Boca.* Now the nicknames that Felinez and I annointed ourselves when we were hot totties seem radickio. But Caterina beams, so I stop blushing. She then instructs the camera crew to start filming the tiny fashionistas in action. "How old are you?" she asks Stellina.

Striking a pose, Stellina bats her lashes and replies, "I don't give out *that* information."

I shrug, and grin in approval. Some of my neighbors gather around to see what's going on. "Lord, what they giving away?" Mrs. Watkins asks, rushing over. She works at the supermarket across the street and becomes so excited at the prospect of a freebie that she almost drops one of the three grocery bags she's juggling.

"We're primping for prime time," Tiara explains matter-of-factly.

Mrs. Watkins beams with pride. "Shoot, I ain't too old to be a model. Y'all should have me in the competition. I would tell them people at Piggly to get Wiggly cuz I'm gone!"

After a few minutes of clicks and more cackling, Caterina motions for the crew to head to the elevator.

145

Mrs. Watkins follows us. "Heard someone in Queens won sixty-three million yesterday," she announces to anyone who'll listen. Mrs. Watkins is referring to the New York Mega Millions lottery. She buys tickets every week. "How come nobody in Harlem ever win?" No one answers her. Meanwhile, Boom the cameraman pans the lens across the graffiti-lined walls. "Oh," I say nonchalantly, "we've been trying to get that cleaned up forever, but our landlord, Mr. Darius, won't do anything."

Caterina quickly changes the subject. "Of all the supermodels, who do you like?" she asks, shoving the microphone in my face.

"The ones who personify feline fatale," I quip.

"What about Tidy Plume?" Caterina asks, which makes me realize she doesn't know what I'm talking about.

"Um, no, she's more like couture confection."

Caterina goes blankety.

"A Barbie doll. Too perfect," I explain, sounding calm, but I'm sweating profusely and worried my underarms may start venting despite the extra applications of Arrid Extra Dry that I glommed on for this uncertain occasion.

"Um, I think that Tyra Banks or Moona—" I start in, but I can tell Caterina's gone blankety again.

"She's the model from Somalia, the SNAPS cosmetics spokesperson? I think she has feline fatale appeal," I continue, realizing that my teacher Ms. London is right. Black models don't get the hype that white models do, or Caterina would be up on Moona, too.

The silence is thick in the elevator, but I'm grateful for the small things at the moment. "Thank gooseness it's working, because yesterday it wasn't," I say, smiling apologetically. When the elevator door opens onto my floor, I shut my mouth like a Venus flytrap at the sight of Chenille. True to her stoic nature, she ignores the camera crew and glumly announces, "I'm going down to Reesy's."

I nod approvingly like a good older sister and quickly usher the film crew inside: Chenille can make her coins, but she is *not* stealing my camera cues.

Once inside, I secretly hope that Ice Très has beamed himself up to my apartment like Scotty in *Star Trek* while I was gone. One look at Angora, however, tells me that's not the case, so I go into my Catwalk house leader mode, initiating introductions all around. Then I hesitantly inform everyone. "We're having a few, um, technical difficulties but hopefully Mr. Darius, the landlord, will keep his appointment to remedy the bathroom situation soon," I say emphatically into the camera.

Suddenly, I feel embarrassed, but Zeus switches on his brilliant smile. "The fashion show must go on," he declares, snapping his fingers.

"I heard that," Aphro seconds as we all head over to the dining room table to get down to Catwalk business.

Zeus takes a black portfolio emblazoned with a zebra lightning bolt decal from his backpack.

"Fabbie Tabby, time to start the meeting!" I yell.

On cue, Fabbie hops onto the table and plops down. Boom and Caterina let out approving yelps, and two cameras zoom in for a close up on Fabbie's whiskers.

"I love the color contrast—turquoise and lime green," I comment on Zeus's skateboard graphics. "No animals in the mix?"

"We'll be getting to that," Zeus says confidently.

After we finish goospitating over Zeus's portfolio, I pass around Xeroxes. "I need your input to create the Catwalk Credo, which will serve as guidelines. Here's what I've scribbled so far."

I watch Zeus's face as he reads my outline: "I dig that: 'As an officially fierce member of the House of Pashmina, I solemnly swear to abide by the directions of my team leader, to represent my crew to the max, and to honor, respect, and uphold the Catwalk Credo.'"

"We also have to make up a list of all the positions we need to fill for our house," I continue.

"Photographer," Zeus says. "I mean, we should be documenting our whole Catwalk process along the way."

"*Brillante,*" coos Felinez.

"I know somebody lethal—he's in my visual display class," Zeus lets on.

"Explain?" Angora asks.

"Lupo," says Zeus, shoving a handful of pink popcorn into his mouth. "Lupo Saltimbocca. He's hyped about becoming the next Francesco Scavullo. He's outta sight."

"Got it," I say, recognizing the name of the famous fashion photographer from the seventies. Scavullo was a star in the *Vogue* magazine stable back in the day. "Okay, so we're gonna set up in Studio C for Tuesday from four to six for interviews. Please let Mr. 'Salt in the boca' know so he can be there or be square."

"*Saltimbocca*—it means 'jump in the mouth,' an expression to use when something is supa-tasty." Zeus chuckles.

"I heard that. Just what we need," adds Aphro.

"That reminds me," I say. "Not everyone is down with our cause. So I think the flyer should put it right out there: 'Only cat lovers need apply.' "

"Let's take a vote," Angora seconds.

"I've also written down the definition of feline fatale style—'adorable and playful but fiercely clever, and pays homage to our catty companions regardless of sex.' I mean gender," I say, blushing.

"*Brillante!*" Zeus says, imitating Felinez. "I'll put a pink cat illustration on the left of the flyer."

"That's outta sight!" I say, imitating Zeus.

"Awright—let's talk about models!" Aphro yells out.

"We're gonna need to sign up seventeen more models," I say. "So far we've got three. And figure ten kids as guest models to open the show."

"One lead designer, one assistant designer," adds Felinez, then explains to Zeus, "I'm the accessories designer, and Aphro's the jewelry designer."

"What about Nole Canoli?" Zeus suggests.

"Nole is down with Chandelier Spinelli," I say pleasantly, since Ms. Lynx has warned us to "behave instead of beehive"—even though I'd like to sting Chandelier.

"Maybe Ice Très—for the second designer?" adds Zeus, swinging his second fashion strike.

Angora's blue peepers rise above the rim of her cat's-eye glasses, and I feel the gnawing disappointment from Ice Très's dis full force. Not that I'm about to drop that tiddy right about now.

In the meantime, Caterina has her own recipe for "reality" television. "How did Chandelier enlist the most talented designer at FI for *her* house?"

Note to fashion self: Caterina's khakis may not be

"crisp," but her behind-the-scenes snooping is bona fried.

"Chandelier is a Gucci hoochie. Some people are impressed by that," Aphro says, venting.

"I, um, don't think Nole Canoli is the only digable designer in school," I offer feebly.

Everyone looks at me like they're waiting for me to drop the winning Lotto numbers.

"Um, I think Diamond Tyler is purrworthy, too," I add.

"Oh, she's the one stressed about her cat, right?" Zeus asks with concern.

"Who don't you like?" Caterina interjects.

"Miss Jackson. She's such a Fendi fiend," Aphro blurts out.

"What Aphrodite is trying to say is . . . ," I begin, pausing to formulate my thoughts.

"She can runway, but she can't hide!" Aphro says with a sneer.

Boom chuckles, lightening the situation.

"We have our own definition of what 'fashion-forward' is." Now I decide to look directly into the camera. "Not everyone is down with that. There are competitors who would rather stick with the tried, even if it's *not* true. We believe when it comes to fashion trends, sometimes you just have to drop it like it's hot. Now drop that—*boom!*"

Suddenly, there's a loud rapping sound on the door. Everybody shrieks with laughter at the timing of the interruption. I shoot Angora a look, however, like *It better be Ice Très*. Much to my chagrin, however, the first face I see when I open the door is the sullen one of Mr. Darius. Amazingly, he is with a repairman, who is carrying a toolbox and a plunger.

I usher them in like they're dethroned royalty. "Kats and Kitties, *this* is Mr. Darius, my landlord."

Mr. Darius steps inside, and once he sees the cameras, his eyes start rolling like pool balls.

"Don't mind the film crew," I say sweetly, regaining my nerve for Operation: Kitty Litter. "They've been filming the building, too! Isn't that exciting?"

Mr. Darius starts mumbling to the repairman, and they hurry to the bathroom. I follow them so that Boom, Jay, and Caterina will follow me.

"The toilet's broke and the hot water hasn't been working," I lament.

Mr. Darius mumbles to me, "Please go."

I trot back to the living room and wait for Mr. Darius to come back with a prognosis, but he proceeds to leave in a hurry, without saying a word.

"Mr. Darius, is the toilet fixed? Oh, did you see the crack in the ceiling?" I ask pleadingly.

"No, no. My wife wait in car. She get angry, I keep her waiting," he says, eager to get away from me.

"Well, maybe she could come up," I suggest. "Have some pink poporn?"

Mr. Darius's kernel of patience with my on-camera charade finally pops, causing him to let out a minor explosion in the hallway.

"We have fizzies, too—ginger ale?" I squeak as he exits hastily down the hall. "*See ya,* Mr. Darius!" I say, shutting the door.

"Bravo!" yelps Angora, clapping loudly. "That's what I call effective Catwalk leadership skills!"

Caterina grins at me, while Angora decides to turn the table, asking, "Who decides what footage you're going to use?"

"The network has final cut," Caterina reveals.

"Are you going to let the competing houses see each other's footage to create more drama?" I ask.

"They'll see it when it airs," Caterina says firmly.

"Do you leak stuff to the media?" counters Angora.

"We do send them footage, or 'items,' in the hope that they'll give us some coverage," Caterina admits.

"What's an item?" Felinez asks.

"Newsworthy tidbits, like the stuff we read in the gossip column in *Women's Wear Daily* or 'Page Six' in the *New York Post*," Angora explains proudly. She *is* the fashion journalism major among us.

"So, you mean there may be something printed about us in the newspaper?" I ask, getting excited.

"Could be. The news editors decide what they'll print or air," Caterina continues. "We're gonna shoot a lot of footage—there'll be plenty of opportunities for media coverage." Then, in her clipped tone, Caterina commands: "Okay, how about some questions now?"

"Abso-fre—" I say, then stop myself mid-word.

"Pashmina, I sense there is tension between you and your sister, Chenille. Does she want to be in the House of Pashmina, too?"

I gagulate at Caterina's candor and start mumbling. "No, maybe she doesn't, but she understands that I'm an, um, aspiring modelpreneur," I say, diverting the drama from my cranky sister. My mother will skin me like a rabbit in a Maxmilian fur trap if I dis Chenille on camera.

Luckily, Angora steps up to the fashion plate. "Not everybody is on board with our agenda. They just think we have it easy. But they don't realize, if a model doesn't plan her career carefully, she'll have nothing more than some pretty pictures and a pocketful of poses when it's all over, and there's no greater fashion tragedy than a marked-down model."

Caterina instructs the camera to go to Zeus for input. "Um, my family isn't totally cool with what I'm down with. I mean, if that's what you want to know," he reveals. The camera keeps rolling, so does Zeus. "I think they'd rather I do something else. But I see modeling as a way to help my family. I mean, my dad works hard. He's a custom tailor and has his own shop, but he could have been a designer, I mean he's got the skills."

"Were you deejaying in the Fashion Café yesterday when everyone was voguing?" Caterina continues.

Now my clunky clogs come in handy—because I kick Zeus on his left Adidas under the dining room table. After a few seconds of silence, Caterina realizes that we aren't going to break from twenty years of covert tradition, not even for our five minutes of fashion footage, so she continues probing with supa-catty questions.

"Who's the bigger threat—Shalimar or Ninja, Jr.?"

"They are not our enemies—merely the competition," I respond calmly. The four of us do the Catwalk handshake on that one.

"What is that you're doing?" Caterina asks.

"That's our Kats and Kitties handshake," I explain proudly. "You know, crossing paws."

After fifteen more minutes of sound bites, we take a snack break, then get back to our meeting. By the end, we've compiled a list of all the candidates we need to assemble for team members and we complete the copy for the flyer I'm putting up on the Fashion Board.

"Ayigght, I'm gonna hook up the cat graphics and the type tonight on my computer, and I'll have the poster ready in the morning. Cool?" Zeus asks, beaming at us.

"Abso-*freakin'*-lutely!" I say emphatically.

After the Teen Style Network crew leaves, we start squealing. "You were fierce!" declares Aphro.

"Really? I felt like a Bazozo," I say jokingly, referring to our Catwalk code for dunce.

"Miss Biggie Grande, you're gonna have to stop with the hoochie shout-outs, or we're gonna end up in the haters' corner," warns Felinez.

"For true," I second, issuing a gentle warning before dolloping praise on Fifi: "You were on *punto*, too," I say, giving her a much-needed hug. I think all that model talk sometimes does bother her now that Aphro and Angora are in the mix.

"Caterina is *très* inquisitive," notes Angora, who is helping me clean before my mom gets home from work, which will be *pronto*.

"Mos def," I concur. "I bet she even knows where all the squirrels in Central Park bury their acorns."

"Well, you definitely put your landlord on blast, that's for sure," Aphro teases.

Zeus looks at us, puzzled. After we brief him on Operation: Kitty Litter, he gets his heckle on heartily. "Well, I definitely think you got his attention. I don't know if that ceiling is gonna get fixed, though," he says, trying to suppress his laughter.

We all laugh so hard that my disappointment about Ice Très's disappearing act melts away. Who cares, cuz I definitely earned my zebra stripes today by snagging Zeus for the House of Pashmina—even if I don't get to keep him all to myself.

## FASHION INTERNATIONAL 35TH ANNUAL
## CATWALK COMPETITION BLOG

New school rule: You don't have to be ultranice, but don't get tooooo catty, or your posting will be zapped by the Fashion Avengers!!

BOYZ IN THE HOODIES

Ever since I was a young fashion thug tying up the laces on my first pair of Adidas Superstars and leaving my mark on my first legit slab of vertical concrete (the 20-foot overpass on Highway 20), I knew I wanted to represent street style for brothers everywhere. See, back in the day, fashion was all about name-dropping, from your hoodie to the bangle on your hot toddy's arm, but today you can jet to Shanghai or South Central and see our raw flavor served full strength. I'm not gonna front—I did snag those style sentiments from a certain delovely. Anyway, as for the new-school definition of a brother: it's anybody who isn't trying to jack up my street cred just because they're making paper on Wall Street or shouting from their seat in the House of Representatives. See, we're all representatives in this thing called life. As for a "house," the time has finally come that I'm going to be part of one that'll make fashion *he*story. Straight up this Catwalk competition at Fashion I is dominated by the delovelies, but I will still represent. If the music business can clean up its act and end the pirating of video vixens to sell

158

records, then the fashion business should stop the propaganda that style is for sissies. But I won't lie: a de-lovely with a style vision of her own (like the aforementioned) is like a virgin slab of concrete. I'll never be able to resist the temptation to leave my mark. So, there's nothing else I can say to the ones tempting me right now except "Tag, you're it."

10/01/2008 10:45:44 AM
Posted by: Fashion Thug

8

"I still can't believe Ice Très stood me up," I bemoan to Felinez, slamming my locker shut. "Wait till I see him, I'm gonna be so shady—"

"I know: it's total eclipse time," Felinez interjects, because she understands my dark side too well.

What I don't understand is why I can't stop *obsessing* about the Fashion Thug—that is, I can't stop until Zeus strolls up with the fabbie flyer we'll post on the fashion board. He opens his black vinyl messenger bag and holds up his handiwork like it's a delicate soufflé. "Think potential Kats and Kitties will dig that?"

"You put the 'fly' in flyer!" I squeal, marveling at our tagline: ONLY CAT LOVERS NEED APPLY.

"Check the groovy graphics on the borders. *Hello!*" adds Aphro.

Angora takes notes on the curlicues. "*J'adore* this typeface. Is it from Font Book?"

"Nah, I designed this jammy myself. We can use it for all our graphics needs—the programs for the fashion show, our little hype handouts, everything," explains Zeus.

"*Major* purr points," Angora concurs.

"Okay, let's tack and roll," I order, grabbing the flyer and Felinez's arm. Aphro is chaperoning Angora to the ladies' room.

"Non-Catwalk business," I inform Zeus with a wink while we stand there whispering among our fabbie three selves.

Zeus smiles knowingly: "I got two sisters. I got you," then jets to his locker in the next row.

"Oy, now I'm getting like Ice Très," I comment to Felinez as we walk to the fashion board. "Winking and blinking."

"What happened?" Felinez asks in an agitated tone.

"What's bothering you, Blue Boca?" I ask, taking the spotlight off myself.

Felinez's apple-size cheeks turn bright red as she explains what happened on the way to school this morning. "Outside the bodega, this fat guy with his stomach hanging out of his T-shirt yells at me, '*Hola*, fat ass!' So I turn and blast, 'Who you calling fat?' He laughs like a stuffed *puerco*. 'I said, *flat*. FAT asses I like, *mami*!'"

"What a jerkaroni," I snarl, comforting Felinez, at least until I see Ice Très helping Shalimar put up *her* flyer. Now I'm the one who needs to be comforted. My mouth open like a guppy's, I read the overly hyped header on Shalimar's poster in disbelief: CALLING ALL FASHION THUGS. HOLLA. Suddenly, that's exactly what

161

I'd like to do: scream and make some noise. "So now she's into ghetto couture?" I hiss under my breath, grimacing at the musical-chair turn of events. Ice Très has obviously become her graffiti guru. Fifi pries the pink tacks out of my hand to prevent me from sticking them into Ice Très's pointy head instead of on the corners of our prized poster. The guilty one grins in my direction, instinctively realizing that he's just escaped the wrath of a killer kitty. Meanwhile, I pretend I can't see the brightness of his rabbit teeth bouncing off the fluorescent lights.

Felinez nudges me back to business. She points to Chandelier's poster—the most blinged-out on the board. "She must have gotten here at six a.m. with the other fashion vampires," I comment as we walk away. "Well, at least we beat Anna Rex and Willi Ninja, Jr."

Against my will, I turn to stare at Ice Très. Shalimar winces at me and points to the meowch pouch strung around my neck on a piece of pink rawhide. "What you got in there—voodoo mojo? Don't think it's working!" she giggles. I ignore her and try to meet Ice Très's gaze so I can level my signature shady glare, but now *he's* pretending he doesn't notice, his head shrinking into his Rocawear hoodie.

"I can't believe I've been *hoodwinked*." I wince, walking away to lick my wounds in private.

Now Anna Rex and Elisa Pound whiz by us, their

poster in hand. "Sorry I'm late," Anna moans to her black-clad disciple. "I had to beg my mother to give me money for Alli."

"I wish I could go get Alli, too," Felinez laments.

"Who's Alli?" I ask her, secretly wondering if she's losing it. That's when I discover the only thing she's trying to lose is weight, as usual. "Alli" is the half-dose of the prescription drug Xenical—a fat-blocker pill—with disgusting side effects I can't repeat.

"This one *is* approved by the FDA, though!" Felinez blurts out. "But I wish it didn't cost fifty dollars a bottle."

"Yeah, well, that's not the only price you pay. Do you really want to become known as Senorita Poops-a-Lot?" I ask. "I hope when we win the competition, you have better things to do with your prize money."

"Well, I hope people show up for our interviews later!" Felinez counters sarcastically.

About that, Fifi is right. "And I hope we don't get any *LOSERS*," I add nervously, twirling a loose strand of hair at my temple at full throttle. "Even if they have been approved by the FDA!"

︿ ︿

At four o'clock sharp, Aphro, Felinez, Angora, and I are the only ones sitting at our appointed table in Studio C. Tapping my meowch pouch against my chest, I order everyone to fill out their membership forms. Then I cup my head in my frozen hands. "If nobody shows up, I'm gonna have a meltdown like five-day-old mac and cheese."

"Well, at least Zeus is down for the twirl. He'll be here," Aphro says, jabbing my elbow. "My lips are chapped. Gimme your lipstick."

Aphro swipes the Baked Brownie Swirl Stick from my hand and pops open the tube. "This ain't frosted, is it?"

"Of course not," I reply.

"Good, cuz I was about to get frosty with you," she hmmphs.

I know that Aphro hates bling-bling on her *boca* because she thinks it makes her lips look too plumpalicious, even though I wish I had a smoocher like hers.

"Speaking of frosty, *chérie*, I'm going to risk my life telling you about a certain blog entry," Angora starts in, intently filling out her form. "Ice Très is waxing his Magic Markers about joining a certain house—"

"Shalimar's. We know," says Felinez.

"He's also hoping that all admiring 'delovelies' consider becoming his design muses. I guess that's what he meant by 'Tag, you're it'?" Angora reflects.

"Delovelies? He's not a designer—he's a dunce," comments Aphro.

"Also on dunce detail—Delilah Diddy waylaid me

164

after textile science today to show me pictures of her cat and her sketchbook," I report to my crew about one candidate too anxious to wait for the scheduled interview rendezvous. "Her style is so predictable, the only things she should consider designing are crystal balls."

"*Je comprends*," Angora says, concurring.

"Oy, maybe we should forget about cat lovers. At this rate, I'm gonna need a CAT scan!" I moan in jest.

Suddenly, there's a loud cackling outside the studio and I look up, hoping the graffiti artist will grace us with his wearable denim art and goofy grin. Instead, I realize it was merely a caco*phony* orchestrated by Chandelier and Tina, who hurriedly walk by, peering into the studio on the fly.

"I don't think he's coming," Aphro snarls, reading my troubled mind.

Now I feel like a dunce—and compelled to share my secret obsession with my crew. "Remember those Pepe LePone peep-toe slingbacks? I saw them on sale at the Shoe Shack, but I didn't buy them? Then I went back the next week hoping they had slashed the price some more, but somebody else had already snatched 'em. Remember how I couldn't stop obsessing about them? Well, that's how I feel about Ice Très, okay."

"So you're saying, you're not really interested in a guy until he's been marked down?" Angora interprets.

"No, that's not it. Pink Head's saying she wasn't

feeling Ice Très till somebody else was!" blurts out Felinez.

I shrug. I don't know what I'm feeling anymore.

"Well, I know Shalimar ain't feeling Ice Très's fashion thuggery. She *must* be peepin' something else—" Aphro starts in, but smacks her lips instead, blotting her freshly applied lipstick.

We all giggle uncontrollably while Zeus appears in the doorway with a supa-shortie in tow.

"This is my man Lupo Saltimbocca," announces Zeus, his flash-ready smile lighting up the studio. Maybe Aphro is right. Maybe I don't think I'm good enough for Zeus. I know that's not what she said, but maybe that's what she was thinking. He's got it made in the shade, while I have to deal with family drama.

Lupo blushes and looks up at Zeus, who is a head taller than him. He has a really big nose and a grin that's goofier than Ice Très's.

"Come on, now. I had to put you on blast. Show them your work," Zeus instructs Lupo, obviously eager for us to give his recruit our feline seal of approval.

Lupo clumsily opens his portfolio, and a pile of photos plops on the floor. I watch him pick them up, hoping he has more luck loading his camera. "These are some of the models I shoot already," Lupo explains excitedly, his big brown eyes getting pop-eyed. I zoom right in on the head shots of Elgamela that landed on the top of the heap, while Aphro homes in on the silver lily pendant dangling on a platinum chain around Lupo's short, thick neck.

"Did you make that?" she asks.

"No, I'm not a designer," Lupo clarifies.

"I know, but it's handmade," Aphro continues.

"Yes, by Agnello. He makes jewelry back in Firenze," Lupo explains in his thick Italian accent. "This is the, how do you say, the symbol, yes, for my region. *Gigli*."

"The lily pad is the symbol for Firenze?" asks Felinez, trying to help Lupo. "We're all taking Italian."

"Oh, bravo," says Lupo, impressed.

"See, we're trying to do more than order ice cream in Italian—that is, if we win," I giggle.

"Gelato, *per favore*!" Lupo giggles, too. "I can help you with that, you know?"

"Ordering gelato?" Felinez asks, her mouth salivating. "Where—here?"

"No, I can help you study Italian," he clarifies.

"Well, that settles it—" I start, realizing what an asset Lupo really is to the House of Pashmina.

"You're in there like swimwear!" Zeus says, finishing my sentence.

"Seriously, though—these photos are hot!" I exclaim, flipping through his portfolio and noticing eight more photos of Elgamela posed in slinky black Lycra

167

outfits against a stark white backdrop. I wonder if Lupo is obsessed with her. Maybe he has already interviewed to be in Chandelier's house just to be close to his model muse.

Right on cue, Zeus adds, "You know that Chandelier wants him in her house, but I told him this is the move."

"Do you know Elgamela?" Lupo asks, turning to me. "For me, she is incredible." Sensing my hesitation, he quickly adds, "You are very beautiful, too. And you." Now Lupo is pointing to Aphro. "I want to take pictures of both of you."

"Oh, you're definitely in with us now," Aphro says, smoothing down her straight bangs.

"We love Elgamela. I mean, she hit the fashion trifecta—tall, exotic—and she can dance," I say.

"Not as good as you," Lupo squeals at Aphro. "I saw you in the café. *Madonna,* you were *marveloso!*"

Now I'm getting the impression that Lupo pulled Zeus's strings for an intro, and not the other way around.

Aphro tilts her head like a peacock. "Well, I try."

"See, Elgamela is friends with Nole and Dame— and *Chandelier,*" I continue, getting back on the Catwalk track.

"Yes, but Elgamela loves me. If we want her, I tell her that, no?" Lupo says earnestly.

Zeus nods behind Lupo's back. "He's the man, I'm telling you—things can be done, tassels can be pulled."

Suddenly, I get hopeful. "Really? Then make it happen. I've got to hand in these sheets," I say, pointing to the formidable stack of empty member forms that will need to be filled out and delivered to the Catwalk director's office by Friday morning.

"Can I come in?" asks Diamond Tyler, knocking on the door.

"I didn't think you would show," I say like a bad hostess, I guess because I'm relieved that she *did* come.

Diamond stands in the doorway, her hands shoved in the pockets of her Free People Reindeer Love parka.

"Girl, don't just stand there. Come on in and take your jacket off. The pawnshop's closed!" Aphro yells out.

"Such great energy. I love her!" gushes Lupo. He's definitely feeling Aphro. Diamond chuckles and plops her cute aqua-and-pink-striped Yak Pak on the floor, the two pandas perched on the front pockets positioned by my pink Mary Janes like they're gonna smooch my toes.

"How's Crutches?" I ask, watching as Diamond squirms on the edge of the chair.

"Oh, great! Now they've got her swimming with this new pussy paddle."

Lupo and Zeus snicker, then burst out laughing. "Sorry," Zeus says, trying to stifle his guffaws.

Diamond earnestly explains about the physical therapy contraption before she veers into her latest source of discomfort. "Did you hear about the sheep on the Grand Concourse?" she asks, turning to Felinez since they both live in the South Bronx.

"No," Felinez responds guiltily. "I didn't, um, count any sheep?"

Lupo giggles. I think that's his calling card, along with the Nikon camera he has taken out of the case and strapped around his neck.

"There are five slaughterhouses right on Tremont," Diamond explains seriously. "Well, one of the sheep escaped with the USDA clip hanging off her ear. She ran right into the street. She could have been killed. I mean, she's escaped death twice. Really."

I try to understand what she's saying, then I get it.

"We're petitioning to get her sent to a farm in Westchester," Diamond goes on, "instead of being returned to the meatpacking district to be killed. The meeting is tonight, so I gotta get uptown."

"I got you," I say, eager to accommodate her busy animal-activism schedule. "Show us what you got, cuz I don't think Aphro has seen your designs."

Diamond gingerly lays her sketchbook on the table

and I turn the pages with tender care. "Sweet," I comment with each passing page. I really do dig Diamond's vibe, even though I can sense that the rest of my crew has doubts about her skills.

"What kind of stuff do you want to do?" Diamond asks hesitantly.

"We're gonna feature regular and plus sizes for the Kats and Kitties," I say proudly. "And we'll open the show with a few fashions for kids, too."

"That's what feline fatale style is all about: *all sizes*," Felinez says.

"I like that," Diamond says, nodding approvingly.

"Yeah, we do too," Zeus pipes up.

"I love all sizes too," seconds Lupo, and the two of them start guffawing again.

"I think I'm gonna have to separate you two till recess," I warn them.

Then I turn my head and mouth to Angora: *I don't think he's gay.* She nods back at me in agreement.

In the meantime, Lupo focuses his camera and starts clicking away. The flash from the Nikon startles Diamond, who puts her head down and tries to cover her face.

"We must document the whole process, I think?" explains Lupo. "For the fashion show, we can have a photo collage on the walls behind where the audience is sitting, no?"

"That's *meowverlous*!" I coo in my British alter ego voice. Zeus and Lupo are making me giddy.

Diamond gets excited too, and pulls out another notebook of design sketches.

"Wow. Now, these I dig. The babydoll dresses—this one with the eyelet bib and the ruffles," I say, tapping the page.

"And you can wear it on or off the shoulders. We could put some cat's-eye shapes beveled with rhinestones around the neckline," Diamond suggests. "And put some cat's-eye tattoos on the model's shoulders?"

"Nice," says Zeus. Judging from the phoenix on his right arm, it's not surprising tattoo sightings would get a rise out of the graphic artiste.

"We could do a whole babydoll segment. That would look great with headbands," adds Felinez.

"For jewelry, I wanna make some necklaces with cat charms dangling from them," adds Aphro.

"Oh, that totally works with this kind of neckline," Diamond says, then turns to Felinez. "I really like the meowch pouches you're wearing."

"Oh, yeah. We want the models to carry those instead of the wristlet clutches everybody else is doing," explains Felinez.

"What's your thought on pom-poms?" I ask.

"If you've got them, you'd better shake 'em?"

Diamond says, shrugging as if she suddenly realizes that she is indeed auditioning.

Zeus, Lupo, and Felinez giggle.

"Well, I think we should give it a twirl, no?" I say to Diamond, hoping she'll say yes. "I mean, I know you can't stay, but we'll see what the cat drags in." What I really want to say is: *I pray that Nole Canoli smells the catnip and careens around the corner any* segundo.

"Is there any designer at FI you dig?" Zeus asks her outright.

"Yeah, your friend Nole Canoli. I mean, he was in my draping class and, well, he's a genius," Diamond says, like she's telling us something we don't know. "Have you asked him?"

"Yeah, I asked him," Zeus admits. "He joined Chandelier's house. She, um, did her interviews yesterday. I saw him there."

I wince, of course, because Zeus has reminded me that we're scrambling for talent.

"I'm happy you came to see us. I knew we had the same style sensibilities," I say sincerely.

"You know what, I can stay," Diamond decides on the spot.

"*Meowverlous!*" I squeal again.

Diamond relaxes into the chair, like she has let go of caring for all the animals in the world except for the desperate felines in front of her. "So, did you get a job?" she asks me, seeming genuinely interested.

"Um, no, but Felinez did," I say, turning to Fifi.

"It's just an internship, so don't be jealous!"

"What about you?" I ask, wondering if Diamond will be able to contribute to our burgeoning demand for design supplies.

"Yes!" Diamond says excitedly; then she drops the doggie bag. "It's at the Animal Care Center on 110th Street. Volunteering, you know."

"Oh, right," I say, then change the subject. "We'll discuss the Catwalk budget later, but I'm getting about three hundred dollars for the first installment."

"*Hola!*" shouts Chintzy Colon, who walks into the studio with a tall blond girl in tow. I've seen the girl in the library, but I don't know who she is, even though it's obvious she hit the genetic lottery and we're talking the Mega Millions jackpot.

"Your flyer was so cute!" the girl coos, interrupting Chintzy. She's even taller than I am, and blonder than Angora. "You won't believe, but my name is Kissa Sami!"

Now Lupo's eyes really get pop-eyed. "You're a model, right?" he asks.

"I will be soon!" Kissa coos. Lupo aims his camera at Kissa and clicks away. She poses without any prompting. "Do you want me to walk now?" Kissa asks, looking around to see who's in charge.

"Yes, please," I command, watching her sashay—sort of stiffly, but with definite potential.

Aphro jumps up and gives Kissa some instruction. "Push your hips forward, then let it flow. Don't move your arms so much." Kissa walks again, this time more assuredly.

"You have beautiful eyes," I say, noticing how her eyes are slanty but blue and icy clear, not hazy like Zeus's. "Where are you from?"

"Finland," Kissa coos, then tells us how psyched she was to be chosen for FI's student exchange program. She goes on to explain how long the waiting list is—longer than the one for a highly coveted Birkin Bag at Hermès (and that one is six years!). "My best friend was crushed—she couldn't come. We dream together to be in the Catwalk competition!"

"Did you make up your name?" Aphro asks, half-joking.

"Oh no. It means 'cat' in Finnish. We have seven at home. I swear!"

"Seven Kissas, or seven cats?" Lupo asks for clarification.

"Seven furry, not seven tall like me!" Kissa giggles, then pulls out pictures from her shoulder bag. "You don't believe."

"Oh, we believe," I giggle, looking at the photos of her most beloved feline—a black cat she tells me is named Kuma. "My mother went to a sushi restaurant and she misunderstood the waiter. She thought he told her that 'kuma' means 'black' in Japanese, but it turns out it means 'bear'!" While the kitty coo-fest continues between Kissa and Angora, a few more students enter the studio.

"I got this," Aphro says, and handles them while I conduct an interview with Chintzy Colon.

Chintzy sits down and smiles on cue. "You must have been upset that you didn't win, um, one of the house leader positions," I begin, broaching the touchy-feely.

"My mother was more upset than I was," Chintzy says, but I wonder if she's merely on spin patrol as usual. "I mean, I'm not sure I could handle the stress anyway, um, now that I'm going to be working—" Chintzy stops like she's spilling the refried beans.

"Where are you working at?" I ask, trying to fend off an attack of Gucci Envy.

Chintzy hesitates, then blushes. "At Grubster PR."

"Oh, so Shalimar hooked you up?" I ask, blushing brighter than Chintzy. Sometimes being right feels worse than being wrong.

"Um, she got me an interview, that's all," Chintzy says apologetically.

"So why don't you join her house, *mija?*" Felinez asks, butting in.

"My sense of style is closer to your vision?" Chintzy says like it's a question, swinging her leg nervously. Now the question on my lips is why she's wearing Cayman Crocs, those ubiquitous holey plastic clogs that should be relegated only to tiptoeing around the tulips.

"I also think your house is the most fun. Everybody else takes themselves so seriously," Chintzy adds for good measure.

"That's true, *chérie*," Angora says, looking up from her interview with Liza Flake, a hairstyling major in the Fashion Annex. "We are just one big furry ball of fun and michief."

Liza smiles at me and says, "I see your sister is in the program now!"

"Yes," I say, then divert the drama by pointing to her photos. "What's that—you did a shoot?"

"Yeah, my first one!" Liza says, excited. "For Elgamela—she's really working hard on getting her portfolio together. I think she's definitely gonna win one of the modeling contracts in the competition."

"We agree," Angora says diplomatically.

"Did you interview her yet?" Liza asks, like she hopes we did. "I told her I was coming here."

"Um, no, but who knows? The night is still young," I say, then divert the drama again. "I love her hair swept up like that."

"We could do upsweeps like this for the show—with chopsticks?" Liza offers.

"Love, *love*," Angora coos. "Did you interview with anyone else?"

"Well, yeah, but I don't want to start any bidding wars," Liza says, running her fingers through her bright red hair.

"Name your price," I say sarcastically.

"I get to pick the lead stylist," Liza quips.

Now I wonder if she's serious, so I put her to the test. "Who do you have in mind?"

"Dame Leeds?"

I can't help but think, we are definitely not picking the lucky numbers tonight.

"We'll take your offer into consideration," I say politely.

"Is that hennafied, Miss Redhead?" Aphro blurts out, breaking the heated negotiations.

"Freakin' yes," coos Liza, lightening up. "Seriously, though, I like what you guys are doing. The every-size concept. My mother is plus size, and she is always on the major frus about the frumpy clothes. Unify—that's what I think."

"My mother is assistant manager of Forgotten Diva on Madison," I add in agreement.

"Oh, I didn't mean anything bad," Liza says, embarrassed.

"Oh, puhleez. My mother knows. Her customers are old school, or else they'd be petitioning for fiercer threads. Trust," I assure her.

"So, are you gonna get back to me for real?" Liza asks nervously.

"We'd love to have you for the hairstyling assistant."

Liza shifts in her chair for a second, then asks the obvious. "What about your sister?"

Angora shoots me a look, and I know exactly what she's thinking: she wants me to heed her mother's advice, which is exactly what I do. "She's so busy with clients from our, um, neighborhood, she's not stressing the extra responsibility."

"Not even for a piece of a hundred thousand dollars and Louis Vuitton luggage—*and* a trip to Italy?" Liza asks in disbelief, spieling off the goodies like a game-show host. "Well, I'm in it for the loot. And that's the truth."

"Well, sometimes the truth is just plain *appropriate*," Angora says, and we all giggle at the inside joke.

Meanwhile, a few more students come in and sit at the studio table, so I turn my attention back to Chintzy, who has been waiting patiently for a grand finale. "But what would you do—in the house, I mean?" I ask her.

"Be your assistant, and I can help with the PR when the time comes. I can also be one of the dressers for the models backstage at the show," Chintzy says, like she's adding on extra helpings of duties for good measure.

Felinez is talking to Mink Yong from her geometry class but still finding time to glare down my throat. Nonetheless, I make a decision. "Okay, Chintzy, let's do it."

"Great!" Chintzy says, sprinkling me with her smile, then reaching over to hug me. Felinez glares at me like she did in kindergarten after I snatched all the pink crayons, which I deemed only for *my* domain, hence my nickname.

"Bye!" Chintzy says, bouncing off the chair and almost right into the bosom of Jackie Moore and a few more designer candidates, all of whom Diamond recognizes instantly.

"Hi, Jackie," Diamond says sweetly. Roger Rivet nods at her and makes it clear that he is strictly business. Frail and tiny, he unzips his portfolio and places a well-manicured (and frosted?) hand on top of it like he's posing for a hand cream ad. The three design candidates take seats as Shantung Jones takes a twirl for Aphro. Roger stares at his hand like he's about to dig for gold under his nails instead of focusing on the fierce fashion model.

"Now, you know you're gonna have to change your hairstyle?" Aphro tells Shantung teasingly, because they're both wearing the same exact dippin' do—an asymmetrical blunt-cut bob with razor-sharp bangs.

"When Naomi wears her hair like that—for me, she looks *bellissima,*" declares Lupo. Aphro hates any comparisions to the British supermodel who whacked her maid with a cell phone and landed herself in an orange sanitation vest—and I don't mean on the runway, okay.

Shantung giggles, her cinnamon-specked eyes sparkling.

"We'll discuss her hairstyle later," pipes up Liza Flake, like she's the head britch in charge. Only problem is, she isn't.

Aphro throws me a glance like, *Is she the assistant hairstylist, or the lead?*

I make a note to my fashion self to handle that skirmish—as soon as we find someone above Liza's level, thank you. Truth is, any distraction is welcome, because I can tell that Diamond is definitely not feeling Roger's designs, and let's just say I'm definitely not ready-to-wear them either.

Lita Rogers's sketches are a little more appetizing. "I like the lace tops and gypsy skirts," Diamond says.

"My family is going to invest in my clothing line as soon as I graduate," Lita tells Diamond.

"Oh, so you got it like that," Aphro says, demi-joking, demi-serious.

Lita shifts her gears into gratitude mode. "I know I'm lucky."

"What's your line going to be called?" Diamond asks sweetly.

"Lollipops," Lita says, grinning proudly. "I've had the name picked out for a while. My father is going to get it trademarked."

"That's tasty," I say politely. Angora's silence, however, is palpable.

"*Chérie*—what say you?" I ask, grinning. My mouth is starting to hurt from all this interviewing.

"There is a famous strip club in Baton Rouge called Lollipops," Angora informs us hesitantly.

Lita's face turns beet red. She flaps her sketchbook shut tighter than a Venus flytrap. "Really?" she asks in disbelief.

Angora nods. "Ms. Harness, our fashion merchandising teacher, is right. Research is everything."

"I gotta go," Lita informs us, still red-faced.

"I'll let you know," I tell Lita, trying to smooth her ruffled fashion feathers. After all, it's still a tasty name, and it's hard coming up with an original name someone hasn't already used for their schemes and dreams.

"Um, I have to go too," Roger Rivet informs us, and I give him the same we'll-be-in-touch spiel.

Jackie Moore looks at us like a deer caught in headlights. She pulls out a skimpy sketchpad filled with swimwear designs. "Yellow bikini," I say, observing the bling-bling string set.

"Are we going to do swimwear?" Aphro asks.

"Um, it's possible," I say, but I can't help but wonder where Jackie is picking up her color cues.

"I'm from Florida," explains Jackie. "It's always sunny—that's why I'm into yellow."

I thank Jackie for coming and scribble a few notes on my pad. Heather Bond is next in the hot seat. After Jackie jets, she sits on the edge of her chair like she's ready to eject herself on my cue. Then she nervously opens her sketchbook for our perusal. "I'm into vinyl. I think that goes with feline fatale—big-time."

"I agree," pipes up Diamond, obviously looking out for the hides of all her four-legged friends.

Aphro, however, has an opinion about that one. "I prefer leather—soft as butter and not Parkay, thank you."

"A black pleather catsuit would be cute for the show," I interject. Although Heather's designs are strictly fade to black, I'm trying to see whether she has any diversity.

"Is black your favorite color?" Diamond asks.

"Um, yeah, I guess it is," Lita says, shrugging and sealing her coffin. She definitely seems more like a design disciple for Anna Rex, even if she doesn't know it.

After two *more* hours of noshing and networking, we decide to wrap up our session like a fashion falafel.

"Thanks for stopping by!" Felinez says giddily. She hugs Shantung Jones so hard, the frail model winces as if her tiny bones are being crushed. "Next time we'll have party hats and piñatas!"

Lupo grins and walks out the door after Shantung. I tap him gently on the back and mouth, *Stay*.

He breaks into a big grin and resumes his posturing.

"Okay, so now that it's just inner crew, I want to get some feedback." I instruct everybody to sit down.

"I can't believe you invited Chintzy into our house without asking the rest of us!" Felinez blurts out.

"Okay, you're right. My bad. But I knew what you were going to say, and I don't agree with you," I say firmly.

"I'm telling you. She's a sneaky senorita!" Felinez says, her face flushed.

"She's going to be our assistant, and she's gonna help with our publicity campaign. I think she's an asset—on some level," I say, kaflustered.

"That's a croc—like those *fea* clogs she was wearing!" Felinez cries. "You never liked her before!"

"Okay, you're pissed. Now you can pick whichever model you wanted out of the—" I count the number of model sheets we've collected and render the final tally. "Okay, we saw twenty-five models so far. I know you want Mink. Kissa. Who else?"

"Jaynelle—and the guy with the corkscrews," Felinez says, still pouting.

"Dreads—that's Benny Madina," I remind her. "Okay, he's in. Who else do you want?"

"Shantung." Felinez folds her arms across her chest and continues to pout. "Never mind, *mija,* you don't listen to me!"

I figure Felinez is cranky because we haven't eaten dinner, so I let it go. "Shantung, of course."

"We still don't have a lead designer," Aphro reminds me.

"Jackie is tacky," I moan.

"I agree," adds Angora. "Yellow is only a fashion color if you're Big Bird. What about Roger?"

"All those hanky hemlines. No, thank you. I wanted to pull out a tissue and blow my nose," I respond.

"Heather 'Pleather'?" asks Aphro.

"Well, at least she's into catsuits. Lita with the dirndl skirts and crop tops was too sickeningly sweet. Yuck," adds Angora.

"So we *still* don't have a lead designer," Aphro repeats.

"I know," I shout, finally losing it. "What do you want me to do!"

"Need a moment?" Aphro snarls.

I take a second to chill before I blurt out, "Look, Diamond can do it. I'm leaning toward her. I'm telling you, she's a gem in the rough."

"Rough is right. You sure she won't crumble under the pressure? I mean, she seems more interested in us not eating lamb chops than in winning a competition, okay?" shouts Aphro. "I mean, no disrespect for her vegetarian plan and whatnot."

"We've got her back," I insist.

"Ayiight," Aphro says, sounding unsure. "You're the boss, Miss Ross."

"That's right, you are," says a familiar voice. I look up and there is Ice Très, darkening the doorway.

I smile at him automatically, probably from smiling all afternoon at interviewees. Suddenly, I feel my throat tighten and announce, "I gotta get some water."

I ignore Ice Très, but he trails behind me. "Can I holla at you for a sec?"

"You've got my undivided attention from here to the water fountain. Let's see if you can hold it," I bark at him.

"I just wanna explain what happened," he says with a grin.

"I know what happened," I counter. "So it's a wrap, falafel, and a shish kebab. Get it?"

"Got it," Ice Très concedes. "Look, I didn't want to mix business with pleasure. I thought if I joined

Shalimar's house, then we could just be friends. Know what I'm saying?"

"Um, no, but I'll be right up," I say, bobbing my head down to sip some water from the faucet. When I finish, I stand back up and announce, "Time's up."

"Okay, how 'bout Friday we hook up? Around six? I'm going to see Zeus spin."

"I was going anyway," I say, not giving in.

"You can stretch me to the limit with your catty stance. I deserve that. But we're cool?" Ice Très asks pitifully.

"Chilly," I say, then run back to the studio to retrieve my crew.

My crew is all ears when I return, except for Aphro, who is all mouth, as usual.

"I cannot believe you agreed to hook up with him!" she snarls. "A five-year-old could have cooked up a better story in his Creepy Crawlers Oven than that one."

"Back to business, big mouth, if you don't mind," I warn Aphro.

"Whatever makes you clever," Aphro hisses, and storms off.

Lupo runs after her, which annoys me. "You'd think she was a runaway sheep with a USDA clip on her ear in need of sanctuary," I say, agitated. "Are you two gonna stand there like dummies?" I shoot at Angora and Zeus, who are posed so still they look like mannequins in a Macy's window.

Angora purses her lips and says, "This dummy is going home. And remember, we've only got till Friday to hand in the membership forms."

## FASHION INTERNATIONAL 35TH ANNUAL CATWALK COMPETITION BLOG

New school rule: You don't have to be ultranice, but don't get tooooo catty, or your posting will be zapped by the Fashion Avengers!!

FASHION 101: DON'T FALL FOR FAKE FENDIS

Ever since I can remember, I have wanted to be head of the class. Perhaps my leadership skills come naturally to me since I'm the oldest of four kids and my mother died when I was six years old. During the difficult years that ensued, fashion became my refuge in what I considered to be a cruel and not-so-chic world that could snatch my mother in such an untimely death. While my father worked long, endless shifts as a male nurse at Brooklyn Hospital, I'd keep the four of us entertained by staging elaborate fashion shows in our tiny living room. (To this day, I think my little brother Socket is the best male model on the catwalk.) Becoming one of the lucky ones granted entry into Fashion International has given me an all-access fashion pass.

First of all, I'm armed with valuable insider 411: for example, did you know it was *not* French designer Paul Poiret who created the narrow, elevated ramp used in fashion shows known as *le podium* in gay Paree, but rather British designer Lady Duff-Gordon who staged the first catwalk-style fashion

show in 1904? Secondly, FI has af-
forded me the incredible opportunity
to stage my own fashion show this year
in the prestigious annual Catwalk competition. (Nole Canoli, I want the
world to know that you are the star
jewel in my fashion crown!) Perhaps
the most important lesson that I've
learned at Fashion International,
however, wasn't taught in any of the
classrooms. Let's just say it's the un-
credited addendum to the course Fashion 101. So listen up, aspiring house
leaders: the secrets to any leader's
success are assembling the most formidable team and always keeping an eye
out for true talent. On the flip side
of the fashion token, never ever fall
for the fake Fendis hiding among us,
or you'll develop a serious case of
toxic schlock syndrome that will prevent you from competing at the top of
your fashion game. . . . That's all
for now. See you at the shows, *dar-
lings*!

    10/05/2008 12:35:00 PM
    Posted by: Gucci Girl

# 9

Aphro is still all up in here about our designer duel at the interview finale. At least Felinez and Angora are trying to squash it like two-day-old beef jerky, which is exactly what it is. Literally. Call me paranoid, but I even think Aphrodite has been blasting her mighty "Biggie" mouth to Lupo Saltimbocca. After all, he didn't stay and watch my back; instead, he ran toward Miss Blunt (Bob) like he was going to live up to his last name and jump in her mouth. Or so I grumble to Felinez, who squeamishly mumbles back at me, "*Mija,* I'm just trying to A-B-C my way out of it, *esta bien?*"

"Pash, I think he tried," Angora says gently, adjusting her powder blue beret one micromillimeter away from her forehead. I'm not surprised that Angora instinctively knows why I'm *really* upset with Lupo. She's got it like that.

"Well, Loopy made it sound like all he had to do was click his camera and Elgamela would wiggle her belly button for him," I whine, nervously shoving my hands into the pockets of the shrunken denim blazer I decorated last night with paw prints from a metallic marker, secretly inspired by Ice Très. On the back, I sewed a CAT JUNKIE appliqué. I know that I'm exaggerating Lupo's claim, but I'm upset that he didn't come through on the promise of procuring the next Cleopatra for our house.

In the meantime, Aphro has agreed to meet us by Stingy Sami's newsstand this morning before we go to school. When she finally arrives, she squints at me like she's looking through the scope of a shooting gallery rifle to knock down a plastic duck. At least it's an improvement from yesterday. After I grunt "Hello," we proceed to forage the newsstand like press-poaching possums in search of any tasty tiddies that miraculously have been fed to the gossip columns by Caterina and her crew about the Catwalk competition.

Sami nods knowingly at us before staring off into space, the bit on his high-tail pipe clenched between his teeth. The newsstand owner has given up trying to stop fashion freeloaders—meaning students from FI—from thumbing mags and rags without forking over a finder's fee. But everybody else has to pay the piper. Once we saw him chase a lady in a wheelchair away after she threw a quarter at him for the pawed-over copy of the *New York Post* she was reading.

"I swear if I see Shalimar's name, I'm calling the

sham police," I hiss, carefully turning every page of the *New York Post*.

After scouring every single newspaper in the newsstand, including the *Daily Tattle*, we finally decide to let it go like disco.

"I can't believe we haven't even gotten an honorary mention yet," Angora says, breathing heavily.

"God, are we not worthy? Are we not worthy?" I moan.

We're not the only early-morning fashion desperadoes. A tall blond fashionista with a short, stubby ponytail, whom I've seen in the hallway at FI, crowds the newsstand and pleads with Sami. "Tell me you have the new *Vogue*. Puhleez?"

We giggle at his apparent fresh-fashion jones because we know it all too well. All of a sudden, the ponytailed pleader looks at me like I just jumped out of the pages of *Vogue*. "Omigod, hello! I'm so preoccupied, I didn't see you standing there in all your kitty fabulousness," he coos adoringly to me.

I'm puzzled pink because I don't think we've ever spoken.

"Sorry, let me rewind. Hello! I'm Bobby Beat. Okay, it's my professional name, because I serve the makeup instead of applying it, or so I've been told," he giggles, putting his hand to his chest.

"Where are you from?" Angora asks, honing in on his accent.

"Brooklyn," Bobby says, giggling again.

"Word?" inquires Aphro. "I'm from the BK, and that ain't no accent I ever heard."

"Oh!" Bobby squeals, hitting Aphro on the shoulder with a flicked wrist movement. "Brooklyn, Michigan!"

Angora sighs sweetly.

"Anyhoo, I've been hoping I'd run into your fabbie felineness, because I couldn't make the interview."

I smile back at him, flattered, as he babbles on.

"I had to do makeup for my sister's friend's test shots. Um, she's sending in photos for the next round of auditions for *You'd Better Work, Supermodel!*" Bobby explains earnestly, which piques our budding supermodel interest.

"She's eighteen?" Angora asks rhetorically, because we know the television show's eligibility rules by heart. We also know that *Supermodel* provides one winner a season with a $100,000 one-year modeling contract with the Snoot model agency.

"Yup, she's a freshman at FIT like my sister." Bobby nods knowingly. "But honey, don't stress it. With those cheekbones, there only one way you won't get a modeling contract from the Catwalk competition." Bobby pauses, and we wait with bated breath until he continues, "If you don't have me as the makeup artist in your house!"

"I hear that," Aphro says, finally lightening up.

"*Chéri*, what about your cheekbones?" Angora asks approvingly. "You look like you could model too."

"Oh, I know, but I can't stand the thought of trudging around all day on go-sees. I'm trying to get paid, *chérie*," admits Bobby Beat. "I know what I want: to be the next Kevyn Aucoin," he continues, referring to the late makeup artist, a graduate of Fashion International back in the day.

"Well, show us your legendary beat," I challenge him.

He whips out his book, which is half the size of most portfolios I've seen so far. Bobby senses my apprehension and quips, "It's the new millennium, *chérie*. Time to downsize."

We all huddle together and look at Bobby's test shots. "I'm very into Booty Dust, applied with a sponge, not a brush," he confides, pointing to the sparkly accents on the eyes, shoulders, and cleavage in the photos.

"I definitely dig that," I comment. "It makes everything pop in the photo."

"Who needs kitty litter when you have glitter!" Bobby says excitedly.

We guffaw grandly while a paying customer with an obvious Chinatown version of a Marc Jacobs quilted satchel steps up to the newsstand to buy a newspaper.

"Knock-knock," Aphro whispers to me.

Sami shoots us a look like it's time for us to take our fashion show on the road.

"Aw, Sami, don't be so stingy!" Bobby giggles, forking over five dollars for the September issue of *Vogue*.

"I thought you wanted October?" I ask.

"I do," Bobby Beat explains, "but I spilled orange juice on my September issue this morning at breakfast, and I hate stains—even on the ads, so I might as well get a replacement while I'm here."

"I read my *Vogue* while I'm sipping orange juice too," I giggle.

"Sipping and flipping!" Bobby coos. "Gucci, Pucci, and Juicy, oh my! By the way, what was that 'knock-knock' at the counter? You weren't referring to knocking me off, I hope!"

Aphro lets out a snort and we explain. "Nah. That's our code word for clocking a designer knockoff!"

"I *love* you tabby cats!" howls Bobby, who goes on to tell us his own code name: *SpongeBob*.

"I *love* you, SpongeBob!" I shout back.

"Now, tell me before I sign on," Bobby says with confidence, "who is the lead designer gonna be?"

The smiles vanish from our faces like we're

busted piñatas at a pity party. "Um, Diamond Tyler," I squeak.

Bobby looks disappointed too. "*Chéries, mon amis,* my new dear friends, she has sparkle potential for sure, but how do you say 'V for Versace'?" he moans, referring to Nole Canoli's online identity.

"That's what I said," hmmphs Aphro.

"Don't you just love the Catwalk blog?" Angora asks, veering away from the ensuing drama.

"Honey, first thing I do when I get up and take the chamomile eye pad off is turn on my Apple and read the blog!" claims Bobby Beat. "I *loved* Nole's."

"Is there any reason you want to be in our house?" I ask to keep the flow going.

"I mean, why not Willi Ninja, Jr.'s?" Angora adds.

"Oh, because I'm a queen, we should stick to-gether?" Bobby Beat retorts. "Is that what you're ask-ing, Miss Blue Beret?"

Angora pales two shades. Before she recovers, Bobby keeps pulling out stitches with his seam ripper. "I have been wielding brushes like Picasso and doing my mother's and my two sisters' makeup since I was potty trained. I *love* being around girls and glam and glitter. Does that answer your question?"

"You checked all the right boxes on the catty ques-tionnaire," I assure him. "Just one more question: what's your real last name?"

"Harmon. My grandparents changed their last name when they got to Ellis Island. It was German, like Harmensnauzer or something. But they didn't want to get dissed. It was right after World War Two and all."

"That's totally cool," I say, reassuring him, though I'm the one who really needs it. Forget about having *second* thoughts about Diamond. I'm having triplets!

Luckily, Bobby Beat babbles all the way to school, and we all stay lost in our own thoughts. I start perking up when he shares the source of his inspiration during his tender toddler years. "I loved all the original divas. Diana Ross, Eartha Kitt—can you believe that purr?" he coos.

Even Aphro warms up to Bobby, telling him about her foster mother's former job at Eartha's estate. As soon as we approach the front of Fashion International, Angora whispers in my ear, "Well, somebody is worthy." At first, I think she's referring to the Dalmation dogs from the technical school across the street, because I see them standing in a pack in front of our school as usual, ogling our roster of groovy girls. Then I realize that she is referring to Caterina and her crew, who are standing around like they're waiting for something to jump off. I notice Shalimar and her chic chortlers huddled together, engaging in a chorus of "Omigod! Omigod!"

"What's with the caco*phony*?" I ask, trying to keep

the situation Lite FM since Bobby Beat is in our midst. "That should be the new tagline of her house—printed right on T-shirts: 'Omigod'!" Nonetheless, I watch, transfixed, as Shalimar bats her Lee press-on lashes while she carries on in her shady corner. Meanwhile, Ice Très is trying hard to make eye contact with me. When that doesn't work, he tries the flip side and bum-rushes me.

"This place is wild," he says, grinning from ear to ear as he gets in my face.

"Yeah, a real urban safari," I quip, wondering what his *punto* is.

"The bet is she ain't gonna show," Ice Très continues, which makes me realize we're not on the same fashion page.

"What happened?" Felinez asks him.

"We're waiting for Chandelier," Ice Très responds.

"Why?" I ask, disappointed he wasn't referring to a famous fashionista sighting.

"Where y'all been?" Ice Très asks, like we're clueless kitties. "You ain't heard?"

"Awright already with the Sesame Street cue cards," I grumble. "Spill the refried beans."

"Snaps, I can't believe you're not on this. Awright, it's like this. Well, let me put it this way: Chandelier's father was indicted for chopping up body parts and selling them!" Ice Très says, delivering the news-breaking blow like the first reporter on the scene. "And at six thirty-five p.m., Chandelier's father was taking the perp walk outside arraignment court for participating in a *lucrative* cadaver operation."

"What, *what?*" I ask in disbelief, forgetting my deep freeze on Ice Très.

Angora shrugs and gives me a look like *Don't blame me.*

"Geez. It's not enough to have your ear to the street anymore. You've got to get down there with your nose," I moan, embarrassed that we've been trumped by the tagger. "I'm *gagulating.*"

Chintzy Colon catches my glance and runs over, eager to serve up every gory detail of the latest drama like they're chorizos hot off her homemade grill.

Between her excited spurts, I gather that Lee Spinelli, a nurse at Mount Morris Hospital and formerly of Brooklyn Hospital, was involved in a black market body parts ring headed by a dentist. "It would take forty-five minutes to take out the bones, then another fifteen minutes for the skin, the upper arm, lower arm, thigh, abdominal area, and more," Chintzy babbles, like she's spouting a recipe.

"Can you believe it?" interjects Angora, who got briefed quickly by peeps on the side.

"No, actually, I can't," I admit. "Is this an early Halloween gag—like somebody's pulling my leg?"

"Nah!" counters Ice Très. "It's on the real. Body snatchers be making *bank*. They be parceling out a whole body and delivering to the highest bidder."

"Like who?" I ask, still not believing the hype.

"Tissue banks—and we're not talking Kleenex, okay. Research facilities—fresh or frozen, you can get a fresh elbow à la mode—or some freeze-dried brains, okay."

Angora picks up the news feed where Chintzy left off. "It's true, *chérie*. Chandelier's father and the rest of the cadaver crew were so busy that they often ate lunch or dinner in the dissecting rooms. He went from earning fifty thousand dollars a year as a nurse to making a hundred eighty-five thousand. . . ."

Suddenly, Aphro gets a shopportunity alert: "That's how come Chandelier started featuring Gucci all of a sudden!"

"Speaking of label dropping—she was so worried about us so-called fake Fendis that she didn't even realize there was one right under her nose," Angora says sadly.

We watch as the crowd outside multiplies intensely. Everyone is completely aghast about the Chandelier blast.

"The pelvis went for five thousand dollars?" Felinez squeals, getting creeped by all the statistics. "*Ay, dios,* I hope mine goes for more than that!"

"I'm sure they'd get at least twenty thousand for your butt!" I blurt out before I realize how insensitive it is. It's bad enough Felinez has to contend with all the stuffed *puercos* in the world who target juicy girls' body parts. "Sorry, Blue Boca. I was on a Tootsie Roll." I wince.

All of a sudden, Mr. Bias, the assistant principal, steps outside and announces loudly, "Okay, everyone, proceed to your homeroom classes. Right *now*, please."

Reluctantly, we all shuffle toward the front door, wondering if we're going to be graced with a Chandelier Spinelli sighting. Even her best friend, Tina Cadavere, is nowhere to be seen. Ice Très taps me on the shoulder and leans close, which gives me the creeps. "Hold on," he whispers. "I'm just trying to tell you something." I figure whispering is in order with this turn of eerie events. "I left you a little something in the stairwell by the Fashion Annex," he coos.

I nod like I know what he's talking about, but I don't. "Look forward to Friday," he says, and jets in front of us.

"What was that?" Angora asks, concerned.

"I don't know but apparently there's a prize for me behind door number three, if you catch my drift," I report, revealing all the details of the secret location. "Now I'm wondering if this is Ice Très's definition of a treasure hunt."

"Speaking of hunted," whispers Angora, pointing to Nole Canoli, who is huddled in the hallway by the security checkpoint. He's clearly trying to hide in plain sight. I can tell by the way he has his back turned to everyone but Kimono Harris, Dame Leeds, and Elgamela Sphinx.

"Doesn't he look a little pale?" I whisper.

"Yeah, even Countess Coco looks a little peaked," adds Angora. "I mean for a Pomeranian, her pallor is off!"

"So is yours," I warn her, then hope she isn't offended.

"I'm still tired from our interview session," confesses Angora. "That was *exhausting.*"

Suddenly, I feel deflated too. "The only item we're getting on 'Page Six' is gonna be about Chandelier, the heiress to a chop shop dynasty!"

"I know," admits Felinez. "But I wonder if she is going to show her face—or fibia—in school again?"

Suddenly, a lightbulb appears over my head. "You think she's gonna drop out?" I quiz, secretly plotting a coup like Haiti's dethroned leader Papa Doc, who we're studying in history class.

Felinez and Angora get the picture. "Or maybe she'll be cut from the Catwalk competition like a dangling thread," says Angora.

Nole Canoli whizzes by us with Countess Coco perched in his Prada bag. He is trying desperately to keep his head down, as if he is shielding his face from probing cameras on a perp walk. We all watch warily as Caterina and her crew march down the hall toward an unknown destination.

"I bet you she's going to Ms. Fab's office," Angora predicts.

Meanwhile, I ponder our possibilities. "Even if Chandelier doesn't drop out, there's definitely too much squeal appeal. I mean, what's she got to offer now: 'Gee, my Dad can get us a fabbie deal on tendons and ligaments'?"

Aphro has had enough. "I'm out," she informs us. Angora attempts to say something, but I put my hand on her shoulder to tell her not to bother. "She can keep stressing me if it makes her happy," I say.

"Let's take the back stairwell, then," Angora says.

"Might as well," I concur. My curiosity has been piqued by Ice Très's mysterious message outside the bottle. When I swing open the door and spot the huge heart shape with Cupid's arrow sprawled wall to wall in the stairwell, my heart sinks like a sunken treasure. It's a message all right: SOS!

"Maybe this is just a clue?" Angora says weakly, her blue eyes popping in utter disbelief.

"He must be sniffing spray paint," I reply, shocked by this blatant disrespect for Fashion International's cardinal rule: don't scribble or dribble on the walls.

We stare at the huge metallic black-and-silver letters left courtesy of the misguided graffiti artist: WAZ-
ZUP, PUSSYCAT? THIS IS 4REAL. ICE TWICE.

"Omigod," Felinez moans.

"Maybe no one will know he's talking about you?"
Angora says hopefully.

"He might as well have hired the Goodyear Blimp
and scrawled my name across the sky. *That* would have
been more subtle!" I wince.

I check my Kitty watch and realize it's time to get
to home period. "Geez," I say, looking back at Ice
Très's handiwork. "A good marker is a terrible thing to
waste."

╭ ╮

By lunchtime, the speculation about the subject of
the tagger's ardor has reached a peak second only to a
Chandelier sighting and the unveiling of the spring
fashions today in the Mercedes-Benz Fashion Week
shows at Bryant Park. "Wazzup, pussycat!" a chorus of
shriekers yells in my direction. I ignore them and run
into the Fashion Café like it's safe passage to the Underground Railroad. "The situation is outta control," I
gripe to Felinez because my nerves are on edge.

"It's not your fault," Felinez says, trying to reassure
me. Somehow she has regained her appetite and is

hovering at the lunch counter, with her arms bent like chicken wings, unable to make a decision about her order.

"Velma, what should I get?" Felinez asks our favorite food attendant.

"Angel hair capellini," Velma shoots back.

"I'll have the same," I say. "This suits our continuing exploration of Italian culture."

"*If* we make it to Italy." Felinez grunts. "I don't know if I can go through a year of this roller coaster."

"Puhleez. A roller-coaster ride is more predictable," I grumble in return. Suddenly, a lightbulb goes on. I take out my Catwalk notepad and begin to scribble some thoughts for our Catwalk Credo. "Strap yourself in and fasten your Gucci seat belt," I read out loud.

"*Très bon,*" says Angora, looking over my shoulder, then adding her tasty thoughts to the Catwalk Credo until we come up with the remainder of the tenet right there on the spot. *Whenever I feel like screaming my head off or jumping out of my chic caboose, I will resist the urge; instead, I will tighten a notch on my fears like a true fashionista.*

"Yoohoo!" shouts Bobby Beat, zooming by us with his food tray poised gracefully at his waist. "Can you believe the drama today? Talk about Zorro—somebody left their mark in the stairwell! I'm so outta here after lunch!" he coos.

I'm relieved that Bobby Beat doesn't know that I'm the secret source of inspiration for our urban Zorro, and I have no intention of telling him. I also instinctively know what Bobby's early departure means. He is one of the lucky seniors who have been granted access passes to the one event we juniors have yet to witness: the fashion shows taking place at Mercedes-Benz Fashion Week.

"Oh, I am so green with Gucci Envy," I admit. Bobby laughs it off. "Oh, look at the credo we're creating. You'll get a copy, of course, at our first official team meeting." My stomach ties in knots as I say that. *Please, God, let me get my team assembled before I'm disgraced*, I silently plead.

Bobby Beat takes the glasses off the top of his head and puts them on to read the credo. "Truly fabulous!" he agrees. I exhale, satisfied that I have at least channeled some of my agitation into something constructive for our cause. And I also managed to snag a bona fide makeup artist for our house. "Okay, I've got to twirl," Bobby says excitedly. "After the shows, I have to get to work."

"When do you work?" I ask, my ears perking up at the mention of a job.

"Honey, I work twenty-four-seven," Bobby says evasively.

"Yes, I should have known, Superman—the glasses were a clue," I coo.

Bobby air-kisses each of us on each cheek, including Angora, who blushes. "Mademoiselle Blue Beret, that's how they do it in Europe—so get used to it!" he advises.

I'm relieved that the static between them was squashed. I would have felt fried if we didn't snag Bobby Beat for our house. When he sails away, Felinez says, "See, not everything is bad. I really like him."

"Yeah, I do too. Let's perch in our catty corner," I say, feeling inspired by Bobby Beat's effusive energy. "If he beats like he talks, then he's the second Rembrandt."

"*C'est vrai!* That's the truth," Angora agrees.

We always sit four tables back from the entrance of the café, which affords us a panoramic view of the floor show, as we call lunchtime antics.

Zeus and Lupo burst through the door, looking wild-eyed—like everyone is today—obviously searching for clues of intelligent life in fashion land. They spot us and sit down to cross paws. "I just wanna give you a heads-up. Ice Très is in Mr. Confardi's office."

"Why do I get the feeling the other platform shoe is about to drop," I moan, mortified that Zeus knows about my situation. I've even given up hope that he's ready to tango with me. Why would he want to? I'm the object of affection of a magic marker gone haywire.

"Pashmina?" Zeus repeats, and I realize he has been trying to bend my ear some more. "I just saw the camera crew coming out of Ms. Fab's office, too."

"You don't think—?" I freeze, wondering if I'm gonna be the source of more shame for my house.

"Nah, nah," Zeus says, waving his hand like a freestyle paw.

I start coughing wildly.

"You all right? *Va bene?*" asks Lupo.

I cough and nod at the same time, then sip some water till I regain use of my larynx. I try to resume eating. That's when I notice a long dark hair resting on my pasta.

"Not mine," Zeus says, running his fingers through his wild wavy hair. "Want me to take it back?"

"Yeah, get Velma to handle this, cuz I don't think that's a hair from an angel," I explain, handing him my plate of capellini.

My cell phone rings and I shriek because I forgot to turn it off. Even a fashion toad would know that today is definitely not the day to break any more Fashion International rules like the one clearly posted on the wall of the Fashion Café: EAT YOUR JELLY, BUT NIX THE CELLY.

Angora covers me while I discreetly grab the phone out of my purse and see that the number belongs to exactly the person I'd like to avoid right now, the prying Teen Style producer, Caterina Tiburon.

"*Tales from the Crypt,* part two?" I moan, getting paranoid.

"Answer it!" Angora orders me.

"Hello, Kaflamma Central," I answer in the voice of my chirpy alter ego.

Caterina doesn't miss a beat. Obviously in her line of work she's seen more than her share of fashion alter egos—or just plain egos.

"I wanted to give you a heads-up," she begins.

"Wazzup?" I query hesitantly, wondering why I am suddenly the recipient of so many heads-up today.

"Tune in to Channel Two news tonight, five o'clock—there might be a segment of interest to you."

"Omigod!" I shriek before I realize what I've said. Felinez and Angora snicker. "Is this about Chandelier?"

Felinez and Angora close in on me like an invasion of body snatchers is about to take place. In her typical cagey fashion, Caterina doesn't give me a straight answer. "It just may be something of interest to you."

"Awright. I'm on it," I say, sick to my stomach as I sign off. Then I tell my crew what Caterina said.

Zeus comes back with a fresh plate of capellini. I push it away. "I'm sick," I confess, reporting the phone call to Zeus. "I think we might be getting the ax."

"You mean, like, cut from the competition, or losing a limb?" Zeus asks.

"Could be either," I say, kaflustered. "Forget about catfights. With these latest developments, I honestly think fashion is going to the dogs—*for real.*"

## FASHION INTERNATIONAL 35TH ANNUAL
## CATWALK COMPETITION BLOG

New school rule: You don't have to be ultranice, but don't get tooooo catty, or your posting will be zapped by the Fashion Avengers!!

YOU'D BETTER WORK, SUPERMODELS. . . .
Today was the official start of Mercedes-Benz Fashion Week in New York City—the only place in the world I would rather be than Paris, Milan, or Firenze next June (opening the Pitti Bimbo show, if I'm lucky—and I think I will be now that I have hooked up with the most purrlicious house in the Cat-walk competition this year!). Anyhoo, back to foundation basics: I waited three years for the moment I could walk into the glamour-fortified tents at Bryant Park with an access pass—instead of hiding in the folds of the tent for a behind-the-scenes peek! More than 100 spring collections will sashay the runways under the over-guarded tents during the course of five days at Bryant Park, and other nearby venues (because not every de-sign house can afford to sell their embryos in exchange for a spot in the park!). The spring shows are held every year in the fall and the fall shows are held in the spring. (Got it?) The fall fashions you are seeing in the stores now were shown earlier this year—that means last spring, when I was merely a junior, so those col-lections were not christened by my eyes! The lag between showtime and

shipping gives the press and retail buyers ample time to manipulate the fashion crystal ball so you will think you've made your own selections to hang in your closet. (You don't honestly believe you have been put on this planet to make your own choices, do you?) Anyhoo, I adore the anticipation, the music, the models, the fashion makers pacing to and fro with scissors, sandwiches, and sponges—and, of course, the goodie bags placed so delicately on each guest's chair! Street-smart fashionistas remove the appointed goodie bag from their seat and plop it immediately into their kiss-lock purses to be on safe side. (Swag looting is on the rise, so guard your goodies with a vengeance, my dears!) More than the goodie bags, I honestly just love seeing inspired fashion brought to life. By the way, I spent more than three hours in line with my fellow senior fashion classmates to get our student access badges with nothing more than my sponges and Booty Dust, which I applied generously to everyone in line. I say, who needs kitty litter, when you have glitter? It's simply all-purpose! Anyhoo, I'm not bwitchin' about the long lines that come with being a die-hard fashionista. I don't even mind that I cannot take off my Dolce loafers right now because my feet are so swollen. I've decided that I'll just sleep with them on.

The other reason why I was so electrified today is because I also met some feline fashionistas with whom I plan to align myself so we can "scratch, scratch" out the Catwalk competition at our school next June! With no disrespect to the creativity I witnessed today at Mercedes-Benz Fashion Week, the Catwalk competition means more to me because I will finally be an important ingredient in a fierce fashion enchilada. Sorry, I must be getting famished again—gotta go get my sponges and Booty Dust out, so I can beat some more faces. . . !

10/10/2008 11:45:22 PM
Posted by: SpongeBob

# 10

Next period, I have model appreciation. I'm so scared that I'm going to be dragged like an alley cat into another scrappy situation that I don't even look up from my notebook in class. "The Trinity of Terror was not a left-wing Palestinian organization but the reign of which three supermodels?" asks the teacher, Ms. Boucle. Her ample chest heaves with anticipation while she waits for a response. "Anybody?" No one volunteers. "Pashmina?"

I feel a poke in my back that startles me back to reality. I look up and see everyone staring at me.

"What, what?" I ask, embarrassed by my trip to the Bozo sphere. Ms. Boucle pushes her thick red glasses up on the bridge of her nose disapprovingly. Ruthie Dragon, who is seated in front of me, raises her hand energetically.

"Yes, Ruthie," Ms. Boucle says, putting her hands on her hips and throwing me a glance like *I'm watching you Pinkie*.

"Um, it was Linda Evangelista, Christy Turlington,

and Naomi Campbell!" Ruthie says enthusiastically. I am so over her. I thought we were on the same fashion page, but she didn't even show up for my team interviews. Then I find out that she's joined Chandelier's house, or perhaps I should say chop shop.

Suddenly, there's a loud outburst right below our second-floor classroom, which faces Thirty-eighth Street. A few students jump up and peer out the half-opened windows to check out the action. Even Ms. Boucle adjusts the extra-wide red lizard belt trapping her waist and waddles over to the scene of an unfolding drama. I sit frozen in my chair, paralyzed by my own fears. Ruthie Dragon turns from the window and shoots me a look like *You'd better get over here and check this out.* I make a fire-breathing face at her like *Don't make me slay you, okay.* I figure the commotion outside probably has something to do with Chandelier. No doubt she's finally gracing us with her notorious presence. And with the chop shop heiress's dumbfounding luck, her father has probably already bribed his way out of prison by donating a few hardened arteries to the Police Athletic League.

"PASHMINA!!"

The guttural scream from outside is so visceral, my veins turn to warm milk. Now everyone in class turns to look at me. I jump up and run to the window. Ice

216

Très stands tall, looking up at the window, waving like he's looking for someone—me. Mr. Confardi hovers by the entrance and barks at him, "A suspension isn't enough? We can head right to expulsion if you'd like. As a matter of fact, why don't you apply to the School of Visual Arts, where your *talents* would be more appreciated!"

"I'm sorry, Mr. Confardi. I just wanted to say good bye to someone real quick before I jet," Ice Très offers in a feeble voice.

"Friday, awright?" yells Ice Très, still waving to get my attention. I stand still like a dummy—a real one—because I can't help wondering, *How did I ever get myself involved in this corny kaflamma?*

"Everybody go back to your seats, please," orders Ms. Boucle. "The show is over!"

Felinez is waiting for me outside class, and I'm so embarrassed that I'm the one who's now walking like a fashion felon on a perp walk. Shalimar is standing squarely outside like she's waiting for me and ready to rumble. In her case, however, that merely means extra-heavy doses of lash batting. She's wearing a brown flowered wrap dress. "I see we've been reduced to wearing consignment shop finds," I say, observing the vintage of Shalimar's nineties-looking Diane von Furstenberg dress.

"She's already handed in her forms to Ms. Lynx's office," Felinez informs me like it's good news.

"So?" I hiss back. Just what I needed—an annoying reminder that I haven't handed in my team membership forms yet.

"So that means she just got a strike since Ice Três got suspended," Felinez says defensively.

"Oh, right," I say apologetically, scanning the Catwalk rules and regulations in my mind: *Any infraction by team members results in an automatic strike, which will be calculated into the judges' tally for your house's final overall score.*

"We should consider ourselves lucky he didn't show up to the meeting, *mija*. That's all I'm saying," Felinez adds.

"Luck is a funny thing, isn't it?" I muse, staring at Shalimar head-on. Shalimar turns away sheepishly. "That also means Ice Três got disqualified as a team member in her house as a result of his suspension. Now I can see it. She's become unglued at her Shimmy Choos."

Angora joins us and, true to her journalistic nature, delivers an update. "Calls from Chandelier were fielded by Mr. Confardi's office. I got that from a reliable source. Even better," she says, trying to look over at Shalimar, "you missed a certain person's Coty Fashion Critics' Awards performance in Ms. Lynx's office fourth period. And I got that from an even more reliable source."

"Crocodile tears?" I ask in disbelief.

"*Au contraire*," Angora tells me.

I gloat for a *segundo*, then turn glum. Shalimar may be shedding real tears, but I am far from shedding my real fears. "We don't have a leg up on the competition yet," I say apprehensively. "What we do have is a head's-up from Caterina that we have to deal with."

"Let's wait for Zeus," advises Angora. "We need all the back-watching we can get in this lipstick jungle." I smile, realizing that she is already quoting quips from Bobby Beat, our latest addition to the House of Pashmina.

⌐ ⌐

As soon as Aphro comes out, then Zeus, we all head uptown to my house. Zeus stays zip-lipped on the subject of Ice Très. But Aphro is anxious to gloat and just can't miss the shopportunity to seal it with a dis. "I told you to watch out for Mr. Blinking and Winking," she snarls at me.

I nod like I'm listening.

"Hi, Pashmina," screams Stellina, running out of the courtyard as if she's been waiting for me. "The cameras were here!" she says, like she's giving me gossip so hot her little fingers are scorching.

"I know," I say with a giggle. At least I can feel proud about one thing: how hyped Stellina and Tiara are about being included in the Teen Style camera crew's visit to my humble abode.

"They were talking to Big Daddy Boom," she continues.

"I know," I say, secretly hoping my on-camera prank doesn't backfire on me one day.

"Can I touch your hat again?" Stellina squeals to Zeus.

"Sure—cuz you have that Midas touch," Zeus answers. He can tell by the look on Stellina's face that she isn't following his drift, so he just smiles and bends down so she can get her paws on his plushness.

As usual, Mr. Darius is in fine form. He and José, his assistant, are assembling the massive mountain of recyling bags that must be left curbside for pickup by the sanitation trucks tomorrow morning.

"Don't you ever wonder where all this garbage ends up?" Angora asks.

"I'm sure Mr. Darius wishes it would just disappear daily," I observe. Suddenly, Angora starts breathing heavily and stops for a second to catch her breath. She takes out her inhaler and we all wait in silence for it to kick in.

In the meantime, I watch Mr. Darius in action. Now he's yelling at one of the homeless guys, who we call Mr. Sunkist because he pushes around a shopping cart that's always filled to the brim with empty soda cans. He spends most of his day taking the bottles and cans to the Piggly Wiggly supermarket across the street to collect the deposit money. "Every week, ticket I get!" Mr. Darius yells at Mr. Sunkist, who has already ripped open one of the recyling bags to plunder discarded bottles and cans.

"He's definitely scary when detonated," Zeus observes, nodding knowingly at the explanation of Mr. Darius's nickname. We head upstairs to my apartment, and I'm surprised that my mother is already there, sipping a cup of her favorite Belgian Blend at the dining room table. I called earlier and told her about Chandelier, and that I was bringing my friends over to watch the news. Maybe this is her way of showing support. "This beter be good," she says, looking at us curiously as we all pile into the living room. Leave it to my mother to know how to make me more nervous than I already am.

Anxiously, we sit down. It's only five minutes till

the five o'clock news. "An invite for ringside seats at Mercedes-Benz Fashion Week couldn't be more coveted than a seat on the gently worn black leather couch in my living room right now," I blurt out, trying to keep the situation Lite FM. "Well, maybe I'm exaggerating just a notch on my Gucci belt. *Not*."

"Chenille, come in here," my mother says, much to my chagrin.

Angora catches my horrified look. "Why don't we just invite the Terminator," I mumble.

Chenille saunters in and flops into the butterscotch leather reclining armchair—the withered cousin of the black leather couch, both pieces snagged on Sixty-seventh Street last summer during our furniture-foraging escapades. Judging by the smirk on my younger sister's face, she would rather be somewhere getting paid to scorch someone's scalp with a hot comb than sitting with us.

"So, I hear you're working the press and curls," Aphro inquires like she's with the Labor Department and verifying hourly wages.

Chenille nods her head as if she's bored with bringing in the Benjies. I wish I knew where she hid her money, because I'm tempted to engage in a sticky-finger stint of my own.

"I made twenty dollars this week," Chenille boasts.

"Do you put in tracks?" Aphro asks. Luckily, Aphro is sitting next to Angora, or she'd get a swift kick from my smug pink suede UGGed foot.

"Yeah," Chenille says matter-of-factly, like she's the extension expert behind Beyoncé's bouncy weave. "If you buy the hair, I'll do it for twenty dollars a track."

"Twenty dollars!" shrieks Aphro. "For that much, I'll put my own tracks in with a hot-glue gun!"

"That sounds like a good investment to me," Angora says sweetly. "After all, hair extensions are career extensions!" Angora is always so nice to Chenille and tries to get me to see her hidden potential, which must be buried deeper than Jacques Cousteau's treasures in the Bermuda Triangle, cuz I sure can't find it.

"Okay, shut up, everybody. *Cayete la boca!*" shouts Felinez as the *Five at Five* newsroom anchors start spouting away.

After fifteen minutes of sitting stiff as a board lest I miss one word, I relax into the couch. Nothing so far about us, or even anything interesting, until one of the anchors announces, "More indictments are expected against the body-cutter ring as new charges are filed by the Brooklyn district attorney's office."

"Omigod, listen up!" shrieks Aphro as we all sit on the edge of our seats.

The anchor turns the story over to a reporter

outside the downtown arraignment court. We watch as a group of men in suits walk in wearing handcuffs.

My mother senses the commotion and hovers over the couch. "Which one is her father?" she asks impatiently.

"Probably the one in the Gucci suit," I say. "How do you say, 'Can I get a refund?'"

My mom doesn't smile at the joke that I cracked for her benefit. She's always complaining about the snobby, cheap customers who return clothing they've purchased but obviously already worn and the way they feign innocence when they're declined because of sweat stains or driblets of red wine.

We're all glued to the television as the reporter does her stiff riff: "Five medical professionals—including nurse Lee Spinelli, embalmer Joseph Ricola, and ex-dentist Michael Minelli, the alleged leader of the notorious body-cutting ring, were indicted earlier today on one hundred and twenty-two counts of body stealing, grand larceny, forgery, racketeering, and other charges. According to that indictment, more than a thousand corpses were harvested from area funeral homes without permission from next of kin. . . ."

"No way Chandelier is coming back to school after this," Angora predicts. "I mean, who would sit next to her at lunchtime watching her cut a slice of pizza with a plastic fork?"

Zeus starts fiddling with his zebra-striped mink hat, which means he feels a brainstorm coming on.

"I see steam rising," I say, egging him on.

"I'm gonna hit Dame right now on the cell. I bet you Chandelier has called Nole Canoli and hit him with the hardness!" Zeus says, lit up like the Christmas tree in Rockefeller Center.

"Wow, that's not a brainstorm—that's a hurricane," I mumble.

"Might as well, cuz ain't nothing on the news but the news," Aphro seconds.

It's true. "We've been watching for thirty minutes and there is not a fashion sighting in sight," Angora reports. "Not even an early Christmas push for *très* tawdry tartans!"

Zeus is talking on his cell phone to Dame Leeds. "Word. That's what's up?" He gives us a thumbs-up sign, which we're hoping means he's managed to snag *scandalabrious* tidbits on the Chandelier crisis.

As a matter of fact, we're so anxious to get our gossip grub on that we almost miss the anchor announcing: "Now we go to our latest inductee in the Smiley Wiley 'Shame on You!' Hall of Fame."

"Hey! Isn't that your building?" yells Aphro, pointing to the television screen. Sure enough, newscaster Smiley Wiley is standing in front of Amsterdam

Gardens. I see Stellina jumping up and down in the background.

"Oh, *that's* what she was trying to tell us downstairs," I say, realizing that I misinterpreted her excitement. It wasn't a blast from the past. She was talking about *today*.

A voice-over continues: "Acting on an anonymous tip, Channel Two learned that landlord Nakheir Darius, who owns the high-rise building complex Amsterdam Gardens, located on Amsterdam Avenue and 114th Street, has been terrorizing his tenants for years with illegal threats of rent hikes and evictions, and postponing basic building repairs, even withholding heat by denying access to the boiler room facilities to repair technicians."

The camera cuts to footage of the lobby, elevator shafts, and then Smiley Wiley, who was obviously camped outside our building today, chasing after Mr. Darius himself. "Mr. Darius, is it true that tenants have gone without hot water for two weeks?" Smiley Wiley shoves the microphone toward Mr. Darius, who shields his face from the camera and motions for the camera crew to leave.

"Get out of here now!" Mr. Darius shouts.

"What about the unauthorized rent increases? Is it true tenants are subjected to ten percent rent increases despite the rent stabilization guidelines enforced by the city council?"

"Get out, you idiot!" Mr. Darius repeats.

Facing the camera, Smiley Wiley says in a deadpan voice, "Mr. Darius's favorite phrase seems to be, 'Get out, you idiot.' As a result, today we induct into the Smiley Wiley 'Shame on You!' Hall of Fame landlord Nakheir Darius. Welcome, Mr. Darius!"

"Omigod, we're going to get evicted," I shriek in disbelief.

Chenille throws me a dirty look like *You've really done it now. We're going to be homeless!*

Surprisingly, my mom's reaction is exactly the opposite. "Well, I hope that gets him off his lazy behind once and for all. Cuz I'm sure not paying this rent increase," she announces.

I realize that Mom has kept more to herself than I thought. "You mean he asked to raise the rent?"

"Yes indeed, he did—and we haven't even lived here a year yet!" she reveals, flashing a rent bill in her hand. "Free market rates, my butt!"

"Oooh, he is low-down," Aphro says, shaking her head.

"That was great," Zeus says, beaming at me proudly.

"Thank God they didn't mention me or the

Catwalk competition," I say, finally realizing that Caterina probably orchestrated the leak to help me. "I wonder how Caterina pulled this off?"

"She probably knows one of the producers," Angora offers. "But who knew that television shame could lead to fame! I love it." Her eyes beam with pride at the producer's handiwork.

Zeus, on the other hand, is anxious to share *his* handiwork. "Well, you wanna hear what Dame Leeds said?"

We're so wrapped up in the drama, we forgot about the cadaver crisis. "Tell, but don't kiss!" Aphro says, slapping him on his arm.

"Nole Canoli did speak to Chandelier," he says, pursing his mouth like he's savoring the tasty tidbit he's about to put on the grill for us. "She's not coming back to school for a while," he says, nodding.

"Ay, *dios mio!*" Felinez cries.

"If she doesn't come back to school soon, she's gonna get disqualified from the Catwalk competition," I say, scanning the competition rules in my head. " 'No house leader is allowed any more than five missed school days in the designated year,' " I read aloud.

"If that's the case, then bring it on," Zeus says. Slick minds think alike.

"Holy Canoli!" I say, licking my lips. Suddenly, I

feel a breath of fresh air hitting my lungs. Even Angora seems like she's breathing easier.

"Wow, doesn't it look like my living room got bigger?" I say in amazement, looking around.

"No!" shrieks Felinez, "but our opportunities have!"

"So, do you Kats and Kitties want to stay for dinner?" my mom asks with a smile. I can't believe Mom is so calm about my Operation: Kitty Litter caper. I thought she would throw me in the frying pan and turn me into a burnt frittata—her specialty.

"I want to stay!" Felinez squeals.

While my mother fiddles around in the kitchen, Chenille goes to help.

"I hope she ain't planning on frying any extensions!" Aphro says, then does her snorting laugh. Obviously the mere thought of being able to snag Nole Canoli for our house has gotten her off my grill.

While we're waiting for my mom to whip up a frozen dinner, we start talking about everything that has been going on with the Catwalk competition. "Wait till you meet Bobby Beat," Felinez says enthusiastically to Zeus, her big brown eyes widening. Then she starts playing with a pink toothpick between her teeth that she pulled out of her meowch pouch.

"Oh, that is tick-tacky," I tell her, slapping her hand. "Next you'll be carrying sausages in there!"

Suddenly, there's a loud rapping on the door. "See, *la policía* are coming to arrest you for that!" Felinez bursts, embarrassed. I freeze like a statue in a wax museum.

"Who is it?" I yell, but no one answers, so I look through the peephole and see Mr. Darius. I press my hand to my chest and mouth my horror to my crew: *It's him!*

Everyone stands alert, like a dressing team behind the scenes at a fashion show.

I take a deep breath and open the door. "Hi, Mr. Darius!" I squeak, like Miss Piggy on helium, much to my chagrin.

Mr. Darius breaks into a forced smile. "I just to tell that we sorry for problems and make sure to fix soon," he says. I'm so shocked that I could almost faint. My mother comes to the door and he gives her a forced smile too. "I come to fix soon—everything."

"Oh, good," Mom says, looking at him matter-of-factly. "I got something for you, too. Hang on, I'll be right back."

My mom motions for Chenille to hand her the rent bill. She then hands the bill to Mr. Darius. "I won't be paying the rent this month. That should make up for all the time we didn't have hot water or heat. And please fix that amount. I won't be paying any increase, either."

Mr. Darius humbly nods to my mother. "No problem."

"Good night," my mom says. Translation of her body language: *We're done here, you fool!*

She closes the door.

"You read him with relish—and a hot dog!" I say proudly.

There's another rap on the door. This time Mom opens it. It's Mr. Darius again. Sheepishly, he hands her the casserole dish he has in his hand. "This my wife make—please enjoy."

"Oh," my mother says, suddenly pleased by all the attention. "What is it?"

"Kobideh kebab," says Mr. Darius. "My wife make."

"Well, thank you," Mom says, softening.

This time, after she closes the door, I squeal: "Thank God! Now we don't have to eat Lean Cuisine!"

I am so hyped by what happened that I can't resist the urge to hug Mom, even though I know she doesn't go in for that sort of cuddly behavior, especially in front of my crew.

We all go the table and eat the food Mr. Darius brought, which is actually pretty tasty. "This is the jointski," Zeus comments. "It kinda reminds me of my mom's cooking. It's similar to Mediterranean food."

I nod like I agree. I'm fascinated by what it must be

like to have parents who were born in another country. "I have to check your mom's cooking real soon," I say, then get embarrassed. I don't want Zeus to think I'm inviting myself over.

"Actually, my girlfriend is a better cook than my mother. On the real," Zeus says, smiling proudly.

Suddenly, I feel like someone just did a touchdown on my chest. I pause for a moment to catch my breath. Angora does too and gives me a look that could easily be translated as, *Well, now you know he's not gay!*

"What kind of food is this?" Felinez asks, chowing down the kebabs and oblivious to my deep-dish disappointment.

"The kind you eat," quips Mom.

After we suck up two bottles of ginger ale, Zeus heads out because he has to go home to Long Island. He lives in Monyville, which is near the "five towns," as he explained it.

"Heading off to Moneyland," Aphro teases him.

"Mos def," Zeus says, yawning with his arms stretched over his head and his hands clasped on top of his mink hat.

I hug Zeus, too, amid oohs and ahhs from Felinez and Aphro. I ignore them.

"From now on, I think we should heed our own advice," Angora starts in. "The time has come to strap ourselves in and fasten our Gucci seat belts."

My mom chuckles and hands Zeus his Starter jacket. "That's original."

We explain to her about the Catwalk Credo. She seems like she's proud of me. What I neglect to tell her is that we haven't assembled our whole team, and that the other four houses are all in place—even if one is about to fall like a house of cards.

## FASHION INTERNATIONAL 35TH ANNUAL
## CATWALK COMPETITION BLOG

New school rule: You don't have to be ultranice, but don't get tooooo catty, or your posting will be zapped by the Fashion Avengers!!

DON'T HATE THE PLAYERS, OR THE FASHION GAME. . . .

Everybody talks about relying on your instincts to survive in the fashion game, but sometimes you should just rely on the facts, okay? You can call me superficial, you can call me shady, but the bottom line is that you call me, period. So when I received a phone call this morning from Chandelier Spinelli, whom I've adored and supported throughout her fashion metamorphosis (stop, rewind; actually, I'm the catalyst behind it), telling me that she was going to take a hiatus from school due to a personal crisis, I felt it was necessary for me to publicly state my game plan. Let it be known right here that I did NOT abandon Chandelier Spinelli in her darkest hour of need. I live with a single parent myself—one who is incapacitated and requires a Hoveround Power Chair just to get around because of her weight problem and because she needs hip replacement surgery, which she cannot afford, okay? So I know firsthand the drama that a parent can put you through. (Everyone feels sorry for single parents, but you should feel sorry for their kids, okay?) I might act fabulous, but that does not mean that I'm not honest about who I am. So let me get out my seam ripper and pluck out some useless stitches: no one cares that when I was six years old I started dressing my Barbie dolls in hand-stitched clothes, each sequin and bugle bead given more attention than the parts for my Tonka trucks. Sure, that will make a good sound bite for the Teen Style Network, but the truth is, the only thing anybody cares about is if you're a winner or a loser. I may not be the most fabulous designer of all time, because we all know who that designer was (Gianni, may you rest in haute couture heaven), but I don't believe that there is another designer currently in the fashion galaxy who is more FABULOUS than I am. Now, that's as honest as I'm ever gonna be. My freshman design teacher, Mr. Rocailles, gave me a piece of advice, which has stuck to me like Velcro. He said, "The fashion business is like musical chairs. When the music stops, you'd better quickly plop your ass on another chair, or you're out of the game." And that's exactly what I intend to do. I'm going to bestow another house with my talent, because I sincerely believe it is my destiny to be a winner in the Catwalk competition. So, please, don't hate the player OR the fashion game!

10/15/2008 9:30:35 AM
Posted by: V for Versace

# 11

When I get to school, there's a message in my Catwalk in-box to report to Ms. Lynx's office. My pulse quickens because Ms. Lynx has never summoned me before. I'm supposed to submit my team membership forms to her office today, "But why is she on my case so pronto?" I speculate nervously to Felinez. The indelible image of Zorro's banned cousin waving wildly as I watch from my fashion tower frightens the froth off my steaming hot cappuccino. "Oh, I get it. I might be joining Ice Très in Style Siberia after all."

"You'd better go now, *mija*," Felinez warns me.

"No way, José," I say. "I have to get cap-happy first."

"*Cuidate*—be careful," Felinez sighs, waving her hand in defeat as she heads off to textile science.

I trot in the opposite direction to sociology but get ambushed around the bend by Willi Ninja, Jr., who's intent on providing a private lesson in the collective behavior of nosy human beings. "Did you stand up for your man?" he asks, posing in a defensive pirouette stance.

"What?" I ask, blushing shades of paranoid pink. I should have known peeps would be offering their own versions of the brou-haha.

"Well, he got suspended because of you—the least you can do is defend his honor," Willi Ninja, Jr., says, provoking my posture.

"Th-that is radickio," I stammer. But the truth is, I do feel guilty as charged.

"Is it, Miss P.P.?" Ninja, Jr., says, eyeing me carefully to see if I'll bend like saltwater taffy. "Better check your in-box. I'm sure he sent you a broken arrow to mend."

"I checked my in-box," I say, now getting paranoid times squared. I wonder if Willi Ninja, Jr., saw the note from Ms. Lynx. That's it—he's probably already peeped the situation!

Willi Ninja, Jr., pivots and turns to get the last word. "Well, all I can say is: one down, three to go. . . ."

It figures the pedigreed poser already assumes he has the Catwalk competition on lockdown, but the battle hasn't even begun. "Don't make me snap my clutch purse!" I call back, marching away defiantly. That's it! I've had it with peeps pushing me around. Time to stop tap-dancing gingerly and bring in the noise!

I send a text message to Zeus: "Make it happen." He'll know exactly what I mean. Then I march right into the Lynx lair.

Sil Lai looks up from her desk and purses her

lips. "You haven't submitted your team membership forms yet?"

"No. Not yet," I say, my voice zooming from squeaky to leaky in seconds. "I had a message that Ms. Lynx wants to see me?"

Sil Lai looks at her computer screen, opens a document, then looks at me with that Botox face, which makes it hard for me to read between her lines. "She's busy. I put you in for fourth period," Sil Lai informs me.

Fourth period? I'll have a catiac arrest before then. I look around the office and see Farfalla, stationed in her cubicle. I wish she manned the reception desk, because I could read her like the *New York Times* style section—backward and forward. But Farfalla doesn't look up, and as usual, she seems buried in work, like an archaeologist at an excavation site.

"I spoke to Mink," Sil Lai says, still stone-faced.

I wait for Sil Lai to drop an Altoid (a minty hint), but *nada*, so I decide to take her probe further.

"I can't believe she joined my house!" I gush, but realize immediately that I sound like I have no self-esteem—and I'm not talking about the clothing label, either.

Now the phone rings and Sil Lai gives me a look like I'm dismissed. Scurrying out of the office, I pop the collar on my Flower Power burnout sweater to ward off the chilly thought of fashion exile.

After sociology, Zeus is hovering on the horizon to give me the heads-up. "Definitely getting used to buzzwords involving body parts," I say, smiling. I stare longingly at his beautiful long dark eyelashes and wonder what his girlfriend is like. Probably a model too.

"It's on—lunchtime at Petsey Betsey," he informs me proudly.

"I knew you'd come through," I say softly. What I really want to say is, *Flotsam and jetsam the girlfriend, because I know you're tickled pink over* moi. *M. O. to the I.*

"You heard? Moet Major has been nominated by proxy vote as the replacement house leader. She's forming her own team, though. Chandelier is definitely out on a limb," adds Zeus, snapping me back to my challenging reality.

"Let's pray I'm not next," I say, shuddering, then spill the refried beans about my current concerns.

He gets a troubled look in his eyes.

"What?" I ask.

"Nah. Nothing." Zeus shakes it off.

I send a text message to Diamond, Aphro, Felinez, and Angora: "Operation: Kitty Litter is in full effect."

Although Diamond Tyler doesn't bring Crutches to school, it should have come as no surprise to me that she is a frequent visitor at the Petsey Betsey annex. "How's Crutches coming along?" the attendant, Bubba Barbieri, asks her. Diamond gives him a detailed update, then segues into her current cause: rescuing Sheepish Sally who was desperately trying to save herself from the chopping block by saying baaah-bye to the wicked city.

When the rest of my crew arrives, Bubba grants us access to the waiting area after administering a warning: "You're not allowed in the pet playground."

Zeus gingerly folds his six-foot frame into one of the bright orange wooden chairs with the giraffe-shaped backs.

"These were hand painted by Garo Sparo and donated to the school," Diamond informs us. "He's one of my favorite designers."

"That's a cool name—is he into birds or something?" Zeus asks.

"No, it's spelled S-P-A-R-O. But he does volunteer at the animal shelter. That's how I got my job. He's an amazing designer. He does a lot of corsetry work— evoking style from the Victorian era," Diamond explains, babbling. It's clear she's nervous—and truth is, so am I. "He's gonna let me intern at his studio," she continues. "I mean, so he says. Maybe later in the year."

"We're not interested in interning," Aphro blurts out, like she's not impressed. "We need jobs paying some real paper, okay."

I smile warmly at Diamond to make up for Aphro's aversion to "freebies," which is what she calls internships.

"Have you found anything yet?" Diamond asks, concerned. But she only manages to irritate Aphro—again.

"You make it sound like we're lost," she says, then gives one of her signature snorts.

Zeus spurts out a laugh. He can't help himself because he's still not used to the Babe squeals that emanate from Aphro's smoocher.

Right now, I'd like to stick Aphro Biggie's head in a trough to cool her off.

At last, Nole and most of his entourage—Dame Leeds, Elgamela Sphinx, and Kimono Harris—enter the Annex. Nole kisses Countess Coco on her nose, then hands her over to Bubba, cozily tucked in her black Prada carrier.

"Okay, Countess, no funny business today with the biscuits. Even Your Highness has to share," Bubba warns the fiery-haired Pomeranian.

Meanwhile, Diamond is fixated on Elgamela's bandage dress in juicy orange, which looks very similar to the French designer Hervé Léger's hand-sewn numbers, favored by Beyoncé. It's probably just a knock-knock, even though Elgamela is so fierce she could wear a dress made out of real Band-Aids and still earn purr points.

"Omigod, Nole, did you make that?" Diamond coos, pointing to Elgamela's mummy-tight curve hugger.

Diamond is obviously wearing on Nole's nerves, because he winces and shoots back, "Don't disrespect Hervé like that. And why would I steal his trademark?"

The delicate designer's face cracks like a cubic zirconia. So much for Operation: Kitty Litter. Maybe sticking my head in the odor-absorbing clay would have been a better idea.

"Today's my birthday. My dad got it from the designer consignment shop near where we live," Elgamela coos humbly. "He just got so tired of hearing me whine about it that he bought it for me!"

Nervously, I clear my throat before I speak to ensure that no squeaky sounds emanate against my will. "Wow, that's nothing like the reject consignment shop near my house," I babble, then repeat the motto plastered in the dingy window of Second Time Around: "Why go to JCPenney when you can save at Secondhand Benny's!"

"That's hysterical," Elgamela squeals back, her exotic accent lilting on the words. Elgamela quickly tells us all about Cherry Hill, New Jersey, where she grew up; it is apparently chock-full of designer-obsessed housewives. "My father owns Chirpin' Chicken on Second Avenue. I work there after school," she goes on. "That's why I smell like chicken half the time. Can't get it out of my pores."

"Really? I didn't know that," Felinez says, surprised.

"What—that you can't get the smell of chicken grease off your skin?" Elgamela asks, amused.

"No!" Felinez tries quickly to divert any more drama. "That you worked, um, as a chicken. I mean, that your father was rich. You know what I mean!"

We all laugh hysterically.

"It's right off Sixty-second Street," Elgamela explains. "Come by any time after school—wings are on me. I'll even throw in a breast and a leg!"

"Awright—as long as you chop it up Benihana-style," laughs Zeus, crossing paws with Nole. Suddenly, I realize that maybe Elgamela is Zeus's girlfriend. *Duh!*

Just then, Elgamela breaks into her dimpled smile, beaming at him. There was definitely no riddle to her rave reviews: she is charmed and dangerous. All of a sudden, Ruthie Dragon, who is out of breath, comes running into the reception area. I refrain from blurting out, *Look what the cat dragged in—a dragon*. Good thing too, because as soon as the traitor catches her breath, she blurts out to Nole, "Sorry I'm late!"

Nole introduces us, but I gently inform him that we already know each other—unfortunately. What I want to ask is why she's here: the haters' corner is in the other annex.

"Okay, so you know why we're here. Dr. Zeus said you wanted to see me," Nole says, wrapping his arm around Elgamela's slender waist.

"We want you in our house," I say, opting for the direct approach, because sometimes the truth *is* plain appropriate.

"Yeah, well, I want Ed McMahon to knock on my door and tell me that I've won a million dollars. I might actually have a shot at that," Nole retorts, staring intently at me.

Despite the barking in the background, the room gets so quiet you could hear a dog biscuit drop.

"Well, have you interviewed with any of the other houses yet?" I ask, stalling for time so I can put on my fashion game face.

"Like whose—Anna Rex's?" Nole asks, challenging me. "Why do you think she wears black all the time? Olives in a jar have more color coordination sense than she does. At least they made sure to get stuck with red pimentos!"

"Puhleez. After she loses, she can always get a job working at Vera Wang," Dame Leeds snarls, leaning his shoulder against the safari mural on the wall, right on the large rhinoceros's behind.

"Why there?" Diamond asks innocently.

"Black is de rigueur for all Wang employees," Angora says. God, Diamond is definitely not earning any karats today.

Dame looks at Angora, impressed, then adds, "Churl, I knew one of the showroom sales assistants. Miss Thing showed up to work one day in pink—and Vera gave her a pink slip to go with her outfit!"

"Speaking of pink . . ." Nole pauses, then pulls a tube of hand cream out of his black leather briefcase. "Do you always wear it?"

He carefully opens the tube of Kiehl's hand cream and moisturizes while waiting for my response. Now I'm afraid to answer because I don't want to blow my shot at snagging the infamous Holy Canoli, as he's been aptly nicknamed by Dame Leeds. I try to conjure up an image of the designing drama queen helping his semi-invalid mother out of her Hoveround. It works.

"When I'm not, I'm thinking pink," I answer, then take my honesty to another level. "I dug what you had to say," I stammer, referring to Nole's much-buzzed-about blog entry. "My mother raises us by herself. Me and my sister. I've got to win that prize money and snag a modeling contract because I can't take the Payless situation much longer."

Now Nole shifts gears. He sits down carefully, like he's afraid the chair is going to break. This is the first time I've ever noticed that he's insecure about his pudgy figure. "Please. Every time we have to buy five cans of cat food, my mother starts her Poorvarotti aria!" he admits. I'd heard that Nole's mother is Italian and his father is black, although I don't get the impression his dad is in the family photo album, if you catch my drift.

"You have cats?" I ask, surprised.

"Why do you think I'm here? You think my Gucci loafers are my most prized possessions? No, it's my Persian cats, Penelope and Napoleon. And of course, Countess," explains Nole, dropping more catty details. "They're both snooty by nature, and Penelope has already had two nose jobs. I mean, she did have collapsed nostrils."

Of course, Diamond backpedals again to talk about Crutches.

Nole nods but interrupts to praise me. "I like your all-size philosophy. I want to design a line like that too."

"What's your line called?" Aphro asks.

"Nole Canoli," he responds, like *What else?* "I'm over people associating me with a deep-fried tube of pastry filled with ricotta cheese. It's time 'Canoli' is associated with *chic*ness."

"I heard that," Aphro seconds, who jumps at the chance to explain the philosophy behind her funky jewelry collection, Aphro Puffs.

"And all this time, I thought your name was spelled like the Afro pick!" Nole snickers. "I was gonna call my company Chic Canoli—and make my logo two Cs like Chanel's—but I didn't want the fashion police coming for me with trademark trauma, okay?"

"Speaking of trauma—have you heard from Chandelier?" I boldly ask.

"You know I have," Nole retorts. "She's down for the body count. What can I say? And all she was trying to do was win the competition so she could get that corporate mentorship at Betsey Johnson, then take over the fashion business to help her brothers and sisters."

Now I feel guilty for bad-mouthing Chandelier. We had more in common than I ever realized.

"It's hard when you're fierce," Nole says knowingly, stroking together his freshly moisturized hands. "Night after night I fantasized about becoming famous, lying there in my bed on sheets with a thread count so low I'm embarrassed to tell you."

"Puhleez—how do you spell Maxicale without

counting to a hundred, hello? I'd sure like to forget," blurts out Dame Leeds.

"So, pink purrlicious one. Does everything match?" Nole asks teasingly.

At first, I don't comprehend, but the image of Hello Kitty watching my butt promptly brings Nole's probe into sharp focus.

"Well, take a guess," I say playfully.

"My guess is you always wear pink ones," Nole says, smirking, then turns to Dame. "What do you think?"

"Sometimes they're purple," quips Dame. "Let's make a bet. Loser buys all of us the first round of gelato in Firenze."

Suddenly, I realize that Nole is baiting me. "So do we have a deal?"

"About the gelato?" teases Nole.

"No, about you joining my house as lead designer," I say firmly. "Do we have a deal?"

"In principle," Nole stalls. "I have certain conditions."

"Shoot."

Nole turns to Diamond. "I'm the lead designer and I get star billing?"

A look of relief washes over Diamond's face. "Please. I was the one who suggested you in the first place. I'd be honored to work with you."

"Male fashions make up at least thirty percent of our Catwalk collection," Nole tells me, continuing the negotiations.

"Done," I say.

"My crew is in: Dame is lead hairstylist, Liza Flake is second. Kimono assists Bobby Beat. Elgamela, of course, is star model. And Ruthie Dragon will be me and Diamond's assistant," Nole says. "*And* my cat closes the show in the bridal gown."

I hesitate for a second, because I would like to slay Ruthie Dragon instead of having her join my house now, but I guess fashion beggars can't be choosers. I have also dreamed about Fabbie Tabby walking down the runway in the Catwalk competition for as long as I've wanted to win it. The truth, though: as long as my show closes with a feline, my vision remains intact, so I find myself saying with a sigh, "Done and done." Immediately I can't help but wonder if I have indeed sold my soul for a shot at stardom. I take some blank team membership forms out of my Hello Kitty tote bag and hand one each to Nole, Kimono, Elgamela, Dame Leeds, and Ruthie.

I think Nole secretly wonders the same thing: I can tell by the way he fingers the blank form, then puts it down on the empty chair next to him and rubs his hands in despair. "Again." He sighs as if he is exhaling the disappointment of the Chandelier drama. But somehow I don't think he wants to admit that to us, not yet. Instead, he switches to his signature smirkiness: "I hate those little cuts I get on my hands from cutting fabric. Sooo not chic."

We all laugh. Even Aphro. I take off my game face and watch with glee as the pets romp around in the playground where Countess Coco is holding court. Five minutes later, I'm clutching the last signed membership forms that I need to fulfill my first official task as a house leader. Now I feel fortified to face whatever drama awaits me in the Lynx lair. One down, one to go. I sigh. Then I make the one announcement I've been dying to make: "The House of Pashmina will have its first official team meeting tommorrow at three-thirty sharp. All team members are required to attend."

⌐ ⌐

Sil Lai still doesn't crack a smile when I hand her my membership forms, but now I don't care. The door to the inner sanctum of the Lynx lair is opened, and Sil Lai motions for me to enter. Puccini, who is resting in his leopard bed, looks up at me loopy-eyed, like he's been daydreaming but I've brought him back to some reality. Ms. Lynx is scribbling furiously with a leopard-patterned pen, so I let my eyes roam over her office walls. It's true what I've heard: all the walls are plastered with photos and magazine tear sheets of her back in her modeling days. I'm not at all shocked at how thin she is in the photos because I'd already heard that she was obviously a much smaller size than her present "diva size" 22.

Now Ms. Lynx looks squarely at me, and her intense dark eyes activate another round of stomach fritters. "Do you always wear pink?" she asks, finally smiling.

I break into a grin but refrain from revealing why I'm so amused: two people have asked me the same question in one day. I hear my mother's voice ringing in my ear, *When something's not broke, don't fix it.* "Well, when I'm not, I'm *thinking* pink," I say, smiling warmly.

"Well, that's why I wanted to see you," Ms. Lynx starts in, causing my stomach to flip-flop. "What I mean is, because you are a house leader, I'm going to need you to be discreet about certain events that have occurred recently. That means *on* camera and *off*, if you follow the bouncing ball?"

"I follow it," I say, my voice squeaking. I'm frozen inside. I wonder who told her that I was bad-mouthing Chandelier. Or is she referring to Ice Très and his misfired Cupid's arrow? Neither of which is going to earn me any purr points—forget about my final tally!

"In any case, gossiping is not encouraged, but now,

with the Teen Style Network being granted full access to the faculty and student body, I find it imperative to encourage everyone to take a proactive approach," continues Ms. Lynx in her commanding voice.

Now I feel dizzy because I'm not sure if Ms. Lynx is reprimanding me or is merely on spin patrol.

"Yes, I feel—I mean, I hear you, Ms. Lynx," I say, nodding cooperatively.

I'm so relieved that I'm obviously still in the fashion game that I take a *segundo* to decompress on the spot. "Um, I just handed in my team membership forms," I announce, like a proud mother who just delivered a big litter of kittens.

"Good. I knew you would," Ms. Lynx says sharply. "Now, I've referred you for a sales position. It's for a new boutique that will be opening in Harlem. The owner is an old friend, and the two of you certainly share a shade in common."

"Wow," I say, gingerly taking the piece of paper from her hand. "Thank you so much."

"Don't thank me yet. She's quite a handful, but as I always say, if you can't handle a designer's roar, you'll never survive in the fashion jungle."

I nod furiously like an obedient lion tamer while the words from Gloria Gaynor's disco hit rush to my brain: *Oh, no, not I! I will survive!*

"Make sure you get your budget forms in to me on time," Ms. Lynx says politely.

I assure her I will, then run to the bathroom to deal with the flood under my arms. Now I know what the expression "dodging a bullet" means, because I feel like I just dodged a fashion missile big enough to topple the Eiffel Tower in gay Paree!

## FASHION INTERNATIONAL 35TH ANNUAL
## CATWALK COMPETITION BLOG

New school rule: You don't have to be ultranice, but don't get tooooo catty, or your posting will be zapped by the Fashion Avengers!!

### THEY SHOOT BLACK MODELS, DON'T THEY?

Like most girls blessed with five feet ten inches of fierceness, I have fantasized about becoming a super-model since I can remember. And I do remember exactly when my fantasy began: I was in kindergarten and stole one of Taynasia's blond Barbie dolls. She was this bourgie girl who lived down the block and I knew she wouldn't miss it, so I took it, and I was right—she didn't miss it. So there I was, sitting cross-legged in front of the television set in the living room, stroking the hair on this stolen blond Barbie doll. All of a sudden, this beautiful brown girl who looked like the Queen of Sheba—or what I thought the Queen of Sheba should look like—came walking out on TV in front of all these people, wearing a skimpy outfit that reminded me of Jane from *Tarzan*. Behind the Queen of Sheba were all these other pretty girls wearing sim-ilar skimpy feathered outfits. Then a guy came out and they all started kissing him and everybody in the audi-ence was clapping. My foster mother happened to come out of the kitchen at the time and asked me, "What on earth are you looking at?" I pointed at the screen to the black girl standing there, smiling like I had discovered the Holy Grail. "Lord!" my foster mother said. "Those girls look like they escaped from a bikini chain gang!" I laughed so hard that my foster mother started laughing too. So you see, that day really stood out in my mind for two important reasons: First, I saw a girl who looked like me and everybody loved her. Second, I found out that I had a very unusual laugh that some compare to Babe the Pig, and it made people laugh. It was years later that I realized the model was the infamous Naomi Campbell and that she was strutting in a Todd Oldham fashion show for his summer collection. I happened to see the same exact footage in the video archives last year in FI's fashion library while I was researching a term paper on the history of black models for Model Appreciation. And thanks to the black supermodels—who, I discovered during my research, reigned on the runway back in the day—from Pat Cleveland, Billie Blair, Beverly Johnson, and Iman to Veronica Webb, Tyra Banks, and Naomi Campbell, I have grown up with the opportunity to do more than sit on the sidelines watching fashion shows on a television screen. And little brown-skinned girls growing up now don't have to steal blond Barbie dolls anymore. We can steal brown ones. (I'm just messing with you. Hopefully, you'll be able to at least ask your mother to buy you one.) Next June, my dream is finally going to come true when I model in my first televised fashion show. It will be shown on the Teen Style Network as part of the Catwalk competition. I also happen to believe that I am the proud member of the house that is destined to win in more ways than one. Well, what I'm trying to say is, brown-skinned girls like me can become a part of fashion history. So next June: LET THE STRUT-TING BEGIN!!

10/24/2008 11:30:45 AM
Posted by: Aphro Puffs

# 12

Caterina and her crew have piled into Studio C for the first official House of Pashmina Catwalk team meeting. Aphro, Angora, Zeus, Lupo, and Felinez are already in the house, so we're waiting for the rest of our team to arrive. Lupo is clicking away, taking candid shots of the Teen Style camera crew as they set up. Caterina turns away. She definitely doesn't dig being photographed herself, so I try to put her at ease.

"Wow—how did you know about the meeting?" I greet her with glee. Naturally, I didn't call to tell her about it because that's against the reality show rules and regulations.

"That's my job," Caterina says matter-of-factly.

"Did you happen to catch the five o'clock news?" I ask carefully, because I know she knows *exactly* which daily edition I'm referring to.

"Oh, no," she says, sounding genuinely sorry. "We were running around like crazy because of the shows."

"Oh, right," I say, embarrassed. How could I think my landlord's induction into Smiley Wiley's Hall of

Shame could trump coverage of Mercedes-Benz Fashion Week? "Well, I wanted to thank you for that, um, heads-up you gave me."

Caterina stares at me blankly, pretending she didn't hear me. Instinctively I sense that I've stepped on the toes of some unspoken producer protocol. That's when it dawns on me that what she did fell outside her line of duty, so I realize I should just drop it like it's hot.

Caterina brusquely changes the subject to fit her agenda. "Is it okay if I ask you some questions on camera before everyone comes in and the meeting starts?"

"Absolutely," I say. Boom and the rest of the crew get the camera equipment and lighting set up pronto. Of course, I should have known Caterina was cornering me for some salacious sound bites. Sure enough, she drops the boom.

"How do you feel about Chandelier Spinelli dropping out of the Catwalk competition because of her father's indictment?" she asks, straight-faced.

Now I feel like a kitten cornered in a bulldog pen. Ms. Lynx's admonition rings in my ears. I decide I'd better choose my words carefully.

"I'm sorry that I won't be getting the opportunity to compete against Chandelier Spinelli. I thought she was a worthy opponent. We, um, *I* hope that she will come back to school again soon." I stop abruptly. As my fashion merchandising teacher says, sometimes less is more.

"What about Ice Très's expulsion from the competition—do you think that was a fair result of his suspension?"

"All's fair in fashion and war," I blurt out, then shriek inside. *Just keep it Lite FM,* a voice inside warns me.

"Knock-knock!" screams Bobby Beat from the doorway. I squeal at his acknowledgment of our Cat-walk code, then introduce him to Caterina and her crew.

"Can we interview you for a second?" Caterina asks him.

"Yes, ma'am!" Bobby Beat says, beaming at the prospect of being on camera, and asks if he can primp first.

"Actually, let me get a quote from you while he gets ready," Caterina says to Lupo, and it's obvious she has forgotten his name. This time Zeus, well, jumps in on that tip, and even explains what Lupo's last name means.

"Why did you join the House of Pashmina?" Caterina asks Lupo candidly.

"Oh, because we have the most beautiful girls?" Lupo says, laughing goofily. He looks over at Aphro, and Caterina asks the cameraman to get a shot of Aphro arranging her folder of tear sheets and sketches for one of her jewelry classes.

Meanwhile, Bobby Beat is brimming with ideas that he can't wait to share with me. "Omigod, SNAPS cosmetics has this new bronzing powder with a hot-pink base for highlighting the cheekbones! I think that would be so fabulously feline for the show. What do you think?"

"Bronze it is," I agree.

"Actually, I'd like to start by bronzing *you*. We can't have you on camera like this—not even for reality television. Honey, as far as I'm concerned, reality is something you create."

Caterina overhears Bobby Beat's bite and zooms right in on us. "Don't look at us, just keep going," she instructs us. Bobby doesn't, well, miss a beat. He whips out his makeup kit and commands me to hold still while he touches me up. Then he starts babbling about the latest booty in the beauty biz. "Can you believe someone just bought a tube of lipstick and mascara for fourteen million dollars from H. Couture Beauty cosmetics?"

"What, what?" I ask in disbelief, but Bobby commands me to keep my mouth shut while he outlines it with Very Berry lip liner.

"The mascara casing has twenty-five hundred blue diamonds and the lipstick casing has twelve hundred pink diamonds," Bobby claims, then puts a tissue between my lips for me to blot. "And it comes with concierge service and complimentary lash and lip refills for one year."

"Well, tell them my lips are available anytime," Aphro offers.

"That's good to know," quips Lupo, breaking out in his goofy grin.

Bobby motions for Angora to come over for a quick fluff with his mighty brush. As soon as I notice that Felinez isn't looking, I mouth to Bobby to offer "Miss Fifi" a lip plumping as well.

"Miss Fifi," Bobby Beat says loudly, "could you bring your booty into my beauty booth, please?"

I shake my head at Bobby, but he doesn't get it. He just makes a face at me like, *What?* I make a note to my fashion self to tell him later to refrain from referring to Blue Boca's body parts.

Now some of the other team members pour into the studio. Between Lupo's flashbulbs and Caterina's camera crew, as Angora so rightly observes, "It feels just like Mardi Gras!"

When Nole Canoli enters with his crew, who are now my crew, Caterina and, well, her crew, really go into full-tilt boogie.

I make another note to my fashion self that I must warn all the members of my team not to gossip about other Catwalk contenders in front of Caterina and her crew. As a matter of fact, I make still another note to add that to the Catwalk Credo, which I will circulate at our next team meeting.

When Boom sticks the microphone close to Nole's face, he brushes imaginary lint off his black Gucci shirt, then adjusts the Prada carrier so Countess Coco's tiny visage is visible for the camera. I wouldn't be surprised if Nole actually knew Countess Coco's better side for photography.

"You were close to Chandelier Spinelli, weren't you?" Caterina asks Nole, blindsiding his, well, good and bad sides.

Nole's cheeks turn so red, it looks like he's having an allergic reaction to kaflamma. "Professionally we were close," he says carefully. It's obvious he is really struggling to distance himself from the aftershock of Chandelier's scandal.

"Have you spoken to Chandelier since her father's indictment?" Caterina asks him.

"Yes, I have, but that conversation is private, and I want to respect her while she is going through a difficult time," Nole says calmly. He then smiles warmly, as if to prove to Caterina and her probing camera that he is not some pushover she can control like a Ouija board. His tactic seems to work, because Caterina backs off and asks him a more relevant question: "Who will be your designing partner for the competition?"

Nole perks up and motions for Diamond Tyler to

join him. Then he introduces her. "Diamond's talent is truly uncut. I mean, she is brilliant but serves up humble pie. She's sweet but salty, tender but tough when she has to be, and she can whip out outfits as sublime as a chocolate-marshmallow soufflé," Nole says, beaming.

Angora gazes at Nole and I can tell she is also impressed with his sound bite savvy. "What's your design philosophy?" Caterina asks Nole.

"Whatever it is I'm feeling that day," Nole admits. "All a designer has is a personal vision, and you have to sell it to yourself first, like a sales associate at Barney's working on straight commission, or else nobody is gonna buy it!"

All of a sudden, Kissa and Mink barge into the studio in a fit of giggles, until they spot the camera crew. I introduce them to help them adjust to the "Smile, so you won't get Punk'd" feeling. It's four o'clock, and at last all members of the House of Pashmina are present and accounted for. We sit down at the long conference table, and I instruct everyone that first we're going to go around the table counterclockwise and introduce ourselves. "Tell us a little bit about your overall career goals and what your position is in the House of Pashmina."

After the introductions, I begin the meeting. I look down at the table at all the faces staring at me and the Teen Style Network hovering in the background and the truth of Bobby Beat's words hits me: *Reality is something you create*. And I created this.

I snap out of my *Surreal Life* moment to begin the meeting. "Okay, everyone, to begin with, I want to welcome you to our first official Catwalk competition meeting for the House of Pashmina."

"And we have you to thank for that," Chintzy Colon says, breaking into her Splenda smile. Then Zeus puts his hands together to clap, and everyone else follows suit.

"Bring it, don't fling it!" Aphro shouts out.

I grin. I love Aphro and wouldn't want to be doing this without her, Angora, and Felinez front and center. Angora winks at me and I wink back. Even Dr. Zeus has come to mean something to me, even if it isn't what I want it to be. I glance at Elgamela, Nole, Dame, Lupo, Liza, Diamond, Kissa, and Mink and realize how lucky I am to have snagged such five-star talent. The clapping dies down and everyone gets real quiet. I instinctively sense that everyone is waiting for me to christen our meeting, so I do just that: "By entering the prestigious Catwalk competition and committing to abide by directions from the team leader," I announce proudly, "each of us is publicly acknowledging that we're in for the roller-coaster ride of our young, style-driven lives. It is my duty to inform you that for the next seven months, you will find it best to strap yourself in and fasten your Gucci seat belt."

Nole snickers, then puts his hand over his mouth and blushes. "Sorry!" he squeals softly.

"By the same token, I humbly ask you to please call upon me or one of your Catwalk crew members to share your fears and concerns so that one of us can prick you back to reality that you are not alone. You can also feel free to reach out to me whenever an obstacle presents itself that prevents you from fulfilling any of your Catwalk duties—or whenever you simply feel like screaming your head off. If you cannot reach me at the exact moment you feel the urge to pull out your seam ripper for reasons other than deconstructing a seam, please get in touch with my assistant, Chintzy Colon. Her number, like everyone else's, is right there on the team membership form, which I'm about to pass out. I am here to inform you that there is no one in this room who can hide in plain sight—not for the next seven months, anyway."

Bobby Beat lets out a scream as if to demonstrate a crew member in crisis. Lupo clicks away like he's coming to Bobby's rescue, which causes me to grin uncontrollably.

"Now I'm going to pass around Xeroxes of the team membership forms. Each of you gets a complete set," I say, passing out the packets I stayed up all night copying at the Kinko's by my house. I glance absentmindedly at Dame Leeds's beaming face. "This way, you have contact information for each team member right at your fingertips, and you can also refer to it in case you forget a crew member's duties—or yours, for that matter. I know the introductions were a lot to take in today."

"Well, I can help each of you remember everything you need to know about me right now," blurts out Dame Leeds. "I do press and curls—not pressing! So see Miss Ruthie when your wrinkles are wearing you down—the ones on the samples, that is, not on your face!"

I can see why Nole and Dame are thick as thieves—they both have endless quips on their lips. Ruthie Dragon, on the other hand? I'm still trying to decipher the connection between her and Nole. She raises her hand and waves at Dame's joke. She is, after all, the appointed pressing person, since she is Nole and Diamond's assistant. I still feel uneasy about having her in the mix, but I realize that every leader must make small sacrifices to accomplish the greater good.

"Now I'm going to hand out another form. It's called the 'I've Got the Hookup' sheet," I explain. "Each of us is bringing more to the table than meets the eye. In order to have a bird's-eye view, I need for you to

266

tell me about your connections. Try to think of anything or anyone in your life that you have access to that could be useful to us as a team. As you'll see on the form, I've made some categories to help you begin this process. One category is 'People I Know Who I Don't Realize I Know.' Under that box, you should write everyone from your babysitter to the boot maker round your way who could possibly could be called upon for a favor that would benefit our fashion show."

Bobby Beat raises his hand. "Now, does the person have to be a style diva?"

"What do you mean?" I ask.

"Well, my mother's best friend, Mrs. Hawkins, works at the Spanx factory right on Steinway, and I know she could probably hook us up with some tights for the show, but she herself wears these dresses that come in prints with the biggest flowers—native to the borough of Queens before the settlers took over Astoria, if you catch my drift and smell the pollen."

One of the Teen Style Network camera crew lets out a chuckle. Obviously, Bobby was describing one of his relatives too.

"That's a very good point you've brought up, Bobby. Maybe we should all acknowledge the fact that a fashionista is someone who is smart enough to judge others by something more than their outfits. And I certainly think that someone who has access to fine hosiery such as Spanx is a person worthy of such consideration," I say, phrasing my point carefully.

Now everyone in the room bursts out laughing.

"No, I'm serious!" I protest. "I'd certainly like to think that attending FI has already provided each of us with an insight into human behavior, even though I know most of us also show appreciation for our unique ability to accessorize by getting on our knees and thanking God every morning."

Felinez smiles at my recognition of her true talent. "Does anyone have any more questions about the hookup list?" I ask. "Okay, so for our next meeting, I'd like each of you to have your hookup sheet ready to be handed in. After I've reviewed them, each team member will be given a complete master hookup list."

Liza Flake raises her hand. "What about if we can't come to the next meeting?" she asks. "I start my internship next week at Vidal Sassoon, and I don't think I'll be able to come."

"That brings me to meetings," I say, nodding. "As a team member, you'll be expected to attend every meeting—that's two a month. No exceptions. If you absolutely cannot make a meeting, your absence must be cleared with your team leader first—that would be me—and we're talking documentation will be asked for. So don't even attempt to offer up an excuse that doesn't come accompanied by serious paperwork—doctor's note, court affidavits—you name it, no document is too official to bring with you if it's going to support your excuse, okay?"

I notice that Liza has turned as cool as an air conditioner flipped to the MoneySaver switch.

I stop to take a sip of water. "Before we continue, I must humbly ask each of you a very important question. Please feel free to collectively answer honestly: how many of you sitting in this room right now really want to divvy up the hundred-thousand-dollar cash prize, gift certificates from Louis Vuitton, the Limited, Radio Shack—need I go on?—*and* go on an all-expenses paid, two-week trip to Firenze, Italy, next June and open the fashion show at Pitti Bimbo?"

I watch Liza Flake's face closely to gauge her response. Like everyone else in the room, she shoots her hand straight up.

"Okay, good, because for a second, I didn't think we were on the same fashion page," I say firmly. "Now let's talk schedule."

I pass out another round of forms. "This is your Catwalk schedule sheet. Every meeting, you will be given an updated one. But right now you must face the fact that your time has become a more valuable commodity than Gianni Versace's gunmetal mesh fabric from the seventies. I've already told you your task for our next meeting. I think that's a good start. Any questions?"

Diamond raises her hand. "When do we talk about designing the collection?"

"Next meeting," I assure her. "I will be given my fashion budget as well as the design challenges we'll be expected to complete. Last year, for example, the five competing houses had to create an ensemble constructed out of biodegradable materials. Also, the collection must contain five categories. That's the same every year."

"I hope this year's design challenge is edible," Nole quips.

"Oh, that reminds me," I say. "On the hookup form, you'll see a category for child models. We are definitely doing a children's fashion segment to open our show—because that's an integral part of feline fatale fashion. So if you know any child models—we're going to have to have them come in and try out—make sure to write down the contact. We really need about ten guest child models—I didn't write on the form, sorry," I say absent-mindedly, perusing the form. "They should be under the age of twelve. That's what's still considered a child these days, anyway."

"What if we don't know any children?" asks Mink shyly.

"That's totally cool—I mean, fine. As a matter of fact, anything on the hookup form is merely a way for us to pool resources. No one is expected to *fabricate* connections of any kind. And please—while I want you to eat, breathe, and live the Catwalk competition until that Big Willie statue is in our possession next June, no one should start hanging around schoolyards under the pretense of luring kiddies for our fashion show! Understood? *Vous comprenez? Capisce?*"

"Scratch, scratch, we feel you!" shouts Benny Madina, the tasty morsel with dreads who was Felinez's male model pick.

"Awrighty, that concludes our business for today. And I just want to say, regardless of what happens over the course of the next seven months, it has been an honor to spend this time with you. I'll never forget it." I really mean it. "So, if we could all join hands before we run and state our Catwalk mission together. This is how I would like us to end every meeting."

I stand up at the head of the conference table and join hands with Felinez on my left and Angora on my right. "If you could repeat after me, please," I say, bowing my head and taking a deep breath before I continue: "As an officially fierce team member of the House of Pashmina, I fully accept the challenge and obligations of competing in the Catwalk competition.

My commitment to my house must always come first so that I can become the fashionista only I can be. Meowch, forever!"

Afterward, Caterina tries to get my attention as she hovers in the doorway before departing with her crew. I excuse myself from Chintzy, who has run over to give me a folder of tear sheets of ideas. "I can't give this my attention right now," I tell Chintzy gently. Now I see what it means to be a house leader: you're really the gatekeeper of everyone's dreams locked up inside in a safe place, waiting to be unleashed.

I go over to the door. "Um, thank you, again," I say to Caterina, even though I know she won't acknowledge what I really mean. "That worked out okay."

But Caterina surprises me. "I'm glad," she says honestly, then switches back her producer gear to drive. "I guess I'll see you around campus."

"I hope so," I say, shifting my gear, too.

Nole walks over with Dame and taps me on the shoulder, then reaches over to give me a series of air kisses on both cheeks. "I made the right decision," he whispers in my ear.

I nod in agreement.

"So did I win the bet?" Nole asks me, amused.

"I'll let you unpack my suitcase in Firenze and examine my panty selection so you can see for yourself," I say, giggling.

Dame Leeds's eyes open wide. "Oh, no you didn't, Miss Thing, cut a side deal! That's a no-no. Put it in the Catwalk Credo—I insist!"

I assure Dame I will.

Now Aphro grabs me to get away from the meeting. "You were fierce," she says, hugging me.

Suddenly, I look at one of my best friends and understand what Ms. Fab was trying to tell me earlier about surviving in the fashion jungle. I look Aphro squarely in her face and tell her, "No, no, *you* are fierce." This time I mean it.

## FASHION INTERNATIONAL 35TH ANNUAL CATWALK COMPETITION BLOG

New school rule: You don't have to be ultranice, but don't get tooooo catty, or your posting will be zapped by the Fashion Avengers!!

GLITTER TO YOUR OWN GROOVE. . . .

As long as I've been a student at Fashion International, I've prided myself on living on the cutting edge and getting to know who I really am underneath the faux fur. The truth is, most of the time I feel like I'm walking on imaginary eggshells. That's probably why every day I try to dress fiercely so I can meet and greet the world in a manner that is much groovier than the way I actually feel inside. What I didn't know is that there are lots of people in the world who are just like me. I discovered this recently because I made an assumption about one such person, only to discover that underneath our different layers of flavor, we are remarkably similar. We each use our passion for fashion to rise above our background, to overcome our shortcomings, to camouflage our disappointments in a world that she so aptly described, if I may paraphrase her, as not so chic and even downright cruel.

I want to publicly apologize to this person for never giving her the benefit of the doubt or for taking the time to get to know who she was underneath her faux fur. As I move forward in my ambitious attempt to manifest my dreams—right now through the Cat-walk competition—I plan on changing my current modus operandi. For starters, every time I come in contact with someone—whether they be a frenemy, a ferocious friend, or an outright foe—I'm going to ask myself, *What are their dreams?* If I take the time to answer that question, then I have a better shot at dealing with the person as a human being. In other words, just like me.

So here's to scratching beneath the surface. May you sparkle madly and glitter to your own groove. Meowch forever! . . .

10/25/2008 12:00:55 PM
Posted by: Feline Groovy

# Glossary

**Abracadabra fierce:** Snap-your-fingers fabulous. As in, "Did you see the paisley jumpsuit that opened the Betsey Johnson spring show? It was abracadabra fierce!"

**Angle for a dangle:** To maneuver a situation or jockey for position. As in, "Don't be fooled by Nole's protestations. He's just trying to angle for a dangle. I know for a facto he's dying to go to dinner with you."

**Back in the day:** Referring to an earlier era. It is a sign of pure respect in the fashion game to pay homage to the players who came before you and paved the way for your future reign.

**Battle:** When one voguer challenges another, in or out of a fashion show or ball.

**Beam me up:** Star Trekkies started this riff. Now fashionistas use it to put someone on blast or to vibe with someone. As in, "Zeus can beam me up anytime, cuz I've fallen for him!"

**Big Willie:** A major player in the fashion game.

Someone who has earned street cred. Can also be a reference to the "Big Willie" statue—the prestigious bronze dress-form trophy bestowed upon the winner of the annual Catwalk competition at Fashion International High School. The award's name was chosen in honor of the school's founding father, William Dresser.

**Blang:** Bling squared. Blinding dazzle.

**Blankety:** Blank. As in, "I tried to tell her he's not feeling her, but she went blankety."

**Bling-worthy:** The opposite of CZ (cubic zirconia) in value and merit. Something or someone who is considered a bona fide "gem." As in, "You're always falling for the CZ. Tadashi is the most bling-worthy banana in the bunch."

**Bona fried:** Bona fide to a crisp. Legit. As in, "Trust me, Ms. Boucle, I have a bona fried reason why I didn't do the homework assignment."

**Bootylicious:** Fierce footwear. As in, "Those Shimmy Choos are bootylicious."

**Braggedy:** Someone who flosses like a broken-down braggart. As in, "Did you hear Chandelier carrying on about her job interview? She is so *braggedy*."

**Bumpin':** Purely fabbie.

**Bwitch:** Phat.

**Cacophony:** Discord. Phony flow. Talking loud and saying nothing.

**Cadeau:** French word for *gift* or *present*. Pronounced "ca-doe." A useful expression for kitties who want to milk it: *"Je voudrais un cadeau s'il vous plaît!"* Translation: "I would like a present, please!"

**Catiac arrest:** When you just can't take it anymore. Much more painful than a cardiac arrest. As in, "If I don't get nominated, I'm going to have a catiac arrest!"

**Catitude:** That special feline quality that leaves the peeps gaspitating and proclaiming, "She's fierce!"

**Catwalk:** A narrow, usually elevated platform used by models to "sashay, shimmy, and sell" designers' clothing and accessories during a fashion show. The British term was originally coined after designer Lucy Christiana, aka Lady Duff-Gordon, staged the first fashion show in London in the early 1900s.

**Chat noir:** French for "black cat."

**Chica-boom!:** Extra special. Extra fabulous. As in, "That dress is definitely chica-*boom!*"

**Churl:** *Girl* and *honeychild* rolled into one. As in, "Churl, please, you'd better be on time or I will drop you like a bad habit."

**Click, dial tone, good-bye!:** Dropping the communication line on someone who is getting on your nerves.

**Coinky dinky:** Coincidence. Can also have a sarcastic connotation. As in, "I got the pink lizard

Shimmy Choo slides for Christmas. And so did you? What a coinky dinky!"

**Coin slot:** The crack between the butt cheeks. As in, "Excuse me, Fifty Cent, can you pull up your pants, please, cuz I'm not trying to insert two quarters in your coin slot!"

**Crossing paws:** Playing your cards right. Making things happen. Hanging out with a purpose. As in, "While you were out lollygagging, I was crossing paws with Caterina coming up with ideas for our Catwalk collection!"

**Crunchy:** Someone who is cute, but not as tasty as a Toll House morsel. As in, "Check out the crunchies. Twelve o'clock dead ahead."

**Crutch:** A best friend or true crew member. As in, "You'd better come with me to the dentist, because I need my crutch."

**Dolce dreams:** When you're pining for more than polyester and only Dolce & Gabbana will do.

**Down for the twirl:** Down for a specific cause. Or, a fashionista ready to rip the runway.

**Drop an Altoid:** A minty hint. A tasty hint. As in, "Who's opening Mercedes-Benz Fashion Week? Come on, drop an Altoid!"

**Ducats:** Loot. Cash. Benjamins. As in, "Just put some ducats in my bucket and we'll be *skraiight*, awright?"

**Extra crispy:** Angry or annoyed. As in, "Don't take that extra-crispy tone with me, young lady."

**Fabbity:** On the fab tip.

**"Faboo is not you":** Despite your daydreams, you are not fabulous.

**Fabulation:** A compliment for fierceness. As in, "Mamacita, that outfit deserves a fabulation."

**Fashion forward:** Taking inspiration from all around you instead of following trends.

**Fashionation:** An obsession with fashion in a good way.

**Fashionista:** A male or female who is true to the fashion game.

**Feeling wiggly:** Feeling jittery, nervous, hyper-anxious.

**Feline fatale:** A girl with catlike qualities—feminine, graceful, mysterious—who also possesses strong instincts. As in, "Ciara is such a feline fatale."

**Flossy:** Someone who is conceited or down for showing off at the drop of a tin bangle. As in, "She's so flossy!"

**Flurry:** Thoughts that circle wildly like a 1950s skirt. As in, "I just got a flurry. Why don't we let the junior models work the meowch pouches in the show?"

**Friend of Dorothy's:** Cute gay boy. The Dorothy in question is the main character in *The Wizard of Oz*.

**Furbulous:** Fabulous on the warm, fuzzy edge. Associated with feline fatale sensibilities.

**Glitch:** Someone who tends to clog the flow. As in, "Please don't bring Taynasia to the party. She is such a glitch."

**Green with Gucci Envy:** Jealous to the max.

**Growing whiskers:** Getting too upset. As in, "Stop growing whiskers and calm down please."

**Gucci hoochie:** Someone who is obsessed with established designer labels and afraid to define their own sense of style.

**Hervé Léger:** French haute couture designer known for his trademark mummy-tight, body-sculpting bandage dresses which are sewn entirely by hand and have been worn by fashionistas from Alicia Keys to Naomi Campbell.

**Horse and phony show:** The act of performing elaborate antics that are merely designed to cover the fact that a scam or sham is being perpetrated right before your eyes.

**Hot off the griddle:** News or gossip so scandalabrious that your fingers are still scorching. "Honey, I got news for you hot off the griddle: Shalimar got nominated as one of the house leaders!"

**Hush-hush on the plush:** On the Q.T. On the DDL (down down low). In other words, the person is telling you: "Just don't say you heard it from me!!"

**Hype patrol:** Publicity push for anything from a media event to a sweet sixteen party to a new designer or a hot new product. As in, "I'm gonna be on hype patrol all week so I can get nominated as a Catwalk house leader."

**Jitters and fritters:** Not your garden variety type of fears; this type of high anxiety occurs when the stakes are high or you're reaching for the sky.

**Joints:** Favorite songs or clothing items. As in, "You got the new PRPS jeans? I already got one of them joints—that wash is *sick!*"

**Kaflamma:** Drama times two. As in, "If we don't get to our Catwalk meeting on time, there is going to be some serious *kaflamma!*"

**Kaflempt:** Upset. As in, "I'm feeling kaflempt today."

**Kaflustered:** Discombobulated. Kaflempt. When you're feeling wrecked about a situation.

**Kanoodling:** Acting smoochy with someone.

**Kibbles 'n Bits:** Loose change.

**Kitten smitten:** Someone who gets the feline's charm. A friend of cats and cat girlies alike.

**Knock-knock:** Catwalk code word for spotting a designer knockoff.

**La dolce vita:** Italian for "the sweet life."

**Lap it up:** To indulge in a good thing like getting compliments, or taking an extra sniff from a cashmere sweater.

**Le podium:** French for runway—the narrow, usually elevated platform on which models sashay during a fashion show.

**Lite FM:** Opposite of heavy or stressed. As in, "Don't let Shalimar see that you're sweating her bankroll. When she does her presentation, just keep it Lite FM."

**Loony spurts:** Fits of temporary insanity. As in, "I can't believe Ms. Lynx left me that nasty voice mail. She must be suffering from loony spurts."

**Major:** Fierce times seven. As in, "That hat is major."

**Manny Hanny:** Manhattan. The Big Apple. Aka: "Make Money Manny Hanny."

**Medi-okra:** Average. Mediocre.

**Meowch pouch:** A feline fabbie drawstring pouch for carrying important essentials such as MetroCards, lipstick, keys. Can be worn on a string around the neck, or around the wrist. Designed and created by Felinez Cartera.

**Meowching:** Gossiping, sharing notes, or cupping your hands together in the Catwalk handshake with a member of your crew.

**"Meowch forever!":** "May the power of feline fatales reign for infinity!"

**Milk Dud:** A party pooper. As in, "She is such a Milk Dud."

**Modus operandi:** Mode of operation. Rolling like that. As in, "Would you check out Tiara's modus operandi? Now, that's what I'm talking about."

**Ma chérie:** French for "my dear."

**Moi:** French for "me." Pronounced "mwah." As in "Are you talking to *moi*?"

**Mos def:** Most definitely. As in, "I'm mos def heading over to Mood Fabrics to check out the latest Gaultier gauze prints."

**"Mother Goose is on the loose!":** Catwalk code warning to watch your back when something is about to go down. The Catwalk crew also use it when they're referring to hiding from the Catwalk director, Ms. Lynx.

**"My pockets are nervous":** When you're fresh out of ducats in the bucket. As in, "My pockets are nervous. Can you spring any Kibbles 'n Bits till Saturday?"

**Numbing the tootsies:** Pounding the pavement. Walking the extra mile to success. As in, "I've been numbing my tootsies for weeks. I know I'm getting nominated for class president."

**Off the hinge-y:** Even more fabbie poo than "off the hook." As in, "That Tracy Reese satin trench coat is off the hinge-y!"

**"Oh, plissé":** "Please, don't try it!" Pronounced "plee-say."

**One Big Face:** A hundred-dollar bill.

**Persnickety:** Uppity. Highfalutin.

**Pink Head:** A friend of felines who worships at the altar of pinkdom. Also Pashmina's nickname and the name of the jewelry collection by Tarina Tarantino.

**Pose-off:** A fashion posing contest. The movements are derived from the posing aspect of voguing. True voguers, however, will incorporate intricate dance movements into the competition or contest.

**Prada or nada:** When knockoffs will not do the trick. The real thing or bust.

**Presto:** Something or someone that is abracadabra fierce. As in, "We need some serious prestos to put on the seats at the fashion show."

**Prêt-à-porter:** French word for ready-to-wear. In fashion parlance, it means clothes that are manufactured as opposed to *haute couture*, which is custom made.

**Pronto soon:** Right now. Same as *tout de suite*.

**Pure fabbieness:** When something is just utter perfection. As in, "Have you see the new Dolce and Gabbana hobo bag? It's pure fabbieness."

**Psycho Twinkie:** An annoying person. As in, "Sharpen your claws, girls, here comes that psycho Twinkie Shalimar again!"

**Purrfecto:** Better than perfect.

**Purring:** Throwing around compliments or bragging. As in, "She's always purring about Dr. Zeus like he invented rhymes. Puhleez!"

**Purrlicious:** Tasty. Exceptionally fabbie. As in, "I think Zeus is purrlicious."

**Purr points:** Rating system on a scale of 1–10 for an object, fashion item, or person with feline fatale qualities. As in, "Did you see the new Fendi clutch? I give it five purr points."

**Purr-worthy:** An object, fashion item, or person with feline fatale qualities.

**Put on blast:** To hype. Also, to call someone out. As in, "Why did you have to put me on blast like that?"

**Radickio:** Utterly and completely ridiculous. "Did you tell Chandelier she looks radickio in those polka-dot gaucho pants?"

**Read with relish (and mustard):** When you really tell someone off. As in, "I'm gonna read you with relish (and mustard) if you don't stop lapping up my props!"

**Runway:** A narrow, usually elevated platform used by models to "sashay, parlay" during a fashion show.

**Sassyfrass:** To say something smart-mouthed.

**Scandalabrious:** Describes a scandal so thick, it's dipped in Crisco, then refried. As in, "Chandelier's father got arrested for chopping up body parts. How scandalabrious is that!"

***S'il vous plaît:*** French for "please." Pronounced, "see voo play." As in, "Why should I do your homework? *S'il vous plaît.*"

**Sham-o-rama:** It's the one place that's always open

for business in the urban jungle: everywhere you turn, there is someone trying to pull the wool over somebody's eyes in the name of getting ahead. Word of advice: don't fall for it!

**Shopportunity:** A combination of favorable circumstances for the purpose of shopping till you drop.

**Snap your clutch purse:** Go off on somebody. Tell someone off.

**Snooty-patooties:** Snobby rich people.

**Spin patrol:** A press release version instead of the real deal. As in, "Chandelier is just serving spin patrol. I know she gagged when her father got arrested for selling body parts!"

**Sprinkle:** To shower someone with tasty sweet nothings. As in, "Stop trying to sprinkle me. Aren't you dating Zeus?"

**Stroking her fur:** Boosting someone's confidence. As in, "I know why you're stroking my fur, but it's not gonna work."

**Super winks:** Deep, sound sleep. As in, "I'm in serious need of some super winks."

**Swag:** The freebies and promotional incentives that are given away in goodie bags at fashion shows and other fashion clothing and product launch parties and events. Acronym could stand for Stuff We All Get.

**"Thank gooseness":** "Thank goodness."

**Thread the needle:** Do whatever it takes to get the job done. As in, "I can't believe you still haven't turned in your illustrations. Just thread the needle already!"

**Tiddy:** Tidbit. As in, "Now, that's a tiddy for your ears only."

**Times squared:** Magnified twice. As in, "There are times squared when I just want to click out my claws and scratch Shalimar's face into grosgrain ribbons!"

***Tout de suite:*** French for "right now." Pronounced "toot sweet." As in, "You'd better whip it together, because we have to be in Ms. Lynx's office *tout de suite.*"

**Très:** French for "very." Pronounced "tray." As in "Zeus is *très* tasty!"

**Twirl:** To battle. Also a command used in voguing battle. As in, "You think *you* got the yardage? Then let's twirl!"

**"Wake up and smell the catnip!":** "Stop daydreaming!" "Stop pretending!" or "Stop sleeping on your game!"

**Whatever makes her clever:** Not stressing over someone else's actions. As in, "I told Taynasia I'd take her to school, but she blew me off. Whatever makes her clever."

**"What's the fuss, glamourpuss?":** "Chill out and stop making a scene."

**Wickster:** Someone who is a tad bit wicked. As in, "Shalimar is a real wickster, so don't lean too close, because she'll singe your eyebrows off!"

**Work it for points on the Dow Jones:** To capitalize on a situation. Or, to prance on the catwalk like your paycheck depends on it!

**Yanking my weave:** New-school equivalent of the old-school expression "yanking my chain." As in, "Knock, knock—stop trying to yank my weave—that's not a real Louis Vuitton bag!"

# about the author

**DEBORAH GREGORY** is the author-creator of the wildly successful tween pop culture phenomenon The Cheetah Girls, winner of the Blackboard Children's Book of the Year Award. The sixteen-book series was adapted into the Disney Channel original movie *The Cheetah Girls,* which debuted in 2003. *Cheetah Girls 2,* the sequel, premiered in August 2006 at number one in its time slot for all network and cable stations, becoming the channel's highest-rated movie in history. Gregory served as coproducer for both films. *Cheetah Girls 3* debuts in August 2008. The franchise spawned a cult following that continues to inspire young girls everywhere to "show their spots and follow their dreams."

Gregory has been a frequent contributor to *Essence* magazine. Her work has also been featured in *VIBE, Heart and Soul, Entertainment Weekly, Us Weekly,* and *Redbook,* where she began her writing career.

Gregory was born in Brooklyn and raised in the foster care system in New York City. She earned an associate's degree in applied science from Fashion

Institute of Technology and received her bachelor's degree in English literature and writing at Empire State College. She lives in Manny Hanny with her beloved pooch, Cappuccino. You can visit the author's Web site at www.cheetahrama.com.